VESTAL MCINTYRE was born and raised in Nampa, Idaho, and attended Tufts University. His work has appeared in *Tin House* and *Open City* magazine, as well as in several anthologies. He lives in New York City.

You Are
Not The One

VESTAL McINTYRE

CANONGATE

Edinburgh · New York · Melbourne

First published in Great Britain in 2006
by Canongate Books Ltd,
14 High Street, Edinburgh, EH1 1TE

Originally published in the United States of America
in 2004 by Carroll & Graf Publishers,
an imprint of Avalon Publishing Group Inc., New York

1

British Library Cataloguing-in-Publication Data
A catalogue record for this book is available on request from the
British Library

1 84195 732 1 (10 Digit ISBN)
978 1 84195 732 6 (13 Digit ISBN)

Typeset in Garamond
Printed and bound in Great Britain by Clays Ltd, St Ives plc

www.canongate.net

For Beeb

Contents

Acknowledgments

Many thanks to Jonathan Strong and Michael Lowenthal, always my first and best readers.

Thanks also to Mitchell Waters, Diane Dwyer, Jose Pita, Amy Madanick, Tom Beller and Joanna Yas at Open City, and Don Weise. I wrote much of this book during residencies at the Ucross Foundation, The Djerassi Resident Artists Program, and the Blue Mountain Center, and I am grateful for their hospitality.

Special thanks to Jeff Wright for helping me escape full-time work and begin writing these stories.

And deepest love and gratitude to Aaron Caramanis.

Binge

"IT ALWAYS FEELS like a waste to bring expensive wine to a party," said Charles. "Cookie won't even look at the label. She'll just stick it in with the rest."

"I'm going to pee really quickly," said Lynn. Charles sighed and leaned against the doorjamb. "Did you shut Kitty in the bedroom?" he asked.

"Yes." Lynn flipped on the light in the bathroom and locked the door. From her purse she took her wallet, and from her wallet she took the tiny plastic bag. She pinched it open, dipped her key in, made a wide-eyed, flared-nostriled face in the mirror, held the key tip to her nose, and snorted. It was her second bump of the night. (She had done one after putting on her lipstick and spraying her hair.) Her expression dropped and she looked in the mirror at the tiny lines around her mouth. Then she smiled. She had a secret.

In the elevator, Charles mumbled things about people who would be at the party. He always complained on the way, then enjoyed himself. In the blurred reflection of the steel elevator door, Lynn saw the burgundy shade of her purposely messy hair. She had made a vague decision three years ago when she turned forty never to dye her hair a convincingly natural shade again.

The elevator door opened to the cold lobby and Lynn felt a surge in her heart, not a chill or a rush of adrenaline, but a surge of well-being. I'm going to a party! It's like a teenager to feel this excited.

Charles went to hail a cab, but Lynn stopped him. "Can't we walk?"

"It's cold."

"It's beautiful. Let's walk."

A dusting of snow had made the pavement sparkly. The cold air on Lynn's cheeks drew the skin tight like cellophane on a dish. She looked up at the stars and the glitter in the air.

"We should go up Columbus and across on Sixty-eighth," said Charles.

When they were in Sydney on their honeymoon, Lynn, who had been waiting for days to see the Southern Cross, had looked up as they were sitting in the grass on a warm February night watching an opera on the Domain, and, in a break in the clouds, seen the four bright stars pointing to the southern horizon. The wind was balmy. Beside them a young couple had fallen asleep in each other's arms. Large bats hung like dark fruit from the trees that bordered the Domain. Lynn clutched Charles's arm when she saw the constellation. "Look!" she said. And he shushed her as he would a stranger.

He had been to the Southern Hemisphere several times before. She hadn't traveled at all in her twenties, other than two pastry courses in Paris.

They turned up Columbus, and Lynn suddenly felt forgiving and generous. She felt her heart open and tasted the numbing chemical in the back of her throat. She put her arm through Charles's, and he smiled down at her.

Charles was an editor who worked at home. Lynn had been the pastry chef for the Mariott Marquis for years; then, upon turning forty, decided to quit working full-time, hire herself out freelance, and use the bulk of her time to write a book on mousses and custards. Restaurants hired her to share her recipes and train their own pastry chefs. That was how she came to work with Elise.

Elise was a beautiful twenty-seven-year-old black woman, tall and elegant with wrists so thin, Lynn imagined them snapping when she bore down on the rolling pin to roll a paper-thin crust. Elise let her hair grow in thick, woolly curls to which she added flecks of gold.

It was hardly a secret that Lynn had a motherly crush on Elise. Even the waiters upstairs teased them about it.

During their hours together, Elise meted out little helpings of cocaine she called "bumps," which kept the two of them working swiftly while they gorged on conversation. "Sometimes I imagine you, out at night in Soho or wherever, with the handsome men you must date, dancing and sneaking to the bathroom to make out and do bumps," Lynn admitted one day. The cocaine made her honest and unabashed.

"Lynn," said Elise, smiling affectionately, "I haven't dated men in a long time."

She was a lesbian, then.

"But you're so beautiful!" Lynn cried.

Elise laughed long and hard at that one. It was one of their little jokes that Lynn was a fuddy-duddy, and Lynn often played it up. This time, though, it had been her honest reaction.

Eventually, the restaurant dispensed with Lynn's services. The economy was stagnant and Elise's desserts weren't showing any improvement, either. Lynn would never admit it to anyone but herself, but Elise was a poor pastry chef. She had no feel for the medium and made everything too sweet. Eventually she would be fired and, in a way, that would set things right. Elise should be aboveground, where she would be adored and where she would eat the perfect desserts made by people like Lynn.

The bag of cocaine was Elise's farewell gift. Lynn had never done drugs alone before tonight.

Now Lynn and Charles stood before the door of Jack and Cookie's apartment, listening to the sounds of the party and waiting for someone to let them in. Shifting from foot to foot, Charles buzzed again. It pleased Lynn that her eyes were watery and her cheeks flushed. She loved how fresh people looked coming in from the winter, like perfectly set panna cotta emerging from the fridge.

At last, the door flew open. It wasn't Jack or Cookie, but some stranger, who said, "Come in. Who knows where Cookie went. I'll take your coats."

"There's the Mastersons," said Charles to Lynn. "Let's say hello. We owe them dinner."

"You go ahead," said Lynn. "Let me get settled."

The Mastersons were nice, well-spoken people with a summer house in Montauk and a badly behaved little girl they had adopted from China. (Swinging a plastic baseball bat, she had frightened away an emerald-green hummingbird that had been thrusting its needle-beak insistently into the honeysuckle on the deck a few summers ago. Lynn wanted to strangle her. Maybe she was better now.) Talking to the Mastersons now would have bored Lynn. Instead she stood alone, tossing little smiles and waves to the people she knew. She rooted her feet to the floor and let her gestures imply she was waiting right here for someone to return.

It had been a year or so since Lynn had been in this four-bedroom apartment with its mauve walls and expensive prints hanging here and there. She and Cookie weren't as close as they had once been.

Cookie had decorated the party with peonies: bouquets on the sidebar, single blossoms floating in little bowls on the table, and a pile of long-stemmed flowers lying on the mantle above the fire. This seemed a cruel display, to let peonies lie there dying. Lynn walked to the mantel, picked one up, and cupped it in her hands, letting its stem dangle. It was the size of a newborn baby's head and the color of white linens, but with pink hiding somewhere under all those petals. Peonies in January; they must have cost a fortune.

A woman a few feet away was smiling at Lynn, as if she knew her secret. Lynn put down the flower and wiped her nose.

The woman walked over and held up the backs of her hands in front of Lynn's face. "It's Dusk over Cairo. You can get it at Duane Reade," she said loudly.

"What?" Lynn took a step backward.

"Oh! Oh my God, you are not the one. I'm such an idiot."

"What?" Lynn said again.

"I'm sorry. My friend told me someone over here liked my nail polish, so I thought it would be fun to find the person. But it's not you."

"It's okay, you just startled me. I do like it, though."

The woman bowed her head. Her eyes were wild. "All right. I'm going back over where I was."

"Oh, don't go," said Lynn, who suddenly needed to talk. "That was funny, wasn't it?"

The woman laughed a breathy, nervous laugh. She was around Lynn's age and had frizzy, poorly dyed hair.

"How do you know Cookie?" Lynn asked.

"Oh, I don't. I'm a friend of a friend. And she left—she didn't feel good, the friend I came with. But now I've been talking to those people over there."

"It's okay," said Lynn. "I'm not accusing you."

"Accusing me! Hee-hee-hee!"

"Have you been shown around the apartment?"

"Yes." The woman's eyes grew wide. "It's so big!"

"Yes. Jack, Cookie's husband, makes a good living."

"I found a dog in one of the bedrooms. Even the dog was big!"

"Henry? Oh my God, that dog. You should see the way he drags Cookie around the neighborhood. I won't go walking with them anymore. She has no control, and she ends up screaming at him in the street. It's just too embarrassing."

The woman's laugh was like the twittering of a bird. Her jaw hung ajar and she nodded as she laughed, which may have just been a habit, but it made Lynn feel egged on in her cattiness.

"I've known Cookie forever, so I guess I can say what I want," said Lynn.

"How long have you know her?" the woman asked breathlessly.

"We went to college together. We were two northerners at a small women's college in Virginia. She bossed me around, but she knew everyone, and she got me in the right kind of trouble."

"Like what?"

"Like, we planned a huge food fight. We spread the word that at 6:40 P.M. sharp on Friday, there would be a massive food fight in the dining hall. So everyone wore old clothes and kept their eyes on the clock. All it took was me tossing a bun across the room, and everything just flew. You wouldn't believe the mess. It was pasta night, too, so just imagine cappellini being hurled against the walls and against girls' blouses. For a while after that, Cookie and I were campus celebrities. They probably still talk about it. Then, senior year, the drama club put on *Othello*. Othello was played by a big white girl in blackface. Can you imagine? Well, by some miracle I got to be Desdemona and Cookie only got to be stage manager. That evened things out a bit. Cookie's still resentful. She won't even go to Shakespeare in the Park. No one hates Shakespeare."

Lynn was gorging on her own conversation and everything she said was scandalous and funny. It was nice to have a foil. The friend laughed harder and harder and put her hand to her jaw.

"You look like you have a toothache," said Lynn.

"What?" giggled the friend.

"You look like Stan Laurel in that movie where he gets a toothache."

The friend dropped her hand and knit her eyebrows, though she continued to laugh. Why had Lynn said that? It sounded mean, and now a short silence was made unbearable by the friend's panting and giggling.

"So, where do you live?" asked Lynn.

"The Lower East Side."

"Oh? How long?"

"Five years or so."

"Wow," said Lynn, "It must have changed a lot in those five years."

The friend laughed a little fake laugh.

"I'm sorry," said Lynn, "that's the conversation everyone has about the Lower East Side, right?"

The friend's laugh became more genuine.

"Where did you grow up?" Lynn asked.

"Long Beach."

"You're kidding! I grew up in Long Beach! I mean, we lived all over Long Island, but my favorite house was in Long Beach. It was before my parents divorced. It was two stories and had a huge backyard with a tire swing. It smelled like the ocean. Once a starling got in the house, I don't know how, it was summer. My mom and I opened all the windows and followed the starling from room to room, but it wouldn't fly out. We got a little hysterical. My mom called my dad at work and told him there was a bird in the house. He said, 'Is it an American eagle?' It's not much of a story. My dad still says that, though. 'Is it an American eagle?'"

The friend laughed and laughed at the stupid story.

"So, what street did you live on in Long Beach?" asked Lynn.

"Um, actually, I grew up in Long Beach, California."

"Oh."

To save herself from feeling embarrassed, Lynn concentrated on a part of the starling story that she couldn't put into words: creeping into the dining room, holding her mother's hand, looking for the bird. Something between a giggle and a scream bubbled in her chest. The shadows on the floor and table, cast by the trees outside, swayed with the breeze. The curtains slowly billowed. Then one of the darker shadows in the corner moved and fluttered and, with a flash of blue, flew through the doorway. Laughing despite her fear that it would fly at her and peck her eyes, Lynn ran with her mother after the starling into the yellow kitchen.

The friend stood quietly while Lynn thought these thoughts. What was she still doing here? Waiting for another story?

"I used to work with this wonderful girl Elise at a restaurant," Lynn began. "She's black. When she was little, maybe twelve or thirteen, she came back from her cousins' house. They lived down the street. The cousins, even though they were middle-class kids in a nice part of Brooklyn, had been talking ghetto talk. When she got home, her mother asked her who else had been at the house.

" 'Why you always ax me that?'—she said 'ax' because her cousins had said it.

" 'What did you just say?' said her mother.

"So Elise said it again: 'Why you always ax me that?'

"Elise's mother slapped her hard across the face. Elise was so stunned, she couldn't even cry. Her mother had never hit her before.

" 'If you ever talk like that again, I'll beat you silly,' said her mother. 'Now tell me, who else was at the house? Who was talking nigger talk?'—that's what she called it: nigger talk.

"Elise could barely get the words out of her throat: 'Why you always ax——'

"*Whap!* Her mother hit her off her chair. Elise ran to her room and cried. She never used that kind of talk again, even alone with her cousins, and her mother never hit her again."

There was a pain in the sides of Lynn's neck behind her ears as she finished telling the story, the pain of trying not to cry at a sad movie. She couldn't imagine anyone slapping that face. And she was sick with jealousy that Elise had a mother. She wanted to be Elise's mother.

The friend looked slightly horrified. "Um, I'm going to get a drink. Do you want anything?"

Lynn smelled a familiar nutmeggy-yet-acrid smell, and was comforted by it until she recognized it. Somewhere Charles was smoking his pipe. She ran to find him.

"Charles, you can't smoke at this party! No one else is smoking, and the smell is so strong!"

"Cookie said I could. And other people are smoking cigarettes."

"Where?"

"Over there. Someone was smoking in the kitchen."

"Oh, Charles," Lynn whispered, "people are moving away from you. Please, at least go to the balcony."

"Go to hell, Lynn," he said. But he walked toward the balcony anyway.

Cookie appeared beside Lynn. She was wearing an orange Halston dress from the seventies and a turban on her head. We're too old for that kind of retro, thought Lynn. It looks like nostalgia.

"Thanks for coming, darling," said Cookie, kissing Lynn.

"Of course. I love your parties. Where's Jack?"

"California. That's why I'm having it."

Lynn watched Charles slide open the door and, clutching his pipe with shoulders hunched, shuffle onto the crowded balcony. She had a sudden vision of the balcony peeling from the side of the building and dropping into the darkness, leaving twisted rods and dangling plaster.

"Should I fuck Jack's assistant?" Cookie asked. "He's twenty-eight."

"Of course not."

"Oh, come on. He's going to London when Jack gets back. He

just told me. He got a better job. So he'll just sort of disappear. And if he's good in the sack, I can look him up after the divorce."

"Just how long does it take to get a divorce in this city?" Lynn asked.

"Huh?"

"Because it seems like you and Jack have been divorcing forever. How long does it take?"

"Jesus. *You're* in a mood."

"No, it just seems endless."

"I'll find you again after you've had a few drinks." Then Cookie turned away.

All right. No more talking to friends. Only strangers.

Lynn ducked past a group of people she knew and went down the dark hallway to the bathroom. A handsome man in his thirties was waiting by the door. He had an expensive hipster haircut with long bangs and wore a fat tie, which Lynn found charming. They smiled a little hello, then he reached out to hold the wall and, in doing so, tilted a framed print. He chuckled and squared himself to the print and gently set it straight. "I'm afraid this building is a little unstable," he said. "It just swayed. They should get that looked at."

"I've been having dreams of swaying buildings," said Lynn.

"Ew," said the man.

"Yes, ever since September eleventh. I'm up in a building like this one and it's swaying and I have to run back and forth around the apartment to steady it. Like my weight is the only thing keeping it from toppling over."

"Fucking September eleventh," said the man.

"I know. I shouldn't talk about it at parties."

He shrugged. "Why not?"

"Well . . . do you want to know something I've never admitted to anyone? Something I've never even put into words for myself?"

"You planned it."

"I wanted more to happen. On that day, September eleventh, I wanted it to keep going. Not that more people should die or anything, just, in the back of my mind, wishing for something that would change everything forever. Does that make me sick?"

"I don't know. I kind of understand."

"But it didn't come. People just died and everything got bad. And now I have nightmares."

"We all need new things," said the man, and Lynn wondered for a moment what he meant.

Someone came out of the bathroom and the man, with an apologetic look, went in. Lynn clenched and unclenched her fists and shifted her jaw. Her teeth didn't seem to fit together right anymore. A minute later, the man came out and bowed his head, holding open the door like an usher.

"Thank you, kind sir," said Lynn as she went in.

She sat down and peed and took out the tiny plastic bag. She turned the little standing mirror on the sink toward her and used her key to do another bump. Almost immediately, her happiness was restored. She had waited too long between bumps. That's why she had gotten grumpy with Cookie. She wished she had Elise here to guide her. What would Elise have said if Lynn called and invited her to this party?

When Lynn opened the door again, the man was still there, leaning against the wall. Did this mean they had been flirting?

"Let's get a drink and find Lizzie," he said.

"Who's Lizzie?"

"My partner, girlfriend, wife-type-thing."

Lynn was relieved for a moment, then thought, What if he wants me to sleep with the two of them? Am I crazy?

Lynn followed the man to the bar where he made a sloppy martini, plopping in several olives and cocktail onions. She poured herself a club soda. Then they found Lizzie, who was sitting alone in the corner of the couch with a plate of cheese and bread resting against her large and perfectly round, pregnant belly. The way she looked up and laughed brightly to her husband—laughed at herself and the cheese and her belly—made Lynn fall in love with her. Lynn sat down, letting her shoulder rest against Lizzie's, and introduced herself.

"I'm being such a pig," Lizzie said. "We thought it was a dinner party, so we didn't eat before."

"You're not being a pig," said Lynn, "you're eating for two."

"I am. And Jeffrey's drinking for two."

"For three!" he said cheerfully.

"How wonderful that you like each other so much," said Lynn.

"What do you mean?" asked Lizzie.

"Just that he can drink when you can't, and you don't punish each other. My husband and I aren't like that."

"Who is your husband?"

Lynn scanned the crowd and found Charles talking to a lawyer friend. "Him right there. In the blue shirt."

"That guy?" said Jeffrey. "He was rude to me!"

"What?" Lynn said in horror.

"Hush, Jeffrey," said Lizzie.

"What happened?" Lynn asked. "Oh, please tell me."

"I was just standing there making conversation——"

"Jeffrey was being annoying," said Lizzie. "That's all."

"How could you ever be annoying! You're wonderful! You're both such wonderful people."

"How do you know we're wonderful?" Lizzie asked.

"Oh, I know! And you're about to become parents. You're going to be such great parents!"

Lizzie looked deeply at Lynn. It seemed that she was trying to decide if Lynn was a prophetess or a madwoman. "I hope so," she said. "I had great parents."

"I didn't," said Jeffrey, fishing an onion out of his cocktail.

"Oh, they aren't that bad." Lizzie gave his knee a firm pat.

"My mother . . . it took her a while," said Lynn. "But after the divorce, we became friends. The rules were all thrown out the window—I was a good kid, anyway—and we were always indulging each other. We called each other 'Shih tzu.' She'd say 'Good morning, Shih tzu,' and I'd say 'Good morning, Shih tzu.' I wonder what she's doing right now. She's probably watching TV with her husband. Isn't that sad?"

"Is it?" said Lizzie.

"Honestly, I'd kind of like to be watching TV," Jeffrey said.

"No!" said Lynn. "You're lying! Being here at this party with all these people . . . it's so . . . fun!"

"It *is* fun," said Lizzie, but she turned away as she said it.

"Would you excuse me?" said Lynn. "It's been so nice talking with you, but I think I might go call my mother."

Lynn rose and went to find Charles, who had moved from where she had spotted him. Lynn's high now took the form of a surging love for her mother and an ache to talk to her. Charles was at the food table delicately eating a tiny, crumbling spinach pie.

"Honey, can I use the phone?"

"For what?"

"I want to call my mother."

"Have you lost your mind? It's nearly midnight."

"They stay up late watching TV."

"Lynn, leave your mother alone."

"It's important, Charles, please."

"I don't even have it. It's in my coat, wherever *that* went."

"Find Cookie and ask her."

"No. I refuse out of respect for your poor mother."

"Charles, why do you always have to tease me?"

"I'm not teasing you. I'm keeping you from making a mistake."

"I'll find Cookie myself, then."

Lynn turned, and the bits of conversation she heard as she weaved through the room made a kind of poetry:

"You think you own me just because you showed me how to eat an artichoke."

"It's not at Sixth Avenue and Tenth Street, it's at Tenth Avenue and Six*teenth* Street."

"I looked at him and said, 'You fuck with her and I'll kill you.' And he looked at me and said, 'You fuck with her and I'll kill you.' And it was, like, closure."

Lynn could have joined any conversation with a quick response or addition, but she stayed focused on her mission. When she finally spotted Cookie, though, she froze. Cookie was in a corner doing a strange dance before a young man. It involved swaying like a hula dancer and lifting her arms in an expansive gesture, a blessing. The organza of her wide sleeves swayed slowly in response. Then she stopped and explained something, then began the dance again. The man stood in rapt, amused attention. He had a long brown ponytail and a small, upturned nose, and was holding a green beer bottle. Lynn realized with disgust that this must be Jack's assistant—the one Cookie was trying to seduce.

In looking around for an escape route, Lynn again noticed the peonies lying on the mantel. Moving quickly, she went to the bar, took the water pitcher, and returned to the fireplace. She gently gathered the peonies, stood them in the pitcher, and looked for a spot to hide them. She placed them on the floor behind a ficus tree (in brushing up against its sharp leaves, she realized it was fake) then folded her arms and looked around. Had anyone seen her? She caught a quizzical look from a man across the room whom she did not recognize. Lynn smiled, gave a submissive nod, and wiped her hands on her pants, a gesture which meant, "Just tidying up; hope you're having a nice time." The man looked away.

Lynn had to hide.

She went down the hallway, thinking that she could take a break in one of the bedrooms, but they were all occupied by party-goers perched on the edges of beds. She ducked into the bathroom for a quick bump, then noticed that the door to Jack's office was closed and a yellow light was shining from underneath. She peeked in and saw something wondrous.

A group of about twenty sat on the floor facing Jack's big leather-upholstered swivel chair which had been placed in the center of the room. In the chair a young woman sat lip-synching to Patsy Cline's "She's Got You," a scratchy version of which was being emitted by the speakers on the bookshelf. The only light in the room came from a jointed desk lamp that someone had clipped to the front lip of the desk and extended toward the chair to serve as a spotlight. It looked like a reaching, yearning, skeletal arm.

Lynn quietly joined the circle. The woman knew every word of the song. That was no big deal; so did Lynn. But the woman also knew every lilt in the voice, every sip of breath between words, every brief, melancholy pause, and she captured all of these flawlessly. Lynn was enchanted.

"You're welcome to join us," whispered the young Indian man next to her with a faint British accent, "but you have to play the game. There are no mere observers."

"What game?"

"Well, at a certain point, when the music speaks to you, you have to perform. And maybe you'll earn The Flower."

Was he serious? Lynn looked into his grave face and realized that he was.

"Um, all right," said Lynn. She knew she would never perform before these people, but she needed to be with them, to sit and be entertained, away from the battlefield.

The song was reaching its end, and the woman held out a hand, that slowly balled into a fist, to the lost love whose tokens she cherished so bitterly.

There was applause, and a few people said in a falsetto, "Again! Again!" like little children.

"Should I do it again?" asked the woman.

The audience answered in a hurrah.

She turned to the deejay in the corner whom Lynn hadn't noticed, a chubby boy with Buddy Holly glasses standing between the record shelves and the turntable. He picked up the needle and replaced it. "She's Got You" began again, and the people were silent.

This time, the woman gave her performance a new turn by lip-synching without moving her lips. The words were conveyed in the slight movements of her hands and in the gathering of her brow. There was a round of applause when everyone realized what she was doing. She still breathed where Patsy Cline breathed. It was brilliant.

The song ended; the woman rose and bowed. A man in the front row stood on his knees and held out a peony. She took it to her breast and bowed again.

"Is that The Flower?" Lynn asked her neighbor.

"Yes. That guy was the last performer. He earned The Flower. And he's given it to her because she was so good."

"Have you performed yet?"

"Yes. I did a dance."

"Did you earn The Flower?"

"I did, but I don't know if I would now. People are upping the ante a little." He seemed so familiar with the intricacies of the game that Lynn wondered if he had invented it.

The deejay put on a Charlie Parker record, and Lynn settled in. She soon found that these were the younger of the partygoers, most in their twenties, interns and assistants at people's companies or nephews and nieces of Cookie's friends. They wore interesting clothes, expensive sweaters with strange cuts, a red belt on a boy over there. Some of them had that look on their faces that reminded Lynn of when she was young and new to New York, a look of expecting a famous person about to arrive.

Just when Lynn began to wonder what had become of the game, a very tall, slender boy stood, or, rather, unfolded to stand. His neck was long and muscular, nearly as wide as his head. Ballet dancer, thought Lynn. His expression was so open that you would look away if he weren't so beautiful. He looked from face to face with blue eyes that seemed to be lit from behind.

"Go for it, Jason!" someone yelled.

Some twangy Indian music was playing, all sitars and thumping drums. The boy stepped out of his shoes and stood facing the big chair. Then he bent forward at the waist and looked at the audience from between his knees. Farther and farther down his head went, until he was bent completely in half. Then he wriggled his shoulders between his knees and put his hands into prayer at his heart.

There were oohs and aahs and a smattering of applause.

He proceeded to glide from one beautiful pose to another, some of which Lynn recognized from the more advanced people in yoga class, while others seemed to be his own. His body bent into symbols, letters from another alphabet. He was spelling something.

Finally, he balanced on his forearms, lifted his legs high, then slowly arched backward until his toes, still in their brown socks, touched his forehead. The music went on without stopping so he had to grunt, "That's it!"

Applause. The deejay took off the record, and the lip-synching girl placed the stem of the peony between the boy's teeth. Only then did he lift his legs back up and fold down into a heaving ball.

"Wonderful, wonderful!" cried Lynn, clapping.

The music changed. Lynn hopped from conversation to conversation. All these kids were so nice, so open compared to the people outside. A woman took the stage and sang along with a familiar Puccini aria—was it *Tosca* or *Butterfly*?—in a voice that was flat and screechy. But the sight of her hunched over, straining for notes and retching out Italian words, filled Lynn with admiration. There was something grand about it. The girl's neck, over the course of the song, turned a deep shade of red.

"Brava! Brava!" cried Lynn before the aria was even over. She had to rally the people, who were unconvinced. The woman's voice cracked on the last, high note, and she looked around and shrugged.

"Brava! Brava!" Everyone copied Lynn's call.

"Where's The Flower?"

"Where's Jason?"

"He left."

"Did he take it with him?"

This was Lynn's chance to save the day, to make her mark with these kids without having to perform. "I know where there are more," she said. "Hold on."

Lynn dashed out to the living room. The party was beginning to thin. The music was quieter, the lights seemed brighter, no one was making drinks anymore. Charles sat sleeping in the corner of the huge L-shaped couch. His lips were bluish from red wine.

Lynn pitied him a little; people probably chuckled at him on their way out. And he was missing the game. But he would hate the game, anyway. He would think it childish, which it was.

Years ago, Lynn had complained to her mother about the little disagreements and disappointments on their honeymoon. Lynn had said, "One reason I married him was to travel," and her mother (who always had a surprising understanding of Charles) had said, "But he married you because he's tired of traveling."

Lynn had to get back to the game. She was having the time of her life! But parties end, and then she would have to go home with Charles. She shuddered, then shook it off.

From behind the tree she chose the biggest and most beautiful peony. Then, quickly, she went into the bathroom. She dipped her key into the bag, but had to steady her hand by clutching it at the wrist with her other hand in order to hold the key tip under her nostril. She returned to the room and the audience cheered as she presented the Puccini girl with The Flower.

"Thank you," said the girl.

"Oh, thank you for that wonderful performance. I was trying to remember which opera it was from."

"I don't know. I just know it from a Maria Callas CD I have."

"Well," said Lynn, "it was certainly shrill and dramatic like she can be."

"Are you okay?" asked the girl.

"Why?"

"You're just kind of rubbing your hands a lot."

"Oh, I am," said Lynn looking down. "I've got that itchy-palm feeling. Do you get that?"

"I don't know," said the girl.

Something was nagging Lynn. Something was asking for her attention. Why was she afraid to give it? It was the strange music coming from the speakers, a solo cello—or was it a viola?—making croaky, mournful sounds. It interrupted itself with a quick trip up and down a scale, an arpeggio, then back to its slow moaning. Then a somewhat cheerier sound joined in, higher in pitch like the call of a duck, making harmony, then breaking off into its own music that clashed with the cello, then rejoining in harmony. It was a clarinet.

Lynn tried to ignore the music and think of something to say to the Puccini girl, but she couldn't. She had never heard this piece before—she couldn't even say what type of music it might be, jazz? classical? ambient?—but it was somehow so familiar! This must mean it was speaking to her, even through her stage fright.

But she must.

Lynn arose—she didn't just stand, she rose—and all eyes turned to meet her. She strode among her audience in long steps, swinging her arms heavily. These were the currents of the oceans, the eddying of climates, continental drift. This was where she must start. Some other instruments joined in, all more or less following their own paths, moving in and out of harmony. Lynn realized she must work. So she opened her eyes wide and went about the room picking flowers. She ducked into the corners and pushed giggling observers out of the way to yank stems that were growing from the carpet. She gathered them into the skirt of an imaginary apron.

The music shifted again, and all the instruments were heaving and sighing together. They were all in accord, in unison, but the sound was violent. Lynn put all the flowers onto the big chair and began kneading them together. She must work! She wiped her brow and kneaded. Some people in the back of the room stood to see her better. She took the mass of dough and threw it in the air, twirled it, stretched it long, and wrapped it around herself like a stole. Then she sank to the floor. She took the dough and rolled it out, folded it, sliced it, then mashed it back into a ball and started over, working faster and faster. Then she crouched over it, making an oven of her body. As if responding to her, the music grew hushed and expectant. Someone began to clap, thinking the performance was over, but others quickly quieted him.

A solo violin wailed out above the din. They were ready. Moving with the violin's weird, seemingly improvised song, Lynn went about the room placing cookies the size of quarters into the air before her observers' faces. Soon they caught on and opened their mouths for Lynn to place the cookies onto their tongues. Lynn accidentally skipped the deejay, and he waved and pointed at his open mouth. She returned to him gracefully, then moved on.

Now other instruments were joining in the violin's song. It began to have a discernible melody. The music was beginning to make sense.

Her audience had eaten; now they needed a spectacle. So Lynn returned to the center of the room, moved the big chair, and stood in its place. She had to squash her fear and embarrassment, and dance. She raised her arms and began to spin slowly, then faster. A few people laughed, but it wasn't cruel laughter, it was the laughter of finding a twenty-dollar bill, or running into a friend in some unlikely spot downtown, lucky laughter. Lynn stopped spinning and swayed, making huge oceanic waves with her body, then explosions. The music was loud and gorgeous, an entire orchestra. At one point Lynn made a circle with her arms above her head, and squatted, ballerina-style. She stopped herself and stumbled out of it. This was something taken from someone else's dance, and her audience recognized it immediately. She had to dredge deep within herself to find her own moves.

She had never danced before. She remembered long ago clinging to a man with sour-milk breath and swaying back and forth drunkenly to the Bee Gees. Swaying was the closest she had come to dancing, and even that she had never done with Charles.

She flew around the room like the starling. Life wasn't always pretty. She struck jaunty poses. She made faces at people. Everyone was enraptured, but she couldn't rest; she had to give more. Her moves grew more and more frenetic until the music broke and she broke and fell crookedly to her knees.

There was tension now in the quietness of the music. The strings were jittery, the horns muttered to each other, and all the sounds began to fade very slowly.

So this is how it ended, without a conclusion. It must have been some introductory piece to a longer work, an overture or a prelude. Now the strings were reduced to a whisper. They sounded hoarse.

Her audience needed words. Some sort of note of introduction to the world they would live in now that they had witnessed her dance, and, at the same time, a farewell because the dance was over. But she didn't know what to say. Then she remembered her other performance, all those years ago when she was their age; maybe she could say something Desdemona had said.

"Farewell," said Lynn in a hoarse voice to match the strings. Then she drew in her diaphragm and projected, "Farewell." At last the words came to her:

> . . . O, now forever
> Farewell the tranquil mind! farewell content!
> Farewell the plumèd troop, and the big wars
> That makes ambition virtue! O, farewell!

These words that had lain dormant for twenty years stirred and marched steadily from her. She smiled and tears clouded her vision—actor's tears. She had to make it bittersweet:

> Farewell the neighing steed, and the shrill trump,
> The spirit-stirring drum, th' ear-piercing fife,
> The royal banner, and all quality,
> Pride, pomp, and circumstance of glorious war!
> And, O you mortal engines, whose rude throats
> Th' immortal Jove's dread clamors counterfeit,
> Farewell! Othello's occupation's gone!

And Lynn realized as she looked from face to face of her blissful observers, this wasn't Desdemona's speech, but Othello's. How had she remembered it?

The strings breathed their last, and there was silence.

Then there was applause and cheering. Lynn stood and bowed. The Puccini girl was so busy clapping that she forgot to give Lynn The Flower until her neighbor elbowed her. She stood and made a great show of laying it at Lynn's feet. "Again! Again!" someone squealed. But Lynn laughed dismissively. They knew as well as she that it could never be done again.

Lynn picked up the peony and left. She stood in the dark hallway and listened to the cheering settle into laughter and talking. The music started again, disco now.

Lynn walked further into the darkness and stood for a long time until she caught her breath. But still her heart raced. Her whole body shook with every thump. Her poor heart—it could just stop beating right now. A feeling of hollowness opened up in her, a yawning gap between her heart and her belly where before there had been joy. Should she do another bump?

She crept down the hall and peered into the living room. It was empty except for Charles, who hugged and rested his head against a cushion. The kids in the office didn't realize, but the party was finished. Aside from a few stragglers in the kitchen, there was no one, not even Cookie.

Lynn looked down at the peony, her prize. She walked across the room and put it with the rest behind the plastic tree.

It was nearly three in the morning. She should be dead tired but, in fact, she was wired. The gap between where she should be and where she was—that was the hollowness. She held up her hand

and watched it shake. She knew she shouldn't do another bump, but the other option, to wake up Charles and go home, was more than she could bear. So she decided to go to the balcony and breathe.

As she moved toward the door she saw, at the balcony's far end among the plants—was it just a vision?—someone was pushing someone else over the railing! She ran to stop him, then froze. Orange organza shimmered, red plastic hoops dangled from a long wrist, a hand disappeared into dark hair that had been released from its ponytail. The two made one figure that swelled and jerked like some awful machine. Lynn wanted to vomit.

Where could she go? Back to the game? No, everything was horrible now. She had to leave.

"Charles," whispered Lynn, shaking him, "wake up. We have to go."

"What time is it?"

"It's late. It's time to go."

"Jesus Christ," said Charles, looking at his watch. "Why did you let me sleep so long? Where's Cookie?"

"I don't know. Let's go."

"What have you been doing all this time?"

"Just talking."

He dropped his head against the cushion again and took Lynn's hand. "Did you have a nice time?"

Lynn rose from the sofa. "Let's go, Charles. Everyone's gone."

"All right, then," he said, and stood. "Where are our things?"

"They must be in here," Lynn said, and walked into the first bedroom. The coats strewn across the bed appeared as the shriveled bodies of those Iraqis on that road. She closed her eyes tight to dispel the image. It was best to go home. She wouldn't die.

They were silent in the elevator. Charles hailed a cab, then sat tall and looked out the window the whole way home. It had snowed again during the party, and the snow had melted. The sidewalk reflected the bleak light from a corner deli. Lynn wished Charles would say something, anything, ask her again if she had had a nice time, complain about someone. Did he suspect that she was high? Or that she had found a man at the party and gone to some dark corner and fucked him? (That ugly word!) The other bedrooms had been closed—were people fucking in them? She had never stayed to the end of a party before. Did they all end like that?

Charles paid the cabbie, and Lynn followed him into their building. He nodded at the doorman without a trace of a smile. Lynn turned away. It was the one she thought of as "The Pug." She couldn't deal with that soft, expectant face.

Why didn't Charles say something? Why couldn't he be that type of man? She could be dying inside!

When they entered the apartment, Charles dropped his keys on the table and headed straight for the bedroom.

"You're angry at me, but you have no reason," said Lynn. "At least I have a reason to be angry with you."

"I'm not angry," Charles said.

"Then why were you quiet the whole ride home?"

"Because I had nothing to say."

"Don't you even want to know why I'm angry with you?"

He said nothing but stood looking off into the corner with his head bowed.

"I'm angry because you were rude to a wonderful man who has a beautiful wife. They're about to have a baby. Everything's new to them. He entered your life for a matter of seconds, Charles, and you managed to be rude to him. How could you! It's a crime! Can't you see that? You have a chance with people, and when you ruin it, it's like you've ruined the world!"

Now Charles looked at her. He said, "Have you lost your mind?"

"Why you always ax me that?" Lynn said. Then, with a hint of a smile (as this closed up the hollowness just a bit) she drew near him and projected: "Why you always ax me that!"

How she wanted him to hit her!

"Good night, wife. I hope you will regain your wits before dawn." Charles went into their room and closed the door.

Lynn moved to follow him, then thought better of it. She paced the circumference of the apartment. There was an itchy craving in her wrists, and she rubbed them, her hands rolling over and over each other until they were raw. She went to the bathroom and tried rubbing her expensive moisturizer into her wrists, but the smell made her sick, so she washed it off. She knew not to look up into the mirror. Don't look! Sure enough, the bright light had bleached her into a hollow-eyed corpse. She looked away and dried her hands.

She went back to the couch and tried to remember the things at the party that had made her so happy. The game, that room full of pretty kids. Now Lynn saw them for what they were: brats. What did they know of the real world? Everyone loved them because they were young and beautiful. They didn't have to search out someone to love them; they didn't have to settle. She had nothing in common with them.

But maybe she had given them a bit of the real world with her dance.

Her dance! In a rush (and this was the very depth of misery)

Lynn recalled her dance and saw what it had been, what *she* had been: an old, red-haired clown. She buried her head in the cushions and wished that she could burrow down into the couch and live there.

Then she leapt up, got the tiny bag out of her wallet (it was nearly empty, just plump in one corner), and went to the bathroom, cast it into the toilet, and flushed. She returned to the couch and flipped from channel to channel. At one point, she decided it would help to have Kitty curled up next to her. But he was shut up in the bedroom with Charles. She crept to the door and, very carefully, without making a sound, opened it. Charles's sleeping breath was not a snore, really, but a high-pitched, alternating wheeze and whine, wheeze and whine.

"Kitty," whispered Lynn, "come here!"

Nothing.

"Come on, Kittykittykitty. Come on, Cookie."

A sudden vision: Cookie came scuttling out of the bedroom on all fours, her dress in a bunch around her waist, her bracelets clacking. Lynn turned away guiltily as if someone had just told her a dirty joke.

Then she tried again: "Come on, Kitty!"

Now a tiny baby came crawling out, that couple's baby, Jeffrey and Lizzie's. It smiled up at Lynn and closed its eyelids like two white petals, and its head became a peony.

Lynn went back to the couch and battled herself for hours as the light through the blinds turned from blue to white. She watched the news. Everyone was shooting each other.

Then a sudden beep sent a jolt through her body. Again and again it beeped. She ran to her Palm Pilot and turned it off and shook it. Why would it make that cruel noise—the alarm she used to remind herself of appointments?

Oh, no. Lynn sat down on her hard little desk chair and became very solemn. She had an appointment this morning with the executive chef of a big hotel they were building in Tribeca. She had forgotten. Saturday morning was the only time they were both free, and he was coming in especially to meet her. There was no way she could cancel.

She showered, and walked into the bedroom and dressed like she would any other morning. Charles slept on. Kitty was curled up on the pillow where Lynn's head would have been.

In the street, everything blazed with a white light. She put on her sunglasses and turned onto the avenue, which was already becoming crowded: people with gym bags going to exercise, couples on their way to breakfast before a day of shopping, vain people in their fluffy scarves, selfish people who would never waste a thought on the suffering of the little woman who squeezed between them.

She descended into the subway just as the downtown 9 pulled in. She swiped her card, walked right on, and sat down. She ought to feel lucky to have a seat and not to have waited, but she didn't.

You are a consultant, she tried. You have knowledge that people pay you for. Expertise. You have dined in some of the world's finest restaurants, and tasted their desserts, and thought, "Mine are better." But these thoughts had the tinny quality of a chipper song played someplace miserable. Love songs at the DMV. Or the waiting room at St. Vincent's ER when Charles cut his hand. He fell in the stairwell back when she lived in the West Village. She waited with him for hours, his hand wrapped in brown paper towels from the bathroom, and the music was awful—crackling Muzak. Charles got four stitches and barely flinched. Afterward he didn't want to go home. "Let's go to the river," he said. "It's sunset."

So they went to the river and stood against the rail and ate Vietnamese takeout under stripes of vivid pink that reached all the way across the sky. Charles said, "Do you know how ugly that color would be in paint?"

She decided to marry him then (the offer had been on the table for months) because, who other than she would ever understand that this was his highest expression of beauty and happiness and love? "Do you know how ugly that color would be in paint?" Back then, there was an exhilaration in understanding him.

"Open your ears, *mes chéris,* Lord Jesus is calling," said a woman slowly making her way down the car, drifting from pole to pole. She must have been Haitian. Her face was as round as a smiling sun in a children's book. Her skin very dark with a sheen to it that Lynn would have taken for sweat if the car weren't so chilly. The woman lifted her chin and narrowed her eyes as if she was singing. "You hate your landlord, you cheat on your wife, you jump the turnstile, you drink yourself crazy. He don't care, *mes chéris.* He opens his arms to you, he takes you in. He cleans you in the warm water, he washes you clean like a baby. Leave the dark and dirty world behind you, *mes chéris.* Look to heaven; the Lord Jesus gives you life. He don't care what you've done, *mes chéris.*"

It had never occurred to Lynn, with all the street preachers and subway evangelists she had tried to ignore over the years, that they actually believed it. This woman who sang out in her deep voice and rich accent actually believed that she had sinned, and that her sins had been erased. She believed that her life had been saved. Why wouldn't she want to tell everyone?

"He's the only one who loves you whether you're rich or poor, black or white. He gives his life for you, *mes chéris,* he dies on the cross to make you new again."

Time travel, thought Lynn. You go back before you made mistakes, before you did anything at all, because everything you do is a mistake. (Did religious people get that part—that everything you do is a mistake?) You go back to being a baby in your mother's arms. There was a lullaby Lynn's mother used to sing at bedtime, so close that it tickled her ear;

> *Sail, baby, sail,*
> *Far across the sea,*
> *Only don't forget to sail*
> *Home again to me.*

How did the rest go?

Lynn's head nodded. Lulled by memories and the woman's voice and the sweet idea of redemption, she missed her stop.

Sahara

LAST SEPTEMBER WHEN the Hope House got shut down by Health and Welfare, and all the other orphans and children of drunks got sent away to other houses, I had nowhere to go. I was too old to be sent to another house. Hope Baker herself, bail paid by Pastor Kern and the Assembly of God on Karcher Road, went to hide with her old mother in Homedale awaiting trial for fraud and embezzlement. So I lived in Pastor Kern's garage and started working as a busboy at VIPs Restaurant on Northside Boulevard. Everyone calls VIPs "Vips" except the people who work there, who've been through orientation. They call it Vee Eye Peas. "Welcome to Vee Eye Peas," says the hostess to the customers who squint to see her in the dimness. "Ya mean Vips?" say the customers. On my first Saturday afternoon there the weather was nice and business was slow, so they sent me out in the kangaroo suit to wave at cars on Northside Boulevard. That's when I got kidnapped.

That first paragraph has a lot of information in it, I know. It has what Miss Mills called "flash." "Move things along," she told me. "Load sentences with images. Give the story *flash*." Nampa Christian Schools sort of donated teachers to the Hope House. They'd come out in the afternoon after their real classes were over. Most of them were awful, but Miss Mills was all right. "Les has a hard time with the speaking and listening," she said once in a note to Hope I wasn't supposed to see, but after I turned eighteen and started working for Hope, I had a big key ring with keys to everything including the filing cabinets. "Les has a hard time with speaking and listening, but he's a perceptive reader and writes with spirit and flash." I took the note out of my file and kept it in the Bible on my shelf. By that time it had been three years since I had had Miss Mills for English, and she had long since moved to Oregon.

I didn't mind working for Hope. I just wandered around with my jangling keys, sweeping floors and fixing faucets. The kids gave me room. Growing up there had gotten easier year by year as the mean kids turned eighteen and left. I had to hide in the tower less and less. It wasn't really a tower, just the landing in the back stairwell between the third floor and the attic, where no one had reason to go. I spent a lot of time up there listening to the mourning doves rustling and cooing in the eaves. If you were old enough not to need anything and didn't cause trouble, you could slip between the cracks. I imagined making the tower my home. I would have dragged my mattress up there and kept my books on the stair above the landing, my knickknacks and pinecones on the stair above my books, and my old *National Geographic*s on the stair above that.

I never went there during my two years of working for Hope, except passing through to put something in storage in the attic. In fact, I forgot all about it until I was living at Pastor Kern's. There was nothing to do after dinner but watch TV, and his kids didn't like me, so I'd go lay on my cot and wish to be back in the tower.

Anyways, I was standing out in front of VIPs waving at cars when suddenly before me appeared a blond girl hanging out a pickup truck window yelling, "Hey!" I had no peripheral vision, so this startled me and I jumped back. She laughed at me. I could barely make her out through the white screen of the kangaroo's smile, but she looked pretty despite her flat hair with dark roots. " 'Scuse me, do you know when the game's supposed to start?"

I shrugged in the cutesy cartoon way a kangaroo would. I didn't know and I wasn't supposed to make any noise while I was in the kangaroo suit.

"You know, the football game between Nampa High and Murphy?" she said.

I shrugged again.

Just then I was grabbed from behind by two or three people and thrown onto my back in the bed of the truck. It knocked the wind out of me, and before I could catch my breath they were sitting on me—one on my chest, one on my middle, and a third straddling my ankles, his hands holding down my knees.

"We got him! Go! Git us outa here!" yelled the one on my chest to whoever was in the cab. We lurched to one side, so I could tell we were pulling a U-turn to head out of town on Northside Boulevard, out to catch I-84, most likely. I couldn't breathe and my heart was racing, but I tried to keep my thoughts calm, so I would know where they were taking me.

They all started whooping and hollering and bouncing up and down on me. "Arright! Yee-haw!" they said, and I knew they must be shit-kickers, farm kids from a smaller town because only shit-kickers would actually say "Yee-haw" spontaneously like that. The kangaroo head had gotten twisted sideways, so I didn't even have the screen to see through anymore, but I could hear two girls squealing in the cab.

"Arright, pass this fucker, Shantel," yelled the boy on my chest. "Quiet, boys, hold still, we don't want 'em to see what we got." The motor gunned, and the three sat still pretending I was a bale of hay. Then they started snorting and chuckling. Then they were whooping again.

"Let's see what we got here," said the one on my chest. He turned the kangaroo head by its nose, and suddenly I could see him. His dark, greasy hair whipped around his narrow face. Along his jaw grew the soft, sparse whiskers of a teenager who no one's taught to shave. He grinned down at me and tapped on the screen. "Hello mister dumbshit fuckin wolverine. I can see you." The sky was perfectly blue behind him. He wore a western shirt, just as I had suspected, too tight like an outgrown hand-me-down. Suddenly his face fell. "Wait a goddamn minute." He turned away. "Move," he said to the one whose tailbone had been grinding into my hip. He shoved him off and fumbled with the cloth over my stomach. "What the hell? This ain't the mascot, this is a fuckin kangaroo. You stupid idiot, John, this is a kangaroo."

"Take it easy, Seth. It's the mascot," came a dullish, muffled voice of John who had been sitting on my middle.

"Wolverines don't have pouches, retard. Look at this." He jerked at the pouch.

"It's the mascot, Seth," said John again, but his voice wavered. He moved into my little window of vision, a pinch-faced, crew-cut boy with dirt on his forehead. He looked at me as if I could help him. I looked away.

"What's going on back there?" yelled one of the girls from the cab.

"This ain't the mascot. This is a kangaroo," said Seth, and then to John: "They're never gonna pay us for a goddamn kangaroo. You just lost us a hunnerd bucks."

"We shoulda gone to the high school," said the boy on my ankles.

"Hold him down!" said Seth, remembering, I guess, that there was someone inside the suit. John sat down, gingerly this time, onto my thighs. "Are you a wolverine?" demanded Seth.

I couldn't say anything. I couldn't get much air into my chest with Seth sitting on it, and I didn't know which answer would put me in more danger. And this sounds silly, but I still felt like I should follow the rule and not talk while I was in the costume.

"Answer me!" He hit the kangaroo head. "Are you Nampa High's mascot?"

I shook my head. The kangaroo head barely moved.

"I knew it," said Seth. "Are you a kangaroo?"

I nodded.

"Shit," he said.

"Let's dump him and go back for the real one," said the boy on my ankles.

The blond girl stuck her head through the window from the cab. I could see from beneath the way the little knob of her chin jutted out smartly. "Look, you guys," she said, "it's too late to go back. The game's about to start. There's no way we'll get our hands on the mascot. Besides, Hank and the rest of those dumbshits don't know the difference between a wolverine and a kangaroo any more than you do. They're gonna be drunk. Let's just try to sell him anyway."

"Yeah!" called out the other girl, the driver.

"And if it don't work," said Seth, "least we got us a kangaroo."

Laughing again, they let their weight settle down on me.

Now I had a few minutes to figure out where we were headed. If we had gone north on I-84 we would have passed Caldwell with its three overpasses, then hit all the apple orchards out toward Sunny Slope. But I hadn't seen one overpass or apple tree, just blue sky and the occasional power line. That meant we were heading south on I-84 past the fields toward Owyhee County, the driest flattest corner of Idaho. Here the fields peter out and all you see is sagebrush, a dry lavender shade of green, stretching all the way to the treeless Owyhee Mountains, which might even be in Nevada, I don't know. No one ever goes there.

This all fit, because the blond girl had asked "When does the game between Nampa High and Murphy start?" They were taking me out to Murphy, pretty much the last town on the edge of farmland.

Nampa always makes fun of Murphy saying they're a bunch of country bumpkins, but Murphy, even though it's a quarter Nampa's size, always beats Nampa in sports, because they have in their district plenty of tough boys who've been working the farm since they were six. So Murphy calls Nampa "faggots" and Nampa calls Murphy "sheepfuckers." There's always some fight. This is common knowledge, even though I didn't go to Nampa High. Hope House is, or was, in the country east of Nampa.

By the bouncing and rattling of the truck I could tell we were off I-84 and on some country highway. Seth and the others had convinced themselves again that the hundred dollars was theirs.

"I say we get some beers and have a party," said John. "Jake has a fake ID."

"Nuh-uh, they took it away," said Jake who had since moved off my ankles and was now sitting to the side, I guessed, with one leg draped across mine in case I tried to move. "They taped it up over the counter at the liquor store with all the others."

"Shit," John snorted and everyone laughed.

"I don't care. I'm proud," said Jake.

Seth was the only one still on top of me, and both my arms had fallen asleep under his weight. They tingled and throbbed down to the fingertips. Sweat stung my eyes.

"That's okay," said Seth. "Christy knows the guys at 7-Eleven. They'll sell to her."

"Do ya?"

"Yeah," Christy, the blond girl said in a short sigh, like a movie star who's been recognized in the street.

"Ya mean we hafta drive all the way to 7-Eleven afterwards?" said Shantel, the driver.

"Yeah," said Seth. "What. You got nowhere to be."

"Turn left here," said Christy quietly to Shantel, then, through the window to the boys: "We're almost there. Tie his hands or somethin. Make it look real."

They rolled me over and all the little aches screamed out. My legs were stiff, my back was knotted and my arms burned. I bit my lip as they bent my arms behind my back and tied my wrists. The rope didn't hurt; it didn't feel tight through all that furry padding, but the tingling and pin-prickling was unbearable.

We drove down a long gravel driveway, then everything—the gravel, the wind, the motor—stopped. The silence was scary and no one moved. Then Christy said, "Arright, me and Seth will do the talking. You guys just hold onto the wolverine. Remember, he's a wolverine."

"No duh," said John, mad that Christy was in command, but Seth punched his shoulder.

"Shantel, you just wait out here," said Christy. "Let's go."

They kicked open the gate and pulled me out onto my feet. The kangaroo suit that had been stuck to my skin shook loose and I began to drip with sweat. The head had fallen forward and I jerked my head back, trying to shake it into place.

"Put his head on right," said Christy, and someone pulled it up from behind. I could see a swimming pool—the circular kind that's all aboveground—and an old farmhouse. We started walking across the gravel toward a group of boys on the lawn which crisply bordered, without even a fence, a furrowed sugar-beet field. A couple of the boys had on Murphy football jerseys. One had on grass-stained football pants and no shirt. They all had silver beer cans. I wondered why they weren't at the football game in Nampa.

"Just deal with Hank," said Christy to Seth. "These other guys are idiots."

I staggered a little in the gravel and hung my head. I felt like I should help them fix their mistake by playing the part.

The minute the football players saw us, they burst out laughing. "Holy shit! Look what those cowboys roped us up!"

"Hey guys. Hey Hank," said Christy, who suddenly was chewing gum.

Seth strode up and tried to sound cool by toning down his hick accent. "So a hunnerd bucks for Nampa's mascot. That's what you told Christy, right, guys?"

Hank, a big, pink bull of a boy whose number was 00, turned to Christy as if they were alone.

"Why do you hang out with these losers, Christy?"

She smiled and cocked her head.

"You want a beer? You want to take a swim?" With a stiff sweep of his arm Hank offered her the whole scene. The guys behind him were cracking up and quieting each other.

"Did you guys win?" asked Christy.

" 'Course we won. We always win. And varsity's gonna win, too, and then there'll be lots of people out here havin a good time. Why don't you stick around?"

"Look, man," said Seth. "We brought you the damn mascot. Just give us our money and we'll leave you to your party."

Hank turned to Seth with an exaggerated look of rage. He was weaving a little, drunk. "You think I'm gonna give you money for that? That's not the Nampa wolverine. That's the fuckin VIPs kangaroo!" All the boys behind him howled with laughter. He half-turned toward them and said, "Fuckin trash doesn't realize!"

"You watch your damn mouth," said Seth.

"Seth, cool it," said Christy. I couldn't see her, but there was a little smile in her voice.

"*You* watch *your* goddamn mouth, ya fuckin goat-roper," said Hank.

"Care to step away from your boys so we can settle this man-to-man?" said Seth, his voice trembling.

"Holy shit," said Hank to his friends, "we're gonna have us a real western shoot-out." They were doubled over, slapping each other on the back. "It's like the last stand at the old Apache O-hi-o."

I had been watching Hank and the football players because I'd have to turn my head to see anyone else. But now I snuck a peek at Seth. His face was purple and churning.

"Seth," said Christy, turning him away by his shoulders, "you guys wait out by the truck. I'll be out in a minute. Go on."

We all turned, Seth muttering "Goddamn faggot," and I was led by the elbows across the grass and over the gravel.

"Gonna kill that sum-bitch. You see that? How he wouldn't come away from his boys to fight me? Goddamn coward."

"What happened?" asked Shantel who was leaning, cross-armed, against the truck.

"They didn't go for it," said Jake.

"I'm gonna get my uncle's shotgun and come back for that sum-bitch!" said Seth.

"You are not," Shantel said gently.

Then, for some reason, Shantel turned to me, took the kangaroo head by the ears, and lifted it off. Everyone looked at me, a little astounded.

The breeze instantly cooled my face, and the sky, huge and pink-streaked, as it was just the top moment of sunset, spread above and around me. Now I could smell alfalfa nearby and farther off, sweet, composting manure. I looked to the horizon to get my bearings. We were deep in Owyhee County, judging by the mountains which were the only ragged little break in an otherwise-flat horizon. There was a buzzing, not of insects as I first thought, but of the transformer on the house. All this old stuff seemed new at that moment.

We were quiet for a while, then Shantel asked me, "So what do we do with you?"

She had the soft face of a mother even though she was only, maybe, sixteen. She was a big girl with short blondish hair, not fat but thick and tall—taller than the boys except for John, who was a sunburnt, buzz-cut lug. John leaned against the truck next to Shantel and they hooked pinkies kind of dutifully, but looked in different directions.

The one I hadn't seen until now, and whose appearance surprised me, was Jake, who had held down my ankles. He didn't wear a western shirt like the others, but a little polo shirt, ripped-up jeans, and round glasses.

Seth was fidgeting and pacing and glancing now and then over the truck toward the lawn. "What the hell is takin her so goddamn long?" He was lean and ugly until you subtracted the greasy hair and patchy whiskers. Then he was good-looking enough.

"Maybe she's getting our money," said Shantel.

"I doubt it," Jake said. "Those guys weren't fooled."

"Here she comes," said Seth.

The crunch of gravel under her feet was too loud for the setting, and seemed was almost musical, like chains or marbles.

"You guys go on ahead," she said, arms crossed tight on her chest. "I'm gonna stay here." To avoid the others' eyes, she looked at me and smiled a little.

"What do you mean you're stayin here?" Seth demanded.

"Hank says that Dana's gonna come here after. I'm just gonna hang out and wait for her."

"Who the hell is Dana?"

"My cousin," said Christy. "I'm supposed to stay at her place tonight."

"I never heard of no Dana."

Christy shrugged and looked back to me.

"So . . . I guess you weren't with us after all." Seth searched out the words as he said them.

"I wasn't with anybody. I'm just . . . gonna wait for Dana." With that, she turned and crunched her way back toward the lawn.

"Well, be sure to fuck the varsity team after you're done with junior!" yelled Seth.

Christy turned. "Shut up, Seth. I swear, you are so immature."

"That's what you're doing, i'n it?"

"Go on. I'll call you tomorrow, Shantel," she said, and walked on.

"Fuckin bitch," said Seth.

Jake shook his head in exasperation, watching her leave. But John and Shantel both watched Seth with looks of real distress on their faces. They were more wrapped up in Seth's humiliation than with Christy leaving, or losing the hundred dollars, or each other.

"C'mon, you guys," Seth said. He grabbed the kangaroo head from Shantel and shoved it back over my head. "Put him in the back. Let's go." I fumbled, trying to climb over the gate and Seth shoved me in. "Let's go!" he yelled. He straddled my chest, digging his knees into my shoulders, and the other two took their places on me.

"Where are we goin?" asked Shantel, revving the engine.

"Just drive."

Night fell as we drove, and John and Shantel were silent.

"Can you believe her?" Seth kept saying. "'*I'm gonna wait for Dana.*' She was supposed to hang out with us tonight." His voice was starting to get hoarse from yelling over the wind.

"That's not right," said Jake. "That's really rude."

"Ain't no such thing as Dana," said Seth. "I bet right now she's fuckin all those football guys."

"You really think so?"

"Yeah. She's a slut."

"Jesus," said Jake.

"You got any money, Jake?"

"I told you I don't."

"What about you?" he yelled into my face. "You got any money?"

I shook my head.

"Roll him over," he said.

They rolled me over, and Seth unzipped the back of my suit. Cool air billowed in and he rustled around in my pockets, finding nothing. All my stuff—my wallet, keys, everything—was in a little unlocked locker in the basement of VIPs.

"Shit. Well, there goes our party," said Seth.

In turning me back over, they let the kangaroo head come almost all the way off. I was glad to breathe the night air and see the stars that the screen had blocked out.

"What are we gonna do with him?" asked Jake.

"Let's dump him here," said John, and my heart jumped into my throat. I didn't want to be alone in the dark night with the coyotes and screech owls.

"We can't just dump him here," said Shantel from the cab. "Let's at least take him into town."

"What're you guys talkin about?" said Seth. "We ain't dumpin him anywhere. He's still ours. I got plans for this kangaroo."

"Really?" laughed John.

"Of course. In the morning we're takin him out to Bruneau Sand Dunes."

The boys started laughing and getting excited, but Shantel said, "Come on, you guys."

They decided to lock me in a shed on Jake's land where his dogs slept. When we got to the end of a dirt road and I heard dogs barking, a wave of fear went through me. The truck stopped, they put the kangaroo head back on, and I was in complete darkness. I tried to hold onto the truck bed, which made Seth happy. "Drag him out, boys!" he said, and they dragged me out.

Jake fiddled with the padlock, and said under his breath, "They don't bite." And when he opened the door, I felt two or three big dogs come out and weave among us, whimpering and begging to be petted. Jake led me into the shed and took off the kangaroo head while the others stayed outside, slapping the dogs on their sides and pushing them down to scratch their bellies. "Just stay here," Jake said. "I'll bring you dinner when I come back." Then he corralled the dogs back in, and the truck sped away.

I wrestled out of the suit with the dogs licking me and turning circles. As my eyes got used to the darkness I saw there were three of them, big droopy-jowled mutts, swatting each other with their wagging tails. I was relieved to be alone with these friendly dogs. Over their water dish was a spigot, and I drank from it and let the water pour over my head. Then I used the kangaroo suit to make a cushion in the corner and sat down. The dogs curled up around me, and we all fell asleep.

When I used to spend the afternoon hiding in the tower, I'd have all these fantasies. In one, a big bearded man like Captain Nemo from *20,000 Leagues Under the Sea* came to the Hope House and adopted me. We lived in his submarine, exploring the depths of the ocean and he gave me a pet octopus. That was a dumb one—the octopus ran around out of water like a little eight-legged dog. But in another one, I went to college and became a scientist who studied bears. I lived in the woods and gained the trust of a clan of bears so they let me hibernate with them, and I spent the whole winter nestled amongst their soft, slowly breathing bodies.

I imagined I was there as I slept with the dogs. Then there was the clicking of the padlock, and the dogs all leapt up. The door squeaked open and Jake was standing there.

"I made you a sandwich," he said.

He handed me a Saran-Wrapped sandwich and threw down a blanket. The night had gotten cold.

"Thank you," I said. I began to eat the sandwich which had bologna and lettuce in it.

"What's your name?" he asked, squatting down.

"Les."

"You go to Nampa High?"

"Uh, no."

"Where do you go?"

"I'm not in school anymore. I didn't go to high school. I lived in a place called Hope House. They taught us classes there."

"The place they closed down?"

"Yeah. How did you know?"

"It's in the paper. They say the lady who ran it is a crook."

I ate quietly for a few minutes, and he watched me. I couldn't see his face, just the silver silhouette lit by a very bright light on the back of the house, which was about a hundred yards up the road. When I finished my sandwich he handed me a Coke, like it was dessert.

"Why'd you live there?" he asked.

Had he been wondering, in that silence, whether he could ask me that? This made me smile.

"Um," I said, "my mom broke my arm when I was in kindergarten."

"Are you lying?"

"No. Why would I lie?"

"It's just, you were smiling when you said it."

"Oh. It doesn't bother me, that's all. It's true, though."

"What happened to your mom?"

"I see her every couple years. It's better that I didn't grow up with her. She moves around a lot."

I sipped the Coke for a while, and he petted the dogs. There was a question that I wanted to ask him, but I couldn't think of how to put it. Funny, we were being so polite after such a strange day.

Finally I said it like this: "So, how do you know those guys?"

"You mean, why do I hang out with them?" he kind of chuckled and shrugged. "They go to my church."

I think there must be two types of people—ones that let things fall around them, and ones that choose. I understood now that Jake was like me, and his friends were something that just fell around him.

"You're here 'cause none of them would want you to see where they live," he added, a little spitefully.

I nodded.

"Well, good night," he said, heaving himself up. "Go lay down," he said to the dogs and they came again to curl up around me. He shut the door.

I was awakened by the dogs whimpering and scratching at the door. I had to pee. Without thinking, I stood up and opened the door and the dogs crowded out. The padlock hung loose on the latch—he hadn't locked it.

The morning was bright and chilly, and I was sore all over and couldn't turn my head. Jake was coming down the road, squinting without his glasses, his hair rumpled. "My mom wants to know if you want breakfast," he said.

"Your mom?"

"Yeah. Come on. Just don't say anything."

I looked down at my dirty, stinky T-shirt, shorts, and bare feet. Jake was already walking back toward the house, so I followed.

"Would ya like some toast?" Jake's mom asked when I entered the yellow kitchen. "I'm sorry. Jake told me your name but I forgot it already."

"Les."

"That's right. Would ya like some toast, Les? It's just toast and oatmeal, kinda simple 'cause we got to get to church early. Don teaches Sunday school."

"You're from Nampa, I heard. Sit down," said Jake's dad. He was eating toast with one hand and going through a pile of pamphlets and workbooks with the other. "I used to buy seed at Franklin's by the railroad tracks in Nampa. Best seed in the valley. Would drive all the way out there. Till Franklin's burned down. Don't mind me, I gotta figure out a lesson plan."

"Ya shoulda done it last night, Don. He always leaves Sunday school for breakfast Sunday morning!"

I ate toast and oatmeal quietly. I guessed that Jake had made up some story about me, some excuse for my bare feet, but I wished he would have let me in on it. Now he was reading the paper, ignoring us all.

"You boys comin with us, or do you want to take the truck later?" asked Jake's dad.

"They're goin with Bill McConnel to his church," answered his mom. "This makes two weeks in a row now, Jake. I'm not crazy about the idea. It's not your church. Next week it's back to normal. Now worsh up before ya go."

After a minute of gathering workbooks and car keys and Bibles, they were gone.

Jake finally looked up at me, then to the clock. "They'll be here soon. You better put on that outfit."

When Seth and the others arrived, they found me locked in the shed, wearing the kangaroo suit, head and all.

"Arright, ya stupid fuckin kangaroo," said Seth, standing in the doorway. "Are ya ready to earn your keep?"

He seemed a little restored, and he jerked me hard as they led me to the truck. I caught a glimpse of Shantel climbing into the cab. She wore a baseball hat, because it was bright out, or maybe because she hadn't done her hair. Her expression was cross and she drove quietly. The boys didn't sit on me now, but huddled up against the cab where they were sheltered from the wind. I lay on my back, just like before. Jake asked a couple of logistical questions: "You go out 78, right? It's past Grand View; there'll be signs." John, the only one who seemed to be wholly enjoying this, kept pestering Seth to reveal what he had planned for me, but Seth just chuckled, "You'll see."

I don't think Seth knew yet.

Bruneau Sand Dunes is a place, deep in Owyhee County, where, for some reason, several huge, white sand dunes rise out of the flat sagebrush expanse. I had been there once before. There's a parking lot and a visitors' center, but I can't imagine they get many visitors.

Now, I know a little about deserts because I did a research paper on desert ecology for my science class when I was sixteen. The thing that makes Bruneau Sand Dunes interesting is that it's a patch of one type of desert in the middle of another type. Southwestern Idaho is high desert, meaning it's very dry, at a high altitude, and is covered by scrubby plants. Sand dunes are normally found in low deserts—the real, pure deserts, like the Sahara. These deserts are the most basic, honest form of terrain there is—the closest to the earth's core. If you scrape away the mountains, the grass, the trees, and scrubby plants, underneath it all, you'll find desert. The way I described it in my paper is that the earth is like a human body. If you take away the clothes, the skin, the muscles and organs, what's left? Bones. Dry as a bone, as people say.

And as the wind blows, eon after eon, and people drive cars and plow the soil, the layers of the earth erode, leaving desert. The Sahara is growing every day. The jungle part of Africa is peeling away, leaving desert.

It's not a very pleasant thought, thinking about deserts. In my paper I pointed out that the two lowest places on earth, the very purest deserts, are named Death Valley and the Dead Sea.

My science teacher gave my paper a C– and wrote at the top "Wordy and inaccurate. Where are your sources?"

Somehow I knew to show the paper to Miss Mills. She took me aside and said, "Les, I'm very impressed with this paper. I read it twice. There are some fascinating ideas here, and I want to read more about them. Next time, though, you should choose a different form. A scientific research paper is not the place. You should put them into a story."

Which is, I guess, what I'm trying to do now.

"Park at the far end, away from that building," Seth said.

"I think it's closed anyway," Shantel answered him.

We parked, and I made a quick scan of the empty parking lot

and the little cinder-block visitors' center before they hoisted me by my arms and pulled me out onto the asphalt.

"Arright follow me," said Seth. "John and Jake, stay behind him so he don't run."

He led us single file—Shantel, then me, then the other two, through the brush toward the dunes. When I tripped over roots and rocks, Seth looked over his shoulder. "Come on, ya stupid thing. Don't lag back." Shantel looked back, too, but her expression was pained. She didn't like this, but she'd see it through because she loved him. John had picked up a long stick that he'd prod me with now and then. In his dumb-boy sort of way, he loved Seth too.

The scrub gave way to soft sand, which was even harder to walk over. Seth led us into the valley between the dunes, farther and farther, veering left when another dune rose ahead of us. We reached a point where, I supposed, all he could see was dunes, and we stopped. There was no breeze here, and the sun had begun to beat down.

"Arright," said Seth. He stood with his hands on his hips, looking up the dunes and catching his breath. "Now we climb up to the top."

"To the top?" said John, who was doubled over, hands on his knees, huffing and sweating.

"Yes, ya fat cow, to the top."

"What're we gonna do with him?"

"If you ask me that one more fuckin time, I'm gonna kick your ass."

"It's just, I don't wanna climb up to the top 'less I know," said John.

Seth punched John hard on the shoulder.

"Ow!" said John.

"Take it easy," said Shantel.

"Are we gonna do this fuckin thing or not?" Seth demanded.

"I'll wait down here," Shantel said sulkily. She squatted and began removing foxtails from her socks. Jake looked away.

"Are we gonna do this?" Seth almost screamed. He turned to me like it was me he was asking. I could see his face clearly in the bright sunlight. All his humiliation from yesterday, and the question of what to do with me was knotted there between his eyebrows.

He shoved me by the shoulders and I fell back into the sand.

"Seth!" said Shantel.

He pulled me up and laughed. "You ready, boys? You caught your breath? Let's go. You first, kangaroo."

I started to climb the dune, heaving hard to lift my big feet. Seth and the other two were close behind me. We had only gotten a little ways up when the sand, with a great moan, began to slide down. We climbed faster, but lost ground, like when you climb up the down escalator at the airport in Boise.

"Spread out! We've got to spread out!" yelled Seth.

We fanned out across the face of the dune, Jake to my right, trudging hard, holding his arms out to balance, Seth and John to my left. The sand was still and we could climb again.

In order to keep my balance, I had to climb fast, almost running. I stumbled once, tearing the knee of the suit, and the sand carried me backward. I could hardly breathe. I took off the kangaroo head and held it by the ear as I climbed.

"Put that back on!" Seth yelled, from behind me. But I didn't.

There were tiny ripples in the surface of the sand. From a distance it had looked blank, but from here I saw that some places it was white as sugar, other places it was gray as ash, and still others, the color of skin. To look at it dazzled me and made me dizzy, so I looked up.

Jake was almost to the top. I heard another great moan to my left and saw that Seth and John were sliding down, still climbing. The dune was depositing the two back down into the valley like spiders you scoop up in the newspaper to set outside. They both hollered in protest.

I turned and ran up to the peak. For a moment I saw the lavender-green flatlands and the highway, so straight it could have been drawn with a ruler. Jake approached me, making the peak give a little, and we slid a few feet down the other side. Everything but sand and sky disappeared again. Jake stopped and the sand was still and silent beneath us.

"You should make a run for it," he said.

"What do you mean?"

"Seth is getting hysterical. You should just go now. Escape." He nodded toward the next dune, and the next, which stood against the sky like men's shoulders.

His suggestion seemed silly to me, like something taken from a movie. "Where would I go? There's nothing."

"Go down and around to the visitors' center," he said.

"There's no one there."

For the first time since being kidnapped I imagined how it would have to end: Pastor Kern in his blue Toyota coming to get me, then me trying to explain to the people at VIPs, then, after dinner, lying down on the cot in the garage, wishing for something to happen. My life restored to the way it was before. It all seemed so horrible.

I climbed carefully back to the peak. "Come on, Jake," I said. He wanted to help me be someone who chose, but he got it wrong. To be someone who chose, I had to go back to the other three, who were standing against the white, shading their eyes to see me.

"I'm trying to let you go!" said Jake.

"Come on. Let's go back," I said.

I turned and trudged across and down the dune, holding the kangaroo head by the ear. The sand made it easy, sliding me down as I went. When I drifted closer, I could see Seth's jaw grinding like a little motor as he tried to come up with a punishment.

Octo

ANGELFISH, BOXFISH, TWO sea snails, striped grunt, surgeonfish, hermit crab—Octo ate them all. He outgrew the sea monkeys Jamie bought to feed him and he started eating the other fish. So Ma and Daddy say it's time to get rid of Octo.

Angelfish was the first to go. It disappeared. Jamie thought it might've got sucked into the filter and died. I've got to clean the filter, thought Jamie. But the angelfish was under Octo's mantle, being eaten. When Octo moved, the next day, there was wide-eyed angelfish, fins gone, jumbled bones, a strip of skin waving in time with the filter's bubbling. Jamie got the net. He flushed the angelfish. He didn't tell Ma or Daddy.

That stupid fish tank smells, said Rebecca.

Shut up, said Jamie.

Friggin thing does smell, said Daddy.

Jamie, if you're going to have an aquarium you've got to keep it clean, said Ma.

But that was months ago. Now Octo's eaten everyone else, too. Now it's just Octo, sitting quietly, thinking.

Jamie tries to get Elsie to help him make seawater, but she

won't. Not in my job description, says Elsie. She's the care provider. Elsie's old and has a limp and can't work. She gets more money from the government if she comes for an hour on the days when everyone else is at work or school. She makes lunch and gives Jamie pills. She's from Queens.

Sometimes she stays longer than an hour if Jamie gets her talking. Like the Monday after the weekend when Jamie first got Octo.

Look, Elsie! said Jamie. He brought Elsie to the tank.

Whoa! She backed up.

Isn't it cute? Octo was teeny-little, swimming around the tank. He was the size of an umbrella you'd put in a tropical drink. He swam back and forth opening and closing his legs like a tiny umbrella.

I wouldn't say cute, said Elsie, getting closer to the tank. But it's somethin. It sure is somethin. You sure you can keep that in a tank?

Jamie told her what the man at the store had told him: that Octo would only survive if the water is kept fresh. Jamie would have to siphon a little out every day and replace it. Otherwise, when Octo squirted ink like he did when Jamie first put him in, he would make the water poison and die. What do you mean siphon out water? asked Elsie. Jamie tried to show her—he started sucking on the siphon to get it going—but Elsie had turned and walked to the kitchen saying, I can't watch this.

That day Elsie ended up telling Jamie about the giant octopus that was displayed at Coney Island when she was little. You had to pay the guy a quarter, right? and he lets you into this tent, this long, dimly lit tent, and the minute you walk in you can smell the rot. Professor Whoever from Wherever is talkin about how he's traveled the world with this exquisite specimen. And laid out on this big piece of canvas was this dead octopus, half rotted away. Musta been fifty feet long.

Was it real? asked Jamie.

Sure it was. If it was fake it woulda smelled a whole lot better.

It must have been a giant squid, said Jamie.

You going to eat that orange or not? It's good for you.

I'm gonna eat it.

Octopus, squid, what's the difference? said Elsie. Jamie tried to tell her but she just went on. And there was the freak show with the man with the stretchy skin and the bearded lady and all of that. Of course that's considered cruel nowadays. They don't have that kinda show.

They don't have it anymore? said Jamie. He was disappointed.

Course not, said Elsie.

Do they still have Coney Island?

You never been to Coney Island? What are you talkin, a kid like you?

No.

Elsie shook her head and picked up Jamie's plate. Where they keepin you?

That day Elsie stayed a full two hours. When she pulled on her coat, she said, What am I doin, staying so long. You think I get paid extra for this? No siree I do not.

That was when Octo was tiny, when he was still satisfied with tiny brine shrimp. Later, when Octo got sea snail #1, Daddy laughed.

Damn thing's goin after its *own* now, said Daddy. Mean mother. Thinks he's a big shot.

It wasn't a little snail. It was giant. Jamie would follow it around the tank. Its soft part made an oval against the glass, and Jamie would watch it up close, seeing its tiny mouth open and close, littler than a freckle, going wow, wow, wow, eating its way so slow around the tank. One morning snail #1 was a bump under the brown web between Octo's two front legs. Octo wasn't moving. The black bars in Octo's eyeballs watched Jamie. You're eating one of the sea snails, aren't you? said Jamie. Octo looked but never blinked. His eyes were always wide open. If my eyes were that wide open, I'd look scared or wondering, thought Jamie. But Octo never looks scared or wondering. He just looks like he knows.

Two days later, in the corner of the tank was a pile of the snail shell in pieces.

That octopus eat one of them snails? said Elsie. She never got too close to the tank. She always scowled when she talked about Octo.

Yeah. I think so, said Jamie. Look. He piled up the pieces in the corner. It's like when I eat peanuts.

Ugh! said Elsie. You oughta get rid of that thing. It ate the angelfish, too.

I'm not getting rid of Octo, said Jamie.

That was the night Daddy said, Damn thing's going after its *own* now.

What's that? said Ma. She was feeding Jacob.

The monster ate one of them snails, said Daddy.

Not a monster, said Jamie.

That thing, said Ma.

I hate it! said Rebecca.

Shut up! said Jamie.

You shut up, said Rebecca.

You both shut up and eat, said Daddy.

I don't see why Jamie gets to keep that stinky thing and I don't get to have a dog! said Rebecca.

Yeah! Dog! said Nancy.

Shut up, said Jamie.

Jamie gets the aquarium because he's the oldest, said Ma. When you turn thirteen, we'll think about letting you get a dog.

That is so unfair! said Rebecca.

Until then, said Ma, there's no use in whining about it.

That is so unfair! I hate this! He gets whatever he wants!

Do not, said Jamie.

Now listen, you two, said Daddy.

Yes*sir*, said Rebecca. You get whatever you want just because you're a boy and you're stupid.

Becca! said Ma.

I am *not* stupid, said Jamie.

All right, said Daddy. He was standing up.

Nancy was crying now.

Rebecca twisted out of her chair. I hate this place! The chair fell over and she ran off.

Becca! yelled Daddy walking after her.

Now, Jamie, settle down, said Ma, moving toward him. Don't cry, honey.

Nancy wailed. Jacob banged his tray.

Jamie, hush, now, please, honey, don't cry. Ma's hands were on Jamie's shoulders.

Judith! Daddy yelled from the other room. Will you shut him up?

Hush, sweetheart.

Nancy was crying.

Judith!

I am not stupid, said Jamie.

Shh-shh-shh.

Now that all the others are eaten, Jamie feeds Octo dead shrimp from the store. Ma lets him.

Octo doesn't move much now. For one thing, he's too big. His legs are the length of the tank, and then some. They reach the far end, then coil against the glass. The coils twitch. He heaves in, stops, then his funnel opens and water billows out, pushing aside the blue gravel till there's a bare spot. Sometimes he gets up and his skin turns into spines and he glides to a different corner. For a few seconds, every part of him is flushed pink, coiling and uncoiling. Then he's still again.

He's bored, thinks Jamie, plopping a shrimp into the tank. He likes eating live things better. The shrimp flutters down and lands on one of the coils. Octo doesn't move, but his eyes now watch the shrimp from across the tank. Nancy kneels down next to Jamie. Sit still, Nancy. Maybe he'll eat it while we're watching.

Octo breathes in . . . breathes out. Two legs begin to uncoil.

Rebecca passes behind Jamie and Nancy on the way to her room, then comes back and looks into the tank. Jamie can see her reflection in the glass. She puts her hands on her hips, all bratty.

Is that thing eating?

Shhhh! say Jamie and Nancy. Octo has turned the underside of two legs toward the shrimp. Now the shrimp starts to inch up Octo's legs, being passed from one sucker to the next, toward his mouth.

I cannot even *tell* you guys how much that grosses me out, says Rebecca.

Octo freezes.

Shut up! whispers Jamie.

Go on, Becca, says Nancy. You're ruining it.

No problem! says Rebecca and she tosses her hair and marches off to her and Nancy's bedroom and closes the door behind her. Then her music comes on, loud.

Octo begins again, slowly passing the shrimp from sucker to sucker.

I don't think it's gross, whispers Nancy.

Good, whispers Jamie.

I like Octo.

Well, I think he likes you, too.

Really? How can you tell?

Well, when he's scared he turns white, and when he's mad he turns red. But now he's his normal color. That means he's comfortable with you. He knows you like him, so he's not afraid.

You mean he can tell me from Rebecca or Ma?

Of course he can, Nancy.

And I'm the only one he likes?

Uh-huh . . . other than me . . . and maybe Elsie.

So can I always watch him eat?

Uh-huh.

Can I feed him?

No. I have to feed him.

Okay.

Without moving too much, Jamie puts his arm around Nancy. Octo freezes for a second, the shrimp already half under his mantle. Then he draws in the rest.

Jamie goes to the bathroom and makes seawater. Before dinner is the only time he's allowed, because no one else needs the bathtub. He fills the tub halfway, adds a teaspoon from the blue bottle to take away the chlorine, then adds a scoop of sea salt, pushes up his sleeves, and swishes the water with his hands. He drops in the little glass hydrometer to measure the saltiness, and leaves it for a while.

During dinner, Elsie calls and tells Ma she's still sick and won't come tomorrow. Ma will have to leave him his lunch and set out his pills again. Elsie was sick yesterday, too.

She's not quitting, is she? asks Jamie.

No, she's not quitting, says Daddy. She's just sick, right, Ma?

I don't think she's quitting, Jamie.

Jamie would be sad if Elsie quit.

Gloria, the care provider before Elsie, had quit. Jamie had fired Rita, the one before Gloria, because he hated her. She was always late and hardly talked to him and made the same thing every day—macaroni and cheese and an apple. I fired her, Jamie likes to say. Before Rita, Jamie used to go to school during the mornings at Empire State Development Center. He got kicked out because of his Fits of Rage. He's glad, though. He couldn't stand going to school with retards. Now that his Fits of Rage have stopped, they might send him back. But he'd rather stay home.

After dinner, he checks the hydrometer in the bathtub. The water is just right, so he takes a bucket to the living room. He sucks on the siphon to get it going and accidentally takes in a salty mouthful. He spits it into the empty bucket. Then he gently pours in some new water as old water runs through the siphon, filling the empty bucket.

Octo watches him calmly. He's used to all this.

Late that night, Jamie has a dirty dream. He wakes up, and he's made a mess. The first time this happened, Ma said that it was okay. His body was supposed to do this, and it was nothing to cry about. She said next time he should go to the bathroom, clean up, and go back to bed. No big deal.

But Jamie can't help but feel ashamed. He holds his privates tight with both hands. The digital alarm clock says 12:23. He feels weak and he wants to cry. He wants to fast-forward time until he's clean again and back in bed and about to fall asleep.

He slips out of bed and shuffles into the dark hall, hunched over, still holding himself. He's careful not to make any noise—he doesn't want anyone to find him. Ma and Daddy's light is still on so he's extra-quiet as he passes their door. They're talking.

I'll take him to the docks at Red Hook and we can dump it in the river. If he thinks it'll survive, he won't get that upset.

Ron, there's no way we're going to do this without him throwing a fit. I just don't think it's worth it.

Well it has to happen sometime. The living room smells like a swamp, the thing is huge. Sure, it was cute for a while, he had somethin to be excited about, he was real responsible about it, but it's gotten way out of hand. You looked at it lately? It's huge! It must be fuckin miserable in that little tank.

I know, I know.

You just explain how sad Mr. Octopus is, Judith. Make him feel bad for keepin it in a tank when it could be out in the ocean with its little sea friends. . . .

Oh, Ron, don't make a joke.

I'm not makin a joke. You explain it to him, and then the three of us will go for a little drive down to the river—Jamie, Pops, and the monster. Simple's that.

That's not going to work! That's not how Jamie thinks. He loves it. He doesn't talk about anything else.

All the more reason . . .

I know, all the more reason to get rid of it. It's not good for him anymore. All I'm saying is . . . I don't know. We just better be ready for a fight.

As Ma says this, her voice is louder and there are footsteps. Jamie runs back to his room and ducks behind the door. Ma opens her bedroom door and the hall is brighter. Then the bathroom door closes and he hears the sink running. Jamie tears off his pajamas, wipes himself with the shirt, and stuffs it under the other clothes in the hamper. He opens the bottom drawer carefully and pulls on clean pajamas. Then he curls up in bed, and pulls the covers over his head, trembling. The bathroom door opens, the light flicks off. I'm made of rock, thinks Jamie. I'm a statue. He holds his breath. Ma's footsteps come down the hall, past her own door, to his.

Jamie? she whispers from his doorway.

He holds completely still.

She pauses. One onethousand, two onethousand, three onethousand. Then her feet pad away.

You can breathe again, but don't cry. Don't cry don't cry don't cry. Four onethousand, five onethousand, six onethousand. Did she close her door?

He hears Ma close her bedroom door.

Don't cry don't cry.

He thinks of the things that usually put him to sleep.

He's in a treasure chest at the bottom of the ocean.

He's a baby chick still in its shell.

• • •

There's a secret about Octo that Ma and Daddy don't know. Octo once escaped from the tank.

It happened at about one o'clock on a Tuesday afternoon three weeks ago. Jamie had been looking at a comic book on his bed, waiting for Elsie, when he heard a loud bump come from the living room. Elsie? he called, but she usually buzzed once or twice to be let in before she used her key. Jamie ran to the living room and saw the tank tipped over on its side and water running across the stand and pouring down, turning the orange carpet brown. Octo was heaving himself across the carpet with his back legs, waving his two front legs before him. His body was pale, almost white. He reached the corner between the bookshelf and the wall, stopped, huddled into the corner and reached up, searching the wall with his front legs. He whipped them around the bookshelf and pulled down some books, which fell open onto the floor.

Oh, no, said Jamie, stomping the floor, not knowing what to do. He ran to the bathroom, started filling the tub with cool water, threw in a scoop of sea salt, then ran back to the living room. Octo had dragged himself along the wall to the sofa, coiled his legs around the sofa's feet, and was stuffing himself beneath.

Oh, no! cried Jamie. He grabbed Octo's body and pulled. Octo turned from white to red at Jamie's touch, and black ink dribbled onto the floor. Jamie had never felt Octo before. Octo's skin was sticky, and as Jamie pulled, he felt like rubber. Oh, please, Octo, let go. Jamie quit pulling, knelt, and started unwrapping Octo's legs from the sofa's feet. Another of his legs coiled around Jamie's arm. Please, pleeeease, Jamie was crying now. Finally Octo gave up. His whole body went limp and Jamie picked him up. He was much heavier than Jamie imagined. His legs dangled as Jamie carried him to the bathroom and put him into the tub. Octo rippled red and white and again squirted ink at Jamie. He lunged away from the running water to the far end of the tub and gathered his legs in coils with the white suckers showing. I'm so sorry, Octo. Jamie hated to scare Octo so. Don't move, just sit still. Jamie turned off the water and ran back to the living room. He knew he had to settle himself down and get things cleaned up before Elsie came, but he couldn't stop crying. Stop crying! he said to himself and struck his fist hard against his thigh. Stop! Stop! Stop!

He righted the tank, replaced the cover and light which Octo had pushed onto the floor, and dragged it, stand and all, into the coat closet. He scooped up the gravel which had fallen onto the carpet and threw it in the kitchen trash. He went to the bathroom to get towels and Octo was still curled up, pale now, with dark rings around his eyes, and the water was murky with his ink. Just stay there. Everything's gonna be okay. Jamie grabbed three towels from the shelf, ran back to the living room, and started mopping up the water on his hands and knees. It stank and everything was still blurry even though he had stopped crying. His nose dripped and he didn't wipe it.

The buzzer buzzed.

Oh, no. He bunched up the towels quickly and threw them into the closet. Then he went to the bathroom and looked at himself in the mirror. His eyes were red and wet and his hair was a mess. He washed his hands, splashed his face, and flattened his hair.

The buzzer buzzed twice more, impatiently.

Okay, Octo, just be quiet. Everything's okay.

He went back to the living room, but before he could buzz her in, he heard Elsie coming up the stairs.

Jamie? What's goin on? You okay?

Jamie undid the latches and opened the door for her. Yeah, I was just going to the bathroom.

You sure? You been cryin? She touched his chin and made him look her in the eye.

Nuh-uh.

Phew. Elsie wrinkled her nose and fanned herself with her hand. That pet of yours stinks to high heaven. I don't know why your parents . . . but she didn't finish because she knew it upset Jamie when she talked bad about Octo. She limped to the kitchen, without noticing the dark spot on the carpet in the corner, or that the tank was missing.

She opened the fridge and bent over. Bologna again? Or beans and franks?

Bologna, please, said Jamie sitting down at the kitchen table.

How's your Mom and Dad?

They're all right.

Yeah? They gettin along?

I guess.

You're lucky, kid, you know that? To have a family that gets along. You should see my family. Get us all in one room, everybody's either yellin at each other or not speakin to each other. One or the other.

We don't always get along. We fight.

Take my little sis Sarah. She hasn't talked to her daughter for two years, *two years,* and ya know why? because she married an Italian Roman Catholic. Two years! You know how long that is? It's torture for both of them, but they won't give in and call the other. I tell her, Sarah, you're missing out on your daughter and your beautiful grandson. He's gonna grow up not knowing you. Why do this to yourself? But she won't budge. So stubborn, just like our father. Mayonnaise, right?

Right.

And mustard?

Right.

Anyways, so she won't budge. I tell her, you're a Jew livin in Bensonhurst. You run the risk. What do you expect? Now if I could show her your parents, maybe that would do somethin. Your mother's Jewish, right?

Yeah.

And your father's an Italian Roman Catholic, right?

He's Italian.

And look, they get along, they got this nice apartment, good-lookin kids . . .

Elsie pinched Jamie's cheek, but he didn't smile.

What's the matter, kiddo? You're not talkin to me.

Jamie had only been half-listening to her. He had thought he heard a sloshing sound from the bathroom, then decided it was his imagination.

I don't know, he said. I don't feel good. I'm sick.

Well go lay down, then. I'll call you when it's ready. You don't look so good. She put the back of her hand against his forehead. Go lay down. Rest. Go on.

On the way to his bedroom, Jamie peeked into the bathroom. Octo was still in the same position, but he had returned to his normal spotted pinkish-brown. Just a few more minutes, whispered Jamie and closed the door.

He lay on his bed, closed his eyes, and listened. Elsie began to sing in the kitchen. Jamie believed in the power of crossing fingers. He crossed his fingers on both hands and tried to cross his toes in his shoes. *Please don't go to the bathroom,* he said in his mind. *Don't even go in the living room. Just stay in the kitchen.* If she found Octo and saw the mess, she would tell Ma and Daddy, and they would hate Octo more than they already did. They might even decide he had outgrown the aquarium and make Jamie get rid of him. He imagined taking Octo back to the pet store. The man would be surprised to see how big Octo had gotten, and he'd say it'd be easy to sell Octo to a new owner. He'd put Octo in a tiny tank, and Octo's frightened eyes would watch Jamie. He wouldn't understand why he was back here. What if the new owner didn't feed him right or change the water? What if Octo poisoned himself? Now Jamie was crying a little, just imagining it.

Elsie's singing burst through the kitchen door and into the hallway. Jamie crossed his fingers so tight his knuckles popped. The bathroom door slammed. Then Elsie screamed. Jamie screamed too. He ran to his doorway to see Elsie backing into the hall, clutching her chest with one hand and holding up her pants with the other.

Elsie! It's okay! He just got out and I haven't had a chance . . .

What in the hell? Elsie tucked in her big shirt and zipped up her pants. Scared the livin . . . Look at me. I'm shakin like a leaf. What in the hell is that thing doin in there, boy?

Don't tell, Elsie, please! He just got out and I had to put him somewhere till . . .

Got out? Oh, God, I have to sit down.

Jamie followed her to the kitchen, tugging on her shirtsleeve. Please, Elsie, don't tell Ma and Daddy. It's nothing really. I just gotta put him back and everything'll be okay.

Quit pullin me, kid. Elsie sat down heavily at the kitchen table and put her palm to her forehead.

You're not gonna tell, are you, Elsie?

Settle down. Just give me a second. You said it got out? What do you mean, it got out?

He just pushed the lid off his tank and crawled out.

Oh, Jesus!

No, it's okay, Jamie wailed. He never did it before. I'll just stick the lid on tighter. Don't tell! Jamie clutched Elsie's arm and shook her.

Would you get off? Elsie pushed him. I won't tell, just settle down, kid. Quit cryin. I'm the one who just got the pee scared outta me.

So you won't tell?

No, I won't tell. None of my business, anyways.

Jamie sat down and wiped his eyes. Really?

Yeah. But you better clean it up. And if they ever do find out, I didn't know nothin and had nothin to do with it. You got that?

Yeah.

And you owe me one, kid. Now eat. I'm leavin. This place is too much for an old woman. Damn near gave me a heart attack.

Okay.

And don't go tellin your mother I left early, either.

Okay.

Don't get paid to deal with this.

After she left, Jamie cleaned up. He sprayed disinfectant on the carpet. He went to the bathroom, dipped the bucket into the bathtub, and nudged Octo toward it. Octo climbed in calmly. Jamie made all new water and used a second bucket to fill the tank. It took all afternoon. Then he tested the water in the tank and, very carefully, poured Octo in. He fastened the lid to the top of the tank with a few pieces of black electrical tape.

Since then, Octo has never escaped, though Jamie sometimes finds him snaking one leg up to press against the lid.

Rebecca hasn't talked to Jamie or even looked at him for two days. She goes through these phases when she's so sick of him, she has to pretend he doesn't exist. If he says anything to her, she gives him a dirty look or just turns and walks away.

This time she's mad because she's tired of sharing a room with Nancy. Jamie's always had his own room, she complained to Ma. Why can't *he* share for a while? Ma told her that Jamie is a teenager and needs his own space and went on about how he spends the whole day at home while she gets to go to school and to her friends' houses—talking like Jamie wasn't listening, even though he was.

Two days went by, Rebecca not saying a word to Jamie. Then, on the third day, Rebecca comes home from school earlier than usual, before Ma and Daddy are home from work. Jamie's watching videos on TV. Rebecca sits down on the far end of the sofa. Jamie looks over. She stares at the TV, scowling.

Hi, says Jamie.

Rebecca looks at him calmly, then turns back to the TV. They sit in silence, then Rebecca says, You know, you could, like, volunteer to share a room with Nancy. It's only fair.

Why should I?

'Cause! You've always had your own room, and I've always shared. I never get any privacy. I can't even talk on the phone in private. I'm either out here and everyone's listening, or I'm in there and

Nancy's crawling all over my bed wanting me to play with her. I have to shut myself in the hall closet to have a simple conversation!

You can take the phone into my room if you want.

That's not enough! I want to have my own room! Look, we can trade off. I can have your room for a few months, then you can have it back for a while, like that.

No. I need to be by myself.

Oh, screw you, Jamie! You get everything you want, and you just can't share, can you!

Screw *you!*

I hate you, you know that? Rebecca yells and throws a pillow across the sofa at Jamie. Sometimes I wish you'd just die!

Shut up! Shut up or I'll tell!

Screw you, you big baby! You are such a pain in my butt.

How am I a pain in your butt? I leave you alone. I don't even *talk* to you!

You don't even *know* how miserable you make me, Jamie. You should hear how the kids at school make fun of me! They say I have a retard brother and it must run in the family. I get that all the time because of you!

Jamie lunges at Rebecca, punching aimlessly. Rebecca shrieks, pushes him onto the ground, and kicks him hard. He pulls her down, and they roll across the carpet, punching and slapping until Jamie's head strikes the leg of the coffee table. He lets out a hoarse bawl and digs his teeth into Rebecca's arm. She pushes and scratches his face until he lets go and curls into a ball. I hate you! she screams. Her voice cracks and she sobs. She hits him again and stands up. I hate you so much!

You're gonna feel bad later for saying that, Jamie whimpers.

No I won't! she says, stumbling away. I'll never feel bad 'cause it's the truth, and I'll never say I'm sorry!

He feels beneath his eye. There's a little blood.

Look what you did! he cries

I don't care! She's standing beside Octo's tank, holding her arm where Jamie bit her. You're such a sissy! I can't believe you bit me! She glances down at Octo. You and your stupid ugly pet. She hits the glass with her fist and Octo glides to the opposite corner.

Leave him alone, says Jamie. He jumps to his feet and moves toward her.

Daddy's getting rid of that thing, you know, says Rebecca, backing away from Jamie into the hallway.

He is not!

Yes*sir!* I heard him tell Ma he's gonna pour Lysol in there and kill it.

What?

And she told him not to and he said it was the only way to get rid of it and you'd think it just died.

Liar! Jamie lunges for her but she runs into her bedroom, slams the door and locks it. Jamie pounds on the door. Liar! You're lying!

Am *not,* comes Rebecca's voice and she laughs meanly. Your stupid pet's dead!

Jamie howls and beats the door.

No response.

Rebecca! You're lying, aren't you? When did you hear that?

Rebecca is ignoring him now. She turns on her music, then starts to sing along. He pounds one more time then goes to his room, locks the door, and lies down, trembling. He thinks back to when Octo ate the hermit crab. It was the last one to go and the only one Jamie actually watched Octo eat.

He had been sitting by the tank watching the crab overturning gravel with its scissor-claws, looking for algae to eat. It was happier, Jamie thought, now that it didn't have to compete with the snails.

Suddenly Octo pounced, covering the crab with his legs and drawing it under his mantle. The crab scrambled under Octo for just a second. Then it was still.

Wow, Jamie whispered to himself, and he thought, Should I have stopped him? But how could I? He was so quick! Jamie had not known Octo could move so quickly.

Now, lying on his bed, Jamie thinks of how Octo fools everyone by being so calm. He spends his life sitting, watching, taking in what's going on, so everybody thinks that's all he can do. Then, when he needs to, he strikes quick like a snake.

Ma knocks on the door. Jamie?

I'm taking a nap, Ma.

Everything okay?

Yes. Go away, please.

Jamie lies on his bed thinking until Ma knocks again and says, Wake up, honey. Dinner's ready.

Okay. Just a minute.

He rolls out of bed, tucks in his shirt, and stands up straight. He walks out, down the hall, and into the dining room.

Jacob is laughing and smearing gravy across his face and kicking the legs of the high chair. Eat right, Jacob, says Ma who's spooning mashed potatoes onto his plate.

Daddy's cutting Nancy's roast beef for her and telling a story from work about how Johnny Rosso's gonna transfer to the

Bronx rather than deal with the district supervisor, who everyone hates.

Mommy, why isn't Rebecca talking? whines Nancy.

Mind your own business, says Rebecca.

Is there something wrong, Rebecca? asks Ma.

No. Tell Nancy to mind her own business.

Jamie! says Ma. What's that on your face?

Everyone looks at Jamie, who's standing in the doorway.

Huh?

You have a scratch on your cheek, honey, says Ma, standing up. You're hurt.

Oh.

Ma holds his chin and looks close under his eye and says, There's dried blood. Who did this?

Everyone's looking except Rebecca who's frowning down at her plate.

Jamie says, Rebecca.

Rebecca doesn't look up.

You two had a fight? Is that what's wrong? said Ma, turning toward Rebecca.

Rebecca shakes her head and says no quietly.

Ma turns to Jamie, who says, We were just playin, Ma. It was an accident.

Ma licks a napkin and wipes hard under his eye. Too much roughhousing. You two should be careful.

Ow! Easy, Ma.

They sit down. Jamie eats quietly while Daddy goes on with his story. Ma alternates between listening to Daddy and cleaning up Jacob, who has settled down now and is shoving one spoonful of mashed potatoes after another into his mouth. Rebecca doesn't look up. Nancy glances from Jamie to Rebecca, then back to Jamie. She begins to cry quietly. After a minute, Ma notices.

Nancy, what's wrong?

Nancy sobs and big tears fall into her food.

Honey! What is it?

Nancy wipes her nose and, between sobs, says, Jamie and Becca hate each other.

Nancy, they don't hate each other, says Daddy.

Mind your own business, Nancy, says Rebecca.

Shush, Rebecca! says Ma, then to Nancy: Sweetheart, everything's all right.

Stop crying and eat, says Daddy.

It's okay, Nancy, says Jamie quietly because he's next to her. Shhhh.

Nancy doesn't stop crying, but wipes her face with her hand and begins to eat again.

Jamie is surprised the next day when the buzzer buzzes at 1:00 and it's Elsie. She hasn't come since Monday, and it's Friday.

Elsie, you're back!

I'm back? Where'd I go? Just been a little sick.

Are you all better now?

I'm a little better. When you're my age you're never *all* better. How 'bout you? You been okay by yourself?

Yeah, Ma's been leavin lunch for me, and I just sit around and watch TV. Pretty boring. I thought maybe you'd quit, and Ma just hadn't told me.

Quit? Nah. Why would I quit?

I don't know. I thought maybe you just got sick of me.

What are you talkin about? Sick of my little friend? Elsie shakes Jamie by the shoulders and he laughs. No way!

Elsie sits down at the kitchen table and Jamie tells her about how mean Rebecca was to him, and about the fight. Telling the story makes his chest tighten and his eyes tear, but he stays calm, even when he gets to the part about Octo: And she told me Daddy's gonna kill Octo. She said he's gonna poison him and not tell me a thing about it.

Poison him?

Yeah. Pour Lysol in his tank and kill him.

Sounds like your sister's making up stories.

You think so?

Jamie, your sister's havin a hard time. You gotta leave her alone when she wants to be left alone . . .

I *do!*

. . . and sometimes you gotta leave her alone even when she wants your attention, ya see? Once you prove she can't make you laugh or cry just like that, she'll start treatin you like a real person. Things'll be okay, kid. Wait and see. Elsie puts her hand on Jamie's shoulder and heaves herself up out of her chair. She goes to the fridge.

Jamie says, So last night I didn't dream about anything but Daddy killing Octo. I spent all morning checking where all the poisonous stuff is, like Lysol, bleach, fingernail polish remover . . . sort of memorizing how everything's arranged under all the sinks.

Why?

So if I find Octo dead, and I see that the Lysol's gone or the bleach is in a different place, I'll know Daddy did it.

Jamie, your dad's not gonna kill it. And if he did, then what? There are more important things . . .

At least I'd know, Elsie. I'd know he did it.

Elsie was quiet. Then she said again, There are more important things, kid. What happens if the octopus dies on its own, eh? I wouldn't be surprised. It's way too big for that tank. It hardly moves anymore. What then? You gonna blame your dad for that?

Not if he doesn't do it.

I'm just afraid you're gonna get all upset and blame him anyways. Just remember, kid, he's your dad. He wants what's best for you and you gotta respect that.

What if he doesn't *know* what's best for me? What if he does what's bad for me?

You gotta respect him still.

That's not fair.

But that's how it works.

Well . . . he doesn't want what's best for Octo. That's for sure.

Ah, what're we arguin over, anyways? says Elsie, setting a bowl of soup in front of Jamie. Your dad's not gonna kill Octo.

But Elsie's wrong. Late that night, Jamie is going in and out of sleep. He can't get comfortable. In his dream he's in tentacles and branches and seaweed. He's holding his breath. Then he gasps, surprised that he can breathe water. Now he's out of his dream and out of sleep and he kicks off his sheet 'cause it's hot. Now he's underwater again, and the difference between being awake and being asleep doesn't make the same sense. He's at a wall of coral and he touches the surface. It's sticky. His hands stick. Then his nose burns at breathing bleach. Or is it just the thought of breathing bleach?

A sound from the living room yanks him out of sleep. He

knows what it is, but he can't believe it—partly because he knew it would happen (and can never believe when those things actually happen), and partly because his head's only halfway out of the dream.

He's out of bed and stumbling down the hall and he hears Daddy's voice. *Shit . . . Shit!*

There's the tank, knocked to the floor, the glass broken in a spiderweb pattern. One big and one small spot of wet are growing on the carpet: the smelly tank water that poured against the wall over the socket, and the ammonia that grows out of a plastic bottle. Daddy's coming toward Jamie. Aw . . . now, Jamie . . . The lights go dark, then flicker back on. Octo is white on the orange carpet with all his legs coiled tight to him, polka-dot suckers exposed. Jamie, c'mon . . . back to your room. . . . The socket sparks and the lights go off, except the hall light. Jamie's mind is crying like a baby, and his body is flying into a Fit of Rage.

Daddy grabs his arms and holds him down. Easy, Jamie! Settle down!

Ma, in her nightgown, rushes in. Ron! What's going on? she asked. She clutches Jamie from behind and he elbows her, but she holds on. Shhhh, she whispers into his ear.

Between Ma and Daddy, Jamie can't move.

What did you do, Ron? asks Ma.

What do you think? he asks. Shoulda done it long ago.

How can you say that?

They think Jamie's too frantic to hear, but he's taking it all in.

Let me go! he says again and again, first screaming; then his voice cracks into a whimper: Please, let me go.

They let him struggle away.

Nancy! yells Daddy, Go back to bed! Nancy, who was standing in the doorway in her nightgown, runs off.

Jamie picks up Octo. His long legs drop limply, almost to the floor. Where are you taking that? asks Daddy. Jamie, sobbing, carries Octo down the hall. Ma follows him to the bathroom and watches him put Octo in the tub and start filling it, adding sea salt bit by bit.

Now, Jamie, what are you doin? Daddy asks from the doorway.

He might live! wails Jamie.

Jamie, your pet's dead. And it's not just me that killed it, either.

Go away! screams Jamie. I hate you! This is the worst thing that ever happened, and you did it!

Don't you talk to me like that, kid.

Daddy steps forward, but Ma stands to stop him. Ron, don't. Just leave him alone.

What, has this place gone nuts, that a kid can talk that way to his dad?

Go away! screams Jamie.

Ron, go. I'll take care of this.

You two are nuts. Ya gonna bring that thing back to life? The thing is dead. And it's happier that way, I'm sure.

No he's not, says Jamie. He might live if we keep him in here. We can take him to the ocean, and he'll get better.

Take him to the ocean? Daddy laughs. But Ma is already saying, Honey, it's all right. We can take him to the ocean.

What did you say, Judith?

Go, Ron! she yells.

No, this is crazy. This isn't right. You think a kid could talk to his dad that way when I was a boy? My Pop woulda smacked me upside the head. None of this coulda happened. This is all so fuckin nuts! An octopus livin in my fuckin living room, stinking up the place, and Jamie thinks it's the most important thing on earth. It's all that matters, right? Even though everyone else hates it and the girls are scared to death of it, right? Now Jamie runs the place. We gotta pay good money to feed the ugly thing, so Jamie don't get upset. Fuckin *nuts!* And if it decides to take a stroll around the apartment while we're at work, no problem! Jamie's in charge now, and the octopus can do what it likes.

How did you know that Octo got out? cries Jamie.

Elsie. How else?

Ron!

Jamie's head drops, and he doesn't move or say anything for a moment. Daddy clenches and unclenches his fists. Then Jamie says in a small voice, so they know he means it, I never want her to come here again.

Oh, honey, says Ma and puts her arms around him.

I don't want her anymore. I don't want any more care providers.

See? says Daddy. Thinks he runs things now.

Judith waves him away.

Jamie turns his back to Daddy and looks down into the tub.

Don't worry, Jamie, says Ma as she turns off the water. Tomorrow morning we'll take him to the ocean and let him go. He'll be okay.

Daddy stomps down the hall yelling something, but no one's listening now.

Jamie puts the bucket on the floor of the backseat, gets in, and braces it between his knees. Nancy sits in the back, too, and Jacob's in his seat between them. Rebecca's in front with Ma.

While Jamie was putting Octo into the bucket, Ma had woken up Nancy and Rebecca and got them excited to go on rides at Coney Island. Jamie knows it's just because Daddy's grumbling and needs to be left alone.

They drive. The avenues are like the alphabet—M, N, O, P— leading to the ocean. They pass housing developments, nice neighborhoods with lawns, Jewish men with hats and beards.

Octo looks deflated. The water is foggy with bits of brown flesh.

Suddenly the signs aren't in English anymore. Nancy asks what kind of writing it is, and Ma says it's Russian and it means we're almost there.

Ma parks and they get out of the car. She puts Jacob in the stroller, and they walk across the lot. The bucket is heavy, so Jamie has to walk slowly, squinting in the bright sun, but he doesn't want Ma to help him. They walk down a narrow alley between two old brick apartment buildings the color of sand. They climb stairs to the boardwalk. Rebecca helps Ma with the stroller. Old people sunning on benches open their eyes just a little to watch them cross the boardwalk. Steam is rising from the sand into the hot morning. The stroller won't go onto the sand, so they all wait on the bottom step while Jamie walks across the beach. Nancy wants to go, too, but Ma says to hush, let Jamie do it alone.

It's hard to walk on the soft sand. Jamie staggers across the beach and climbs onto a jetty made of big rocks extending out into the ocean. He hugs the bucket to his chest. It smells bad, but then ocean air gusts the smell away. Jamie hobbles from stone to stone down the jetty, careful not to slip.

About halfway down, he stops. The water looks deep, with sand churning up from the bottom. He puts the bucket down on a flat stone and sits down beside it. A big wave comes and soaks his foot. The water is freezing cold. Much colder than Octo's tank.

But it's okay, because Jamie knows that Octo is really dead. Daddy killed him. Slowly, he tips the bucket. Water trickles, then pours out, then Octo slides out like a lump of trash. He plunges into the water and sinks out of sight. Bye, Octo, says Jamie.

He imagines Octo coming back to life down there in the dark. Filling back up like a balloon, spreading his legs and crawling to deeper water. He imagines it, but his heart isn't in it. He's just telling himself a story, like Ma and Daddy do, to settle him down.

He leaves the bucket there because he doesn't need it anymore, and returns to the others.

They all walk down the boardwalk toward the amusement park. They stop at an open-air restaurant for fried-egg sandwiches and Tater Tots, and sit on a bench watching the ocean while they eat. Nancy and Rebecca are talking about the rides, but Jamie doesn't listen.

People are jabbing umbrellas into the sand and setting up lawn chairs. Two black women in bathing suits wade in the water up to their knees. They laugh and shift from foot to foot, hugging their arms to their chests.

When they're done eating, Ma gathers the trash and says, Well kids, ready for the rides?

Nancy and Rebecca ride the bumper cars, but Jamie stays with Ma and Jacob. The park is getting crowded. He feels nervous. He's not used to being around people.

Ma laughs at Rebecca speeding around in her tiny car, and at Nancy butting heads with a teenage boy. Look, Jamie, she says.

Yeah, I see.

They go to another ride, where Nancy and Rebecca spin around in cars shaped like bumblebees. The cars go up and down and Nancy shrieks and giggles. After they get off, Rebecca says that she's bored with these kids' rides. She says she wants to ride the roller coaster. Ma says okay, but it's the last ride 'cause Jamie's tired.

Jamie can't know this but, down on the beach, Octo has washed up onto the sand. He lies in a brown tangle of legs until a wave comes and rearranges him, taking two legs and setting them like clock hands. Then another takes him farther onto the sand and turns him upside down so if you looked, you could see the little beak in the middle where all the legs meet.

Two little girls, twin sisters, are digging with pink plastic shovels. One notices Octo.

What is that thing?

I dunno.

They walk over and look down at him.

It's like a sea animal or something. *¡Mira, Mama!* she calls to their mother.

¿Mama, qué es esto? asks her sister. She takes her plastic shovel and gives Octo a shy prod.

Their mother, sitting in a lawn chair, lifts her sunglasses. *¡No lo toques, mija!* she yells.

Ew, says the first girl. That thing is so gross.

But what is it?

I dunno.

¡No lo toques! calls their mother.

• • •

There are two signs at the roller coaster: one has an arrow and says YOU MUST BE THIS TALL TO RIDE THE CYCLONE, the other says NO SINGLE RIDERS.

Oh, no! whines Rebecca. Nancy's too little, and I can't go on by myself. She looks up at Ma.

Don't look at me, laughs Ma. I've got Jacob.

Rebecca turns to Jamie. Jamie, will you go with me?

Jamie kicks at the dirt.

It'll be fun, Jamie. Please? Otherwise I can't go at all.

Jamie is silent. He doesn't want to go.

And I *really* want to go, says Rebecca

All right, he says finally.

They walk between the rails and give the man their tickets. There are only four other people riding. They climb into the middle car, the man locks down the guard rail, and the cars begin ticking forward slowly.

Thanks, Jamie.

Jamie doesn't respond.

I'm sorry I fought with you and stuff. I'm sorry I scratched you. . . . And I didn't mean it when I said I hated you. I was just mad.

The car lurches into an incline.

Jamie says nothing. He isn't mad at her, and wishes she'd just leave him alone. He watches the blue sky as they climb up and up.

And I'm sorry your pet's dead. I really am. I'm sorry about everything. Jamie? Come on. Please say you forgive me.

But suddenly they're roaring down. Their hearts leap into their throats and they both scream. Rebecca's scream has a laugh in it, but Jamie's is pure terror, like he's facing death. He grabs Rebecca's arm tightly and doesn't let go the whole ride.

ONJ.com

THE FOLLOWING TALE concerns a lost world that I lived in and some of its residents whom I knew personally. It shocks me how recently this world existed, and how quickly it vanished when the economy soured. It was the world of advertising, graphics, and the Internet at the turn of the twenty-first century, and its former residents are now unemployed, or differently employed, or clinging to a thread of a job by working long, hard hours where they used to play online poker and make long-distance calls. Untold numbers have suffered the ultimate indignity: being forced to leave New York. And although darker and more recent events make it less and less likely, all are awaiting a recovery and a return to the good old days of short hours and fat checks.

I am, at least.

But on to our story: It was a Monday morning, and a young graphic designer named Olive plodded down the fluorescent-lighted hall, murmuring greetings to her coworkers. Then she stopped. Sitting in the cubicle outside her office—*her* cubicle, where *her* freelancers worked—was a handsome man, around her age, late twenties, swiveling back and forth in the chair like a bored kid. Olive had forgotten that she had scheduled a new freelance Web designer for that day.

Now, most freelancers, on their first day, either arrived nervously, smoothing their dark blue interview suits or, more often, sauntered in wearing T-shirts and tattered cargo pants, even shorts in the summer, revealing how fresh they were from college or San Francisco. Not this one. He wore a fitted orange-and-brown gingham shirt, expensive jeans, and smart black shoes. His black hair was brilliantined and combed back from his squarish brow thirties-style—unfashionable and terrifically flattering.

Olive drew herself up (he hadn't seen her yet) and glided into the cubicle, holding out her hand. "I'm Olive. We'll be working together."

"Craig," he said. His hand was big and warm. "I love your glasses."

"Thank you," said Olive, pushing them up. "Um, just let me put down my stuff and I'll get you started."

She went into her dark office and hung up her coat. As soon as the door sighed closed, Mary, a copywriter and Olive's office-mate, said in her high-pitched, breathy voice, "Your freelancer is cute." Mary was typing at such a speed that she must have been e-mailing a friend. She typed copy at a pained rate, required absolute silence, and took frequent breaks to do yoga in the corner.

"He's gay," Olive whispered. "He just complimented my glasses."

"Oh, darn," sang Mary, as if to a kitten.

Olive's own spark of disappointment had already cooled to relief. For one thing, it would be easier to work with him. Also, she had a special interest in gay men. This is a cluttered little corner of

Olive's personality. Allow me to illuminate it, using imagination and facts that I picked up in conversation from Olive herself:

Let's say that two days earlier, Olive made a short list of life-decisions, or resolutions. It was a quiet Saturday afternoon, and she was sitting at her kitchen table watching a flock of pigeons, black specks following a senseless, beautiful choreography of loops and falls, expanding then contracting like a single life-form that came in and out of focus against the brilliant swatch of sky framed by a high-rise apartment building and an Episcopal church. Beyond them, through a corridor of dull-hued masonry, she could see the spires of the Queensboro Bridge.

Here are the decisions Olive wrote, perhaps on the back of an envelope:

- *Go out with K J & F less*
- *Go out below 14th St more*
- *Draw*
- *Say what I want*
- *Make a gay friend*

Some footnotes: K, J, and F were Kelly, Jill, and France, three friends she had picked up at various former jobs. Advertising friends, a class whose population increased as school friends and one-on-one friends dwindled.

To "go out below 14th Street more" meant to continue to have an active social life but to edge away from those bars in the East Twenties and midtown, where she went with Kelly, Jill, and France and where the men were rich, drunk, and dumb. It was too easy. They were men of whom, if she saw them in the street or on television, she would say, "I would never kiss them," but whom she kissed anyway. Dumb guys who just knew a few tricks—an expensive haircut among them—to fool her. Below 14th Street were the East Village dives she used to know in her art school days, as well as the upscale lounges that had sprung up since. Maybe this was her niche. Or, maybe she should make it her niche. Because the East Twenties was just a younger version of the Upper East Side, and the Upper East Side was just a richer version of her parents.

Next, her resolution to draw meant pulling her art box from under the sink (which she did later that afternoon), unscrewing the crusty lid off the india ink pot, and making some fast, wild line drawings on paper with a brush and diluted ink. In years past she had made these every day, and her walls had been papered with strange, meaningless symbols.

Now her walls were nearly bare. Her apartment was beautiful. She was a graphic designer.

But note the next resolution, lest it seem that Olive was merely longing to recapture her art-student self: "Say what I want." If her goal was to go back in time, she would have resolved to say less, not more.

Our Olive, her newest advertising friends would be surprised to know, used to be a quiet person. Inwardly, she used to wail, laugh, sing, yearn for people, throw tantrums, while outwardly she sat pleasantly quiet, not brooding, but projecting something thoughtful, unthreatened, demure maybe, but silent. That's what she imagined, anyway, to project into the minds of the other art students, the people on the subway, the girls in step aerobics, but in reality it is hard to say what these residents of the past took her for, as quiet people attract less attention than they imagine, except, maybe, from other quiet people. Over the years she had opened up, partially as a result of realizing that the world was less awesome and its citizens less complex than she had assumed. That is what five years in advertising had taught Olive.

So no, for Olive to "say what she wanted" would take her farther down that road from quietness. What she wanted was not to recover something lost in herself, but to go through a minor self-reinvention—one that would make her happy (because she was not happy), yet leave her utterly recognizable.

But this last resolution, to make a gay friend—what could that possibly mean? Olive must have had a high-school friend, a chubby, sensitive boy the jocks called "pansy" and "fag," with whom Olive took drama classes and rolled on the bed laughing—she can't remember at what—until she thought she'd pee. Someone who confided in her his pangs of guilt and loneliness and in whom she confided the endless hurts she suffered at the hands of her parents and teachers and less-sensitive friends—hurts she folded and swallowed, somehow believing that her multiplied suffering would someday configure into revenge, on her parents at least. A friend who begged her to stop swallowing these hurts lest her soul be poisoned. A gay man who now lived on the West Coast, whom she still loved dearly, and e-mailed frequently, yet whose physical distance made a meaningful friendship impossible. Surely it was he that Olive resolved to replace.

No. I don't believe Olive ever had that gay friend. She had had some gay friends over the years, but never that one.

She saw, though, how other women related to their gay friends—the purity and fun; the sense of an outward-looking friendship, one based on aesthetic pleasures, people-watching at cafés, and gossip. That distinguished the straight woman/gay man friendship in her mind: looking outward. No hidden attractions or silent contests, but, rather, appreciating the world together wildly, then criticizing it bitterly, for these seemed to be the same thing to gay men, and she liked that. No dependence; she could go for two weeks without calling and he wouldn't even notice. Then she could cry on his shoulder for three days straight over a breakup, and he'd cheer her up.

She was being silly, she knew. Unrealistic. But on paper was just the bullet point—just the start. "Make a gay friend."

This would explain why she was not really disappointed when this handsome and stylish Craig complimented her glasses. (Incidentally, Olive treasured compliments on her glasses above others because she felt especially worthy of them. She had gone through a hundred small wire frames at the shop, narrowed it down to five, and then, just for fun, tried on a pair of thick green tortoiseshell frames, something a rich old Italian woman would wear. They were astonishing. She loved them. Dramatic, desexualizing, Fellini-esque, but very, very New York. Noteworthy, and Craig had noted them.)

(And as long as I'm dealing with Olive's appearance, I should also mention her heavy-lidded, sultry beauty. While Mary, blond and waifish, was considered more beautiful by the other women at the agency, Olive, with her substantial Latin thighs and her thick chestnut hair, was a favorite of the men.)

Olive looked through her piles and files, and realized she was unprepared to begin the project for which she had hired Craig: to create a mass e-mail featuring a link to a magazine subscription site. She would make the graphics and he would do the necessary programming.

"Craig," she said, emerging from her office, "it's going to be a little while before we can get started. In the meantime, why don't you do a little research of existing sites to get ideas?" She explained the basic concept of the advertisement.

He nodded. "Sure . . . sure . . . excellent."

She slipped back into the dark and read the copy she had to work with. The morning was spent toying with the project, then being interrupted again and again by account managers with other tasks.

"Craig"—she thrust her head out the door close to noon—"I'm sorry to keep you waiting. There've been some interruptions."

"Don't worry about it. Freelancers never do anything on Mondays. People never get their shit together until Tuesday."

He used rude words prematurely, but his eyes sparkled and made it charming.

"That's true. I'll remember that. Should I send you home till tomorrow?"

"Only if you want," he said. "I'm happy to get paid to sit here."

"Great. Thanks."

Mid-afternoon, Debbie, one of the senior account managers, burst into Olive's office.

"Olive," she whined, "this looks like shit. There're white lines between the graphics and the drop shadows." This was Debbie's technique—the sneak attack. Burst in, bark you into submission, into promises of rapid reparations, then ask how your weekend was. "I need you to get on this fast. The client's on my ass."

Say what you want, thought Olive. "Debbie, I have a lot going on. The blues aren't due on that till Thursday. I'll get to it tomorrow."

Debbie's expression shifted from startled to outraged when Mary emitted a low "*Shhhh*."

"Let's talk in the hall," said Olive. She and Mary had worked out elaborate, somewhat monastic rules about conversations in the office, and two to five in the afternoon was the Great Silence.

Debbie led Olive out the door, and they had a suffocating five-minute conversation, none of which need be repeated here. Then Olive made one of her frequent trips to the ladies' room where she locked the door and opened the painted-over window just to breathe a little and hear the traffic.

The agency, it should be noted, was in an old, narrow office building on Park Avenue South, just above Union Square. It was not a glamorous agency. It did not produce innovative print ads or television commercials. It dealt in direct mail, or junk mail, and its e-mail equivalent, commonly referred to as "spam." And although this was a lucrative business, you wouldn't know by the space. Drop ceilings. Brightest White walls. A row of cubicles lined the long hallway, where the bottom rung and the freelancers worked; doors between the cubicles led to small offices that the "creative talent" like Olive shared; then, across the hall from these, behind frosted-glass walls, lay the account managers' offices—larger, with windows. The light that filtered through the frosted glass was the only natural light to be had, except in the bathroom.

Calmed, Olive walked back to her office. She felt somewhat awkward because Craig had overheard her unpleasant conversation with Debbie. But, then again, she had held her own.

"Olive, what's your full name?" Craig asked.

"Olive Navarro Jacobson. Why?"

"I'm at a numerology and tarot Web site. It does your numbers for free if you type in your name. Just for fun. Olive . . . Navarro . . ."—he typed and rolled the double *r*—". . . Jacobson. That's quite a name."

"Navarro's my mother's maiden name. Cuban."

"Wait a minute!" gasped Craig, "ONJ!" Then, gazing up at Olive in mock awe, he sang, *"Would a little more love make you stop pretending? Would a little more lo-ove make a . . . happy ending?"*

"What's that?" asked Olive.

"Oh, come on! *Got to believe we are ma-gic, nothing can stand in our way . . ."* He swayed to his own music.

"Olivia Newton-John?"

"Yes, ONJ. You share her hallowed initials."

"All right, whatever," Olive chuckled.

"Don't shrug her off, Olive, she's a genius. Here, I'll print out your reading. What's your sign, by the way?"

"Libra."

"No! It's too eerie. You share her sign as well."

"Why Olivia Newton-John?" Olive asked.

"Oh, don't disappoint me. Are you one of the many who can't appreciate the genius? I sensed more from you. Maybe it was just the glasses."

"Well, I love *Grease* . . ."

"Don't talk to me about *Grease*."

"Why? She was great in *Grease*!"

"Of course she was great. But if she hadn't shone so brilliantly"—his throat seemed to constrict—"she wouldn't have faded so fast."

Craig was right. The next day, Olive had her shit together and the project was under way. He was fast—too fast, almost—completing the subterranean machinery before Olive could make all the surface visuals. He typed wildly, using the three or four fingers of the self-taught computer geek rather than the ten of a business-class graduate. He sang softly to himself as his hands flew talonlike over the keyboard.

At six-thirty Olive extricated herself from a meeting to find that Craig had already gone. There was a yellow Post-it on her door. "ONJ—check out my work—I mailed it to you—see you tomorrow." Next to these words stood a little cartoon woman, standing proudly, hands on hips, atop a pile of magazines and stacked coins. It was done in black pen, except the woman's glasses, which were in green. Clearly it was she, standing atop the spoils of their little enterprise. Her heart erupted in vain, childish pleasure.

"What are you grinning about?" cooed Mary.

Olive showed her the drawing.

"Cute!"

"Isn't he so great?" said Olive, sticking it to the border of her computer screen.

"I wish I got to hire freelancers," said Mary.

Olive gave a noncommittal, "It's not usually so much fun."

But the truth was, she loved that she got to hire freelancers. She loved the process of requesting one from the account manager, being approved, meeting the new ones, welcoming the repeats, orienting them to the task at hand in words deprecating to the project, to direct mail, and to business in general. Most of all, she loved that she was a good "boss," if that word can be used; she knew for a fact that her freelancers accepted jobs with her over others at better agencies. She made direct mail bearable.

But until now, she had shown a different side with the permanent staff. With them, she praised the agency and its product in that grating corporate language I won't quote here, lest it turn the reader against Olive. And it is unnecessary, since Saturday's "Say what I want" resolution. Although she hadn't realized the scope of the resolution, she now felt liberated from having to feign respect for her business. She would do her job well, but she wouldn't pretend that direct mail was a good thing in this world.

She had tested this, to some success, in the meeting from which she had just been freed. On the wall was projected a letter from Eastern Capital to its credit card-holders offering them additional insurance, in case their cards were misused. This was something of a scam, as the card-holders didn't have to pay for unauthorized charges to begin with, but that was all in the fine print. About ten people were in the meeting, half of them account managers, but for some reason it fell to Olive to read aloud the text of the letter. The heading, in big green letters said "*Another offer from Eastern Capital you'll never believe.*" But Olive read, "Another offer from Eastern Capital you'll never *read*," Everyone chuckled, and Olive continued with the letter.

Now, nailing a videocassette of *9 to 5* to the CEO's door, this wasn't, but with her little joke, Olive had succeeded in saying what she wanted. She had spoken what they all knew: No one reads junk mail. She was careful to make some comments later in the meeting to show that she was still "on board," but was her heart in it? No. Was she a pretender? No.

Over the rest of the week, Craig took every opportunity to make Post-it cartoons of ONJ. Sometimes, as in the first, it was clearly

dark-haired, toothy Olive. Other times it appeared to be Olivia
Newton-John, only, wearing green glasses. Craig was an excellent
cartoonist. Olive stuck the drawings to her computer screen, until
there were too many and she began to feel embarrassed. Then she
made a file folder called "ONJ" and stuck them inside.

We open the file to see rows of ONJs yearbook-style: Here's one
of the Olivia Newton-John variety, wispy hair, headband, green
glasses, pirouetting on roller skates à la *Xanadu;* here's our Olive
sleeping with a keyboard as a pillow, glasses folded on the desk
beside her; here's a close-up of Olive's face, a good likeness, actually,
with a bubble that says, "Go home. Bye-bye."

On Thursday afternoon, ahead of schedule, they finished the
project. The offer looked perfect. The graphics were immaculate
and all the links worked. The account manager was pleased.

"Can I buy you a drink after work?" asked Olive.

"No, I have plans," said Craig. "And tonight's a school night,
for you, anyway. I'll meet you after work tomorrow—then we can
get really shitfaced."

So it was agreed. The bar at a French restaurant in the West Village. Craig's idea—Olive had never been there.

The next morning, Olive e-mailed Liz, the human-resources
lady, telling her that Craig had done "top-notch" work quicker than
expected and was a thoroughly pleasant person to work with. She
cc'd the account manager, who sent a concurring e-mail.

She went home to change after work and was a little late to the
restaurant, but Craig was later still.

Over the first martini, they covered a little background information they had never had time to reveal at the office: where they
were from, parents' marital status, number of siblings, etc. They

touched on the project, and Olive told Craig about the human-resources e-mail. He thanked her.

He seemed a little bored, and when the second brim-full martinis were placed into the little puddles left by the first, Craig took the reins: "Let's play a game. It's called Suit Yourself. I'll explain the rules as we go along. Ahem. Olive, would you rather kiss Mary full on the mouth, with tongue, or spend an entire evening with Phil?"

"Phil the network guy?"

"The same."

"Ew, well I'd rather do neither, but I suppose I have to choose one, right? I'd kiss Mary."

Craig arched his eyebrows, smirked grotesquely, half-shrugged, and said, "Suit yourself."

"What, you'd spend an evening with Phil? That'd be like torture. At least the kiss would be over in a second."

"Two rules," said Craig. "One, a question can never be repeated, meaning that you can't ask me the same question I ask you. We may choose to offer this information for the sake of conversation, but that is our prerogative. And two, the questioner always responds to the answer with the sentence 'Suit yourself.' The bitterer the better. Your turn."

"Okay. Craig, would you rather . . . eat a bug . . . or screw Phil?"

"I would rather eat a bug, Olive."

"Suit yourself."

"Oh, come on."

This time she hammed it up: "Suit yourself."

"Lovely."

The game progressed, Craig leading into dirtier and dirtier territory. But Olive showed a certain penchant for the game. And

Craig was surprisingly well acquainted with the agency's staff members for the short time he had spent there.

"Craig, Dearest, tell me . . . would you rather eat Debbie's ass, or jerk off every male staff member?"

"To ejaculation?"

"To ejaculation."

"Very tough, very tough. I would rather jerk off every male staff member."

Olive delicately placed her hand to her chest, wincing sourly. "Suit yourself."

Craig applauded. "You're a natural, Olive, a bona fide natch!"

As the third martinis are being poured, let us step back to consider the scene. Unlike the other young women here, Olive is not wearing a little black dress. She is wearing a strange acrylic sweater with geometric shapes trapped in one bold, horizontal bar across her breast. It is a thrift-store sweater, which would be unfitting if it didn't fit her like a glove, and if her slacks weren't so smart, pointing to the irony. Craig wears suit pants with no back pockets and a black shirt. In short, they casually wear carefully assembled outfits and make the most attractive pair at the bar.

But what, an outsider might wonder, *are* they? Their laughter is too bellowing to be that of a cautious new, or weary old, romantic couple. Are they the straight woman/gay man alliance Olive had envisioned? No, they are not observing the surroundings with an appreciative or critical eye, their eyes are fixed on each other's. They have too much to talk about to be recently acquainted friends. They must, an outsider would conclude, be old friends, cousins even, long separated, catching up.

The restaurant is one of the seeming thousand mid-range

bistros that have sprung up in Manhattan recently, but which, unlike the others, abandons the hackneyed antiqued brasserie mirrors for more of a hunting-lodge atmosphere. Behind the bar hangs one of those lush still-lifes with opulent vegetables amid folds of velvet and a goose, draped languidly, as if in repose. As if its recent butchering were a mere inconvenience, a little jostle before bedtime. And a red pool table, unused, the balls racked and ready, separates the bar area from the restaurant. This pool table is absurd. As if this weren't Manhattan; as if space were free.

"Do you mind personal questions?" Craig asked.

"Love 'em," said Olive.

"It's a somber one."

"Okay."

"Have you ever thought about suicide?" he asked.

What a strange one this Craig was! He avoided the common mid-range of polite conversation, either ducking under with crass jokes and paltry observations, or sailing overhead, with equal fervor, into discussions of lofty, meaningful things. And Olive was beginning to realize that he wouldn't drop the mock-grand, bordering on British, way of speaking he used at the office. The line between his ironic and real personae must have been worn away years ago from frequent crossings.

"Of course. Hasn't everyone?" answered Olive. "Not recently, but all through art school. I was so miserable at SVA, I wanted to throw myself down a stairwell. At the same time every day, the same stairwell, going to the same class. I'm surprised I didn't do it one day. All it would have taken was a little . . . woop!" and she simulated, as well as she could on a bar stool, launching herself over a banister.

"And what kept you from doing it?" asked Craig.

"My mom. Imagining my mom hearing that I was dead. What about you?"

"Mine was a little earlier. I was happy in college, for the most part—relieved. Junior high, though, I felt like the world was boring and hateful. I was thirteen and I felt like I had seen it all, and it was hateful. For me, the scene was to be at my reading desk, with a pistol. *Young Werther*-like."

"And what kept you . . . ?"

"Something I learned in science class. Octopuses are incredible creatures. They're very complex and not fully understood, but scientists know that they can sense chemical things through touch." He paused. "That means they have a sense that we don't have. Something outside of our five senses. Each little sucker along their legs moves independently, and each has this extra sense, like being able to taste with your fingertips, and having a thousand fingertips. But something different . . . molecular . . . I can't compare it because we don't have it."

"How did this save your life?"

"Just knowing that there was an entirely different sense, completely unknown to us, sort of gave the world back its mystery."

"There's always a specific reason, for you, isn't there? You always have a story."

Craig smiled, apparently relishing the possible birth of an argument. "If you look into things, Olive, there *is* always a story!"

"I don't buy it."

"Look, I have the advantage of posing the questions tonight. But if you look into your experiences, you find links to specific origins."

"Hmmm."

"And if there isn't a story, make one up."

And so on.

Martinis the fourth.

". . . It's impossible to generalize," said Craig, "but generally, gay men are damaged, dangerous people. They feel wronged and are looking for vengeance. And they're obsessed with youth and beauty to the point of, all of them, feeling old and ugly."

"But you just said that they were all stuck in a prolonged adolescence," said Olive.

"So? That doesn't contradict."

"I think you're full of shit. The gay men I have known, if they feel 'wronged,' then it's made them kind, not evil."

"You've got to be careful, though," warned Craig. "Straight women don't get the full picture. You know, there are some gay guys who collect these female friends—wild women, drunks, fat girls who wear Versace. They don't treat them as friends. They treat them as playthings. Their only real affection is for other gay men. I see it all the time. It makes me sick."

"I don't think we know the same gay guys," said Olive.

The mood was lightened by a new round of Suit Yourself, using the people at the bar, and then, perhaps feeling the evening winding down, Craig asked, "In one word, what is the one constant of your life?"

"No fair," said Olive. "I've been the first to answer all these questions. You go first."

"Okay . . . Hmm, I actually didn't have an answer prepared." He paused. "Insomnia."

Olive considered that for a moment. Then she thought of her own answer. "Loneliness."

There was an audible lull in the neighboring conversations that made Olive feel stupid.

Craig said nothing, but gave a pout and squeezed her hand, right there, atop the bar, between their martini glasses. His was empty.

"On that note," said Olive, standing, "let's get out of here. Whoa!" She held the bar for a moment.

"Snuck up on you, huh?" said Craig. "You're not gonna finish this." He swigged the last of her martini and stood to go. "Oh, I almost forgot. I have a gift for you."

"Really?"

Craig pulled a CD, still plastic-wrapped, from his coat pocket. "ONJ's *Totally Hot*. I consider it her finest hour. It's available only on import."

"Craig, you're so sweet!" Olive gave him a little hug. "You're just what I wanted."

"What?"

"Nothing. I can't wait to listen to it."

The air outside was brisk and, after their good-byes, Olive decided to walk home. It was a long walk, but it energized her and cleared her head. As she ate some cold chicken and listened to her messages, she realized it was only ten-thirty. Kelly, Jill, and France were at a bar just around the corner, so she brushed her teeth and went to meet them.

She found them beneath the fronds of a large palm in the corner of an expansive, high-ceilinged, but nonetheless claustrophobic-making space, all three flushed nearly to the shade of their cosmopolitans. The men, it seemed, had been here since after work. Shirtsleeves, suspenders, and sweat marks Olive considered repugnant evidence that they lived too far away to go home for a quick change. She offered to buy France a drink if she were willing to brave the crowd at the bar. France accepted. Olive held out a twenty, but France reached past it to snatch a fifty.

"Fifties are the new twenties," she said and was swallowed by the crowd.

Kelly and Jill proceeded to brief Olive on who was here, but as we know, she had already talked and listened herself silly tonight. She was in the mood to watch, to sail overhead on invisible strings like Peter Pan on Broadway and view them all from above. And then float out the window and over a bluish and shimmering London . . .

Staggering in her heels like a bad drag queen, France returned with Olive's martini. On and on Kelly and Jill talked. Olive pushed up her glasses often, pulled back her hair, cleared her throat, but she couldn't shake the feeling that she was in a steam bath crowded with mannequins. Eventually she excused herself to the ladies' room, and left.

At home, Olive put on the Olivia Newton-John CD and lay on the couch. It seemed inane seventies pop, and she only half-listened as she recounted the night's events. Her dizziness subsided now and she began to drift away. . . .

On Monday morning, there was an e-mail from Craig. It was an ONJ cartoon: ONJ standing, arms at her sides, swaddled in an eight-armed hug from a cute blue octopus. Cheek to cheek, they both smiled blithely, eyes drowsy under elevated eyebrows. Underneath the drawing it said, "ONJ is not lonely."

Within a week, Craig was back at the agency. Olive stumbled onto him in someone else's cubicle.

"You're back."

"Yes, thanks to you."

"Craig, I really appreciated that e-mail. It was so nice. Really."

"Don't mention it," he said. "Actually, I'm making a Web site dedicated to you."

Olive winced. "You're not."

"Oh, don't worry. It's just the cartoons and stuff. There's no explicit references to you."

Still, Olive balked.

"I won't give out your telephone number or anything. It's just for fun."

"All right."

"ONJ.com—I'll let you know when it's up."

Later that morning, disaster struck. Olive and Mary were called to the office of McNab, the head of the agency. A month earlier, the office-mates had collaborated on a project—an e-mail credit-card offer for Eastern Capital. "Time's running out on a great offer," said the headline against a fuchsia screen. Underneath sat a fat black bomb with animated sparks springing from the fuse. When the recipient clicked on the bomb, the offer "exploded" onto the screen: "Congratulations! You've been selected . . ." etc.

Two days ago, the offer had been sent to over 100,000 people.

By unfortunate coincidence, on the same day, a teenager some-where in the heartland had created a computer virus that spread quickly across the country via e-mail. In the media's near-immediate warnings, it had been dubbed the "Sweetie" virus because the sub-ject line of the e-mail was "Hey, Sweetie!" and when one opened it, one read the words "You're screwed!" before one's hard disk was erased.

Suddenly, the public was doubly wary about e-mail from strangers, and clicking on a bomb was unimaginable.

Although the account manager had approved the project, and although the client had gone so far as to call Olive's bomb idea "exciting," Olive and Mary, it became dreadfully apparent in the course of their meeting with McNab, were being blamed. "Of the ten percent of recipients who opened the mail without deleting it out of fear," McNab informed them, "ninety-two percent exited and deleted the mail immediately upon seeing the bomb. Eight percent actually clicked on the bomb. Do you know what that means? Only 800 people opened the offer—slightly fewer, it turns out, than reported the e-mail to the FCC." There was a tremor of rage in McNab's bullfroggish voice, and Olive pondered technology's annoying ability to immediately put numbers to these things.

The meeting was long and dry. Olive and Mary said nothing. McNab never raised his voice and drew no conclusions. He explained the situation in exhaustive detail, and then sent them to their room.

They walked quietly down the hall, Mary having already broken into deep *Ujjayi* breathing. Once secluded, Olive turned to her, hoping to commiserate, but Mary walked directly to the corner and stood on her head. Olive would have to seek solace elsewhere.

She went to Craig's cubicle. "I just got chewed out by McNab."

"This calls for a business lunch," Craig replied.

"I agree. I'll get some petty cash and chalk it up to 'creative strategizing.' After lunch, I'll call my headhunter."

(Olive was always in loose touch with her agent. Like everyone her age, in her business, she hopscotched from job to job almost semiannually. I may have given the impression she had been with the agency a long time, but it was only *her* version of a long time—just under eight months.)

They had a bottle of Muscadet with lunch. She began recounting the meeting to Craig, and he laughed until tears glittered in his lashes. Fueled by his laughter, her retelling shifted from tragedy to comedy, and she realized that this shift was exactly what she had hoped he would facilitate.

Eventually, over dessert, Olive said, "Enough shop talk. I have a question: What is the most degrading thing you've ever done for money?"

Craig leaned forward. "Well," he said deliciously, "after college, during a short stint in the Peace Corps in Honduras—"

"I had no idea!" Olive interjected.

"I became . . . what's the word? . . . acquainted with the drug trade. On two trips home, I had a little . . . extra baggage."

Olive considered him searchingly.

"A condomful of cocaine up my ass."

"You're lying!"

"The first time it was easy. It sort of . . . lodged up there and I just felt a little . . . ripe, but not uncomfortable. But the second time, I just couldn't keep it in. I finally had to poop it out and put it in my medicine bag. I thought, 'If they catch me, they catch me.' They didn't. And you?"

"Well, it's not on my résumé," said Olive, "but I used to do graphics for porno Web sites. You know—banners with two-celled animation of women giving blow jobs." She *O*ed her lips and moved her head back and forth, chickenlike.

"Of course."

"I enlarged the cocks."

"For real," said Craig. "Can you enlarge mine?"

"No."

"By the way, what do you think of *Totally Hot*?"

Panic gripped Olive's heart. "I love it," she said.

"What's your favorite track?"

"The first one," she almost asked.

"You haven't listened to it, have you!" Craig seemed genuinely angry.

"I'm so sorry! I was drunk that night—I fell asleep listening to it. After that I forgot all about it."

"Olive! I can't believe you!"

"I promise I'll listen to it carefully tonight—as soon as I get home—I'll let you know tomorrow how I liked it."

Craig was silent.

Olive was irritated. She shouldn't have apologized so much. She was letting him inflate the incident's importance. It was childish. But gloom was settling, and she didn't want the lunch to end unpleasantly.

"These dessert forks are adorable," she offered.

"They are," Craig agreed.

"I kinda want to steal one."

"You should," he said mildly. "You could sneak it out in your cunt."

Olive's expression dropped. "Oh . . . that's not nice."

"What?"

"For you to say that. It's just weird."

"Oh come on. I was kidding."

Olive didn't know what to say. Craig's neck reddened and his Adam's apple ducked up under his chin—a swallow—then reappeared.

"I was just talking about shoving stuff up my ass," he said.

"But you offered that. You introduced it," said Olive. "Besides, that's such an ugly word."

"Cunt? Oh, jeez! Get over it."

They sat unhappily until a perceptive, white-aproned waiter dropped the check.

The headhunter was as resourceful as usual, and within a month Olive was enduring yet another obligatory late-afternoon good-bye "party" in the conference room. In addition to the usual cupcakes, some male staff members, realizing (Olive assumed) this was their last chance to hit on her and hoping to warm her up for after-work drinks, had brought several bottles of champagne. Sure enough, before the clock struck five, she had three somewhat-pleading offers from doughy men who didn't realize they had drunk more than she, and had lower tolerances. She gently repelled them.

Mary, who avoided the party until the last minute out of either an unspoken affection or hatred—Olive would never know—finally arrived and gave Olive a bony hug.

"We'll have to do margaritas sometime," said Mary. "I have this great place in Chelsea."

"Sure," said Olive, not mentioning that tequila made her vomit.

The party ended and Olive rode the elevator down alone with her box of stuff.

She would never meet Mary for margaritas, and it was with mixed sadness and relief that she realized she would not take with her any friends from this office—only Craig.

The evening following their "business lunch," Olive had sat down at her kitchen table with a cup of steamed soy milk and amaretto to think about the *cunt* comment. Had she overreacted?

Craig's profane suggestions were characteristic and usually charming, and until that moment, Olive had encouraged them with her laughter. Her reaction to the word *cunt* had probably startled him as much as the word itself had her.

So she decided to let it go, and the tension faded as Olive made regular visits to Craig's cubicle during the weeks leading to her departure. She listened to *Totally Hot* and cultured opinions on the different tracks, but left it to Craig to broach the subject and, as Craig had apparently made a similar decision, the silly album became the one ingrown hair, if you will, in an otherwise smooth and pain-free friendship.

In any case, Craig had moved on from Olivia Newton-John, and was now passionately advocating Christine McVie to an uncaring world: "Sure, Stevie is the sex witch but, if you listen closely, Christine is the *soul* of Fleetwood Mac. People say her voice is muffled—I say she knows the art of subtlety. Is there an ounce of subtlety in Stevie's bleat? Christine wrote 'Warm Ways,' Olive!"

"I don't know 'Warm Ways.'"

"Well, it beats 'Rhiannon's' ass any day of the week. And 'Gypsy' is just a gyp."

"How many times have you used that line, Craig?"

"Let's see, that makes four. And I'll have you know it went over marvelously the first three."

And so, a month after the Eastern Capital explosion, a week after the good-bye party, Olive was in a nicer office being paid more to do more interesting work: print ads for magazines. Actually, the position was more administrative than creative, but Olive was pleased nonetheless. She was in charge of routing projects through her department, and of hiring the appropriate freelancers. And, delighting in the idea that Craig was part of the "team" the new agency took on when they hired her, Olive scheduled him almost every day. However, they were both so busy in their new positions that they didn't get together outside of work until the weekend following Thanksgiving.

They started at ten with martinis at that same French restaurant in the West Village, perhaps meaning to re-create the hopeful, friendship-launching atmosphere of their first visit. From there they went to the holiday party of one of their new coworkers—Carmen, a stylish and self-assured Photoshop pro, who seemed capable of an event. They arrived at eleven, a full two hours later than the advertised start-time, but were not late enough. The unknown variable to the party's equation, husband Ned, negated Carmen's charms. The apartment was tasteful but too well-lighted, exposing the sparseness of the crowd which was made up of Ned's dour teetotaling siblings down from Westchester, and Carmen's coworkers—those generous enough to persist in hope of some payoff, but whose white-knuckled holds on glass stems were evidence of inner fight-or-flight struggles. Carmen herself was wasted.

Olive considered this a prime opportunity to practice her ruthless new approach to parties: She guzzled one drink, said some hellos, peed, plucked Craig from a circle of strangers, and moved on.

They were silent in the stairwell, out of respect to Carmen's fallen image, until Olive ventured, "Nice place, though."

"Sure," replied Craig. "Ned's cousin Madeleine was a riot. She kept referring to Washington Square Park as the place where the Knicks play, and no one would correct her."

Olive grimaced. "She was talking about the Knicks?"

"She was."

They emerged into the cold, arranged their scarves, and stood looking up and down the street.

"I wish we had another party to go to," said Olive.

"Well, look around. I think there are quite a few parties we could go to."

Indeed, on this one block of West Twelfth Street, lined with cute brownstones and naked trees lit so lovingly by streetlamps that they could have been a backdrop, there were several people hurrying along with paper bags showing the logos of liquor stores and bakeries. One woman tended to a white poinsettia as her companion checked building numbers.

Olive grinned and nodded and they fell in line behind a troop of gift bearers. They paused as their leader buzzed, then filed into the building, up the stairs . . . and this was more like it: a low-ceilinged apartment clogged with semi-attractive Upper West Siders. "Hi! Hi! Glad you could come," said the host, nodding them in.

"I only wish we had a gift!" whispered Olive to Craig, who agreed.

Two overdressed bartenders standing behind a table gave silver shakers one-stroke shakes, then poured out frothy somethings. The only light came from huge tangles of white Christmas lights hanging in the corners stalactite-like. Simple yet effective, thought Olive.

They got their drinks and made a plan to explore the party separately and rendezvous at the bar.

After some minutes of floating, Olive moored herself near a man and two women who were surveying the crowd somewhat regally, but who smiled when they saw her.

"I don't know, it just feels sort of slapped together. I mean, look at the lights," said the man.

"The Christmas lights?" said Olive boldly, "I think they look nice."

"Yeah," said an Asian woman, "But compared to last year . . ."

"Chuck shouldn't have made him do it," said a white woman, to the others' assent.

"I wasn't here last year; I just came with a friend," said Olive.

"Well, see baldy over there?" With his glass the man indicated a tall, thick-lipped man whose glossy smile resembled the flavored wax lips from Halloweens past. "That's Dan. He works with us. He's an editor."

"A few months ago he started AA," said the white woman. "He came to my office and apologized for anything he might have done to offend me when he was drunk."

"Me too," said the man, "only he had never done anything to apologize for."

"He apologized to everyone, regardless. It's something you do in AA," said the Asian woman.

"Anyways, Chuck is his lover . . . I'd point him out, but I don't see him. Dan begged not to have the Christmas party this year—too much temptation—but Chuck wouldn't give in. And now look at poor Dan."

"Drunk," said the white woman.

"He looks pretty sober to me," said Olive.

"Exactly," said the Asian woman. "That's how he always looks when he's drunk. Hey, don't laugh."

"I'm not laughing," said Olive, "I'm just smiling."

"Why?"

"Just because I always gravitate toward the critics' corner. It's a good thing."

"Well, that's us."

They introduced themselves. The hour is too late and tipsy for new names, so I'll stick to genders and ethnicities.

The criticism continued and Olive watched Dan the Host, beads of sweat glistening atop his bald crown, feign interest in a story which he could probably only half-hear, as one of the gigantic (rented?) speakers stood at his left shoulder. She thought what an awful thing it is to host a party (she had never done it)—to throw open your doors to a deluge (or, worse, a trickle) of ingrates who want to drink your booze and then comment on *your* degree of drunkenness. If it's no fun, too bad: Your own party is the only one you can't leave. She made a drowsy self-promise to be always a partygoer and never a thrower.

A movement to dance in the center of the room was slowly losing steam. Olive caught Craig's eye at the bar—it must have been meeting time—and gave a slight nod that meant, "Come here after you get your drink; these people are entertaining." Then she raised her empty glass to add, "And bring me one, too." By the time Craig crossed the room to where they stood, he had put away half his drink.

"Of course, Chuck hardly drinks," the white woman said. "He just goes on his occasional crystal binge."

"I myself am just getting over a debilitating addiction to crystal," said Craig, joining the circle. "Crystal Gayle."

Olive introduced Craig to the critics.

"So you two are party-hopping tonight?" asked the white woman.

"We are," responded Craig. "The first was a positive snorefest . . . then this one"—his eyes wandered archly—"the next should be really good. It's at that French model, what's-her-name's. The crowd should be semi-famous and the dress and hors d'oeuvres, *haute,* very *haute.* Oh, what *is* her name, Olive?"

"I don't remember either," she giggled.

"Well, we'd better remember before we get there."

"Where are you from?" the Asian woman asked Craig.

"Illinois, why?"

"Oh, I thought you might be British. I couldn't tell."

"That's just his fake accent," blurted Olive. "It gets worse the more he drinks. It's Madonna-like, wouldn't you say?" These last words were an attempt at mimicry.

A brief, truly emotive look flashed across Craig's face. It was jarring, as if he had cast aside his handsomeness for a moment and she saw his real face before the veil fell again. She had seen this once before: when he realized she hadn't listened to *Totally Hot.*

Thinking she had embarrassed him, Olive gave a mock-penitent "*Awww*" and half-hugged him for the audience, a sloppy apology at best, and he retorted generously, "Can I help it, Olive, if you did not enjoy the privilege of being raised on *Masterpiece Theatre?*"

Conversation continued, and Olive forgot about it, but allow me to leave her for a moment and look closer into those eyes that flashed mysteriously. Craig was not embarrassed. Even if embarrassment was a threat to him and not a plaything, a ball he would rather catch and toss back than dodge, why would he be embarrassed in front of these drab publishing people? People who considered *New Yorker* staff writers celebrities? No, she could have embarrassed him all night, and he would have delighted in it.

His expression instead bespoke a rushed rewriting of his version of Olive. She didn't get his main joke—the one that he had assumed she had gotten from their first conversation. Hadn't she loved—

imitated, even—the grandiosity, baroque in its silliness, that she now reduced to a "fake British accent"? He felt what the nice people call *disappointment* but what he calls *betrayal*.

Craig interrupted someone to say, "I'm getting another drink. Anyone want one?"

"I've barely started this one," said Olive.

"I'll have a scotch," said the man.

"Me, too," said the two women, offering their glasses.

"Why don't I just bring over the bottle?" said Craig.

"If they let you," muttered the white woman.

A few minutes later, Olive caught a glimpse of Craig arguing with the bartender. She turned her back to make the image go away and concentrated on what was being said.

"Your friend's stepping on people's toes," said the Asian woman.

"Oh, he's just like that," said Olive. "He doesn't mean anything."

"No. He's literally stepping on people's toes."

Olive turned to witness Craig crashing through the crowd, leaving a wake of looks that could be described as withering had they been at all heeded. He held a whiskey bottle aloft.

"That was intentional!" he insisted once he and Olive were in the stairwell pulling on their coats. "I was trying to get those stodgies to move around a little. No one was mixing anymore, much less *dancing*."

As if summoned by the word, a muffled beat descended from above. Craig smiled and pointed up.

"All right. One more," laughed Olive, "but be nice and stick to club soda."

They climbed two flights, found the humming door, and knocked. A pretty, pierced woman answered.

"We're here!" sang Craig.

"Hi," she said.

"We brought you a little something." From his coat pocket, Craig produced a small porcelain bowl full of little shell-shaped soaps.

"Oh. Thanks." The woman took the bowl gingerly as if it were very hot. "I'll give it to . . ."

Craig and Olive entered. There were maybe thirty club-kid types in the room, the music was almost deafening, the sweet smell of marijuana filled the air . . . but no one danced. Instead they all faced the deejay in the corner. Some people nodded their heads to the beat. No one spoke.

Craig and Olive immediately knew they were much too old for this party, even though everyone was about their age.

On their way to the door, Craig said to the woman, still holding the bowl, "Can I have my present back? Kidding! Happy holidays!"

The woman wrinkled her nose, and they passed into the hall.

"One more! That one didn't count!" insisted Craig, hooking his arm into Olive's and dragging her down the stairs and into the street.

"I think I've had enough fun for one night," she said. "Where did you get that bowl?"

"Let's follow those people over there . . . a good late party." He was pulling her arm too hard. She freed herself and they followed the last of a trio entering a narrow brownstone. Olive was surprised to find herself suddenly in a foyer with terra-cotta walls and boots in the corner. This was a residence; one of those brownstones which had escaped being divided into apartments. A tall man, maybe fifty, with a salt-and-pepper beard was greeting by name the people Craig had followed in. There was no one else in the room. Then the man turned to Craig and Olive.

"Hello. Have we met?"

"Oh, a while back. I'm Craig and this is Olive."

Two old women wandered in from what may have been a parlor, still bidding good-bye. They retrieved their coats from a rack. There were very few coats there. Olive had the awful realization that they had walked into a family's home at the tail end of a very intimate gathering.

"Are you friends of Anthony's? Or Kate's?"

"Kate's," replied Craig taking off his coat, "although she won't own up to it. She associates us with a very rough time."

"Oh?"

"You know," Craig said under his breath, "the abortions . . . the Oxycontin . . ."

The man's eyes widened, and the two departing women interrupted just then to say good-bye.

"Craig," Olive whispered furiously, "what the hell are you doing? Let's get out of here!"

"It's an adventure," he said without turning toward her. "Let's go this way. I smell wine."

He took a heavy step forward and the man freed himself from the women to stop him. "Hold on, let me get Kate for you."

The man disappeared into the other room.

"Come on, Craig. This isn't funny!"

"Quit freaking out, Olive. I can do this."

Olive turned to see the two women standing at the front door, watching timidly. When she turned back, the man was bringing in what seemed to be his college-age daughter, followed by several other family members. The girl regarded Craig and Olive silently, then turned to the man, shaking her head. "I don't know them," she said.

"Just *who* did you say you were?" asked the man, gathering his beard in a gesture more menacing than thoughtful.

"Kate! How could you?" Craig pleaded as Olive slid toward the door. "Remember Tulsa? The bingo game? I saved your life!"

"Call the police," said the man, nudging Kate into the other room.

"No, *we're* calling the police! That little bitch owes me money! Olive, hand me my phone."

The man marched toward them, pointing to the door. "Get the hell out of here!"

Olive darted into the street, with Craig behind, stumbling, as he had been pushed by the man. "This isn't over, Kate! I *know* you!" Craig called out as the door slammed.

Olive stood there, stunned, and was not given the chance to regain her senses before she was again being dragged down the street.

"Oh, my God," cackled Craig, "that was *so funny*!"

"It wasn't funny!" said Olive.

"I know it was scary, but think of the story it'll make!"

"No! It was stupid and mean. Would you stop pulling me?"

She jerked to a stop, sending him staggering forward. He recovered himself and spun around, puffing. His face was red and veiny. He took one step toward her and shoved her by her shoulders. She fell back, sitting hard onto the pavement. She stood and brushed her coat off, watching him in disbelief. He was crouched, breathing like an animal. She began to laugh.

"You . . . are so . . . *fff*——" (she said this slowly and deliber-
ately, so he would know that she was still deciding where the sentence would go, but however it ended, it would be irrevocable)
"fired."

"What?"

"You are fired!" she said, happily amazed at herself. "Don't come
to work on Monday. I never want to see you again." Still laughing
incredulously, she started to turn away.

"You . . . are so . . . *fat!*" Craig yelled with the same inflection.

"That just shows what a lame ass you are!" she said.

"What?"

"Thinking that *fat* is the worst thing you could call me." She
turned and, with a casual air, walked away.

That is, essentially, the end of our story, for I couldn't decide whether
I should chase her down and apologize, or try to provoke further
delicious confrontation, so I did neither. I watched Olive walk down
that cute little block on West Twelfth, then disappear around the
corner, and I never saw her again.

I will, however, imagine my way back into Olive's little world
yet again, in order to preserve the mood and form of our story and
bring it to its right completion:

Olive spent the rest of the weekend worrying that I would
ignore her dismissal and show up at work on Monday. But I didn't.
Nor on Tuesday. And on Wednesday she started to relax and settle
into the fact that I was gone.

But on Thursday there was an e-mail from me, subject line: "I
Deserve to be Shot." It read, "Dearest ONJ, I was a brute. Can you
forgive me? The Web site is up. Love, Craig."

There was a link to ONJ.com, which Olive clicked without really thinking. The computer muttered and a large "ONJ" appeared on the screen, with the *O* wearing green glasses that danced back and forth. Beneath this, it flashed "Loading . . . Loading . . ."

But then a sick feeling stirred in Olive's belly, and she wondered, did she want to see this Web site? Would it be a cute reminder of our friendship that would send her back into my arms? Or would it be some obsessive payback in the form of weird cartoons? Or would it erase her hard drive!

Olive made her decision, and I know this because the window that counted visitors to my Web site remained at zero for weeks and weeks, until I finally took it down.

She pushed "Cancel."

Dunford

THE MORNING HIS wife and son flew to LA was bright, so Mark Dunford took work off and drove to the beach on the south shore. The tide was out, and the tidal plain stretched far off toward the shimmering horizon. Paisley-shaped lagoons and sandbars looked like huge bays and islands viewed from miles above. The sand was the color of pale flesh. A family was leaving, quickly crossing a land bridge, holding down their flapping hats. The wind would have snatched off their hats and carried them up past Mark, over the dunes. He would have liked to have seen that.

He crossed the land bridge to a great sandbar and walked out across the tidal plain. After minutes of trudging, leaning into the wind, he reached the surf where plovers darted back and forth, always an inch ahead of the foam, poking their beaks into sand. Transparent crabs tiny as spiders scurried about. They disappeared into the sand with every footfall, then reappeared after the foot lifted. Mark felt like a giant.

He looked up and was startled to see two girls in bikinis lying on a sand island like beached mermaids. Weren't they cold? He walked slowly ahead because it would be obvious if he changed his course to avoid them. He could hear their voices, but only hard sounds, the Ts and Ks. The tones were lost to the wind. When he drew close enough to make out their words, they began to whisper. They're making fun of me, he thought. I'm the creepy man alone on the beach. He jammed his hands in his pockets and picked up his pace. He couldn't resist glancing over his shoulder after he passed, though, and he saw that they were still looking. He felt a little thrill. Maybe they weren't making fun of him; maybe they were admiring him. Some girls liked older men. After all, he used to be handsome, and he still had most of his hair, and his wide shoulders had not been completely blunted by years at the computer. He lifted himself tall, and all the little pains in his back and shoulders evaporated. Other men he knew were optimistic, why wasn't he? How would things be different if he had been optimistic over the years? Maybe he'd be thousands of miles away, single and happy. Or maybe he'd be here, but still in love with Susan and sharing in what she and their son Pullman shared.

He walked for a long time, dreaming. Then he found himself trapped by the tide at the end of a sandbar. He took off his shoes, rolled up his pants, and waded through the icy water. He laughed. His pants were dry-clean only, but he didn't care. On his way back to the car, the girls and their island were gone.

2

Mark always stayed up after Susan and Pullman had gone to bed, watching whatever was on. It didn't matter, because all he cared about was the commercials. After midnight they ran ads for escort services. One showed beautiful girls sunning on the deck of a sailboat. You could see their hard nipples through the fabric of their bikini tops. Another had a woman in a tight evening gown stepping out of the back of a limousine. She wore stiletto heels with straps that crisscrossed at the ankle. "Why be alone?" a sexy voice asked. "Call Society Escorts." There were only about ten of these commercials that ran over and over again, but they only got better with each repetition. Here's the part where the pretty Chinese girl blows me a kiss, Mark would think, and she'd appear. He named some of the girls and imagined the dirty things they'd say in bed.

Mark usually fell asleep on the couch and slept there all night.

So he had the number memorized. He called as soon as he reached the car because if he waited, he'd lose the nerve.

"Society, Charlene speaking."

"I'd like to make an appointment for an escort," Mark said confidently.

"Are you currently one of our clients?"

"No, I'm not."

"All right, sir, let me explain a little bit about us. Society Escorts is a listing service for professional escorts across Suffolk County. We're available twenty-four hours a day, seven days a week. We are very selective and we screen our escorts thoroughly, but they work as independent agents, meaning their rates and services are determined by them alone."

"I understand," said Mark.

"Great, then why don't you tell me what kind of girl you have in mind."

Mark balked. He wanted to ask if he could just have one of the girls from the commercial, but that seemed stupid. "Well, I hadn't really thought about it."

Charlene laughed. "Hair color? Body type? Race? We work with lots of different girls."

"Could I look at pictures?"

"Certainly. We have an excellent Web site. Do you have a pen?"

"Uh, my computer is down. Can I just come by?" Mark didn't want to go home. He wanted to meet Charlene face-to-face.

"Yes. We're in Centereach, though. Is that convenient?"

"Perfect."

The office was in an industrial park, and the sign in the window said *Society, Inc.* He tapped on the glass door and Charlene buzzed him in then came around the desk. She was overweight and seemed like a mother. "You must be the one who called from the cell phone. I didn't catch your name."

"John," he said, and shook her pillowlike hand. The office had fluorescent lights and drop ceilings. There were large chrome-framed prints of tropical flowers on the walls.

"Have a seat," said Charlene. She seemed completely at ease. "We have two different books you can look at. I'll start you with this one, and you just take your time."

She placed before him a Naugahyde-bound photo album, and turned to her computer. He opened the album carefully and scanned the first page "About Society Escorts," catching the phrase ". . . served the community since 1991 . . ." He turned to the first spread. On the left was a sheet that said "Melody" in grainy computer calligraphy, then listed Melody's measurements, age, likes, and dislikes. On the right was a head shot of Melody. She had frizzy bleached hair and crooked teeth. Pages of snapshots followed with little air bubbles trapped between the photos and the plastic sheets. She appeared in different outfits—a cocktail dress, a bikini, cutoffs and a T-shirt—posing in the same backyard, apparently, on the same afternoon. Melody had sloping shoulders and impossibly round breasts. Her face was pale and her body tan. Last of all, Melody was pictured swimming nude in the pool, looking over her shoulder at the camera. Her buttocks were a white blur through the waves.

The phone rang, and Charlene rose. "I'm going to grab that in the other room. You just take your time."

Mark examined one pretty young woman after another. He could pay any of them to have sex with him. But he couldn't tell if he desired any of them. He was looking for one of the girls from the commercials.

Charlene returned. "My son," she chuckled. "He wants to have all his Little League friends over."

"I have a son myself," said Mark.

He liked Charlene. She helped men buy what they needed. Did her son know what she did for a living? But maybe the phone call hadn't been her son at all, but another john, and she didn't have children, and her name wasn't Charlene.

"Could I look at that other book?" Mark said.

He opened it to a girl with a familiar face. She had rich, shoulder-length brown hair and a spray of freckles across her nose and cheeks. She didn't narrow her eyes like the others, like a porno star, but gave a vulnerable stare with her lips hanging. He recognized her, not from the current batch of commercials, but maybe one of the old ones they had discontinued.

"I'd like to see this girl—Tanya," Mark said.

"Isn't she lovely? And a great personality; I think you'll enjoy her. When would you like to see her?"

"Now. Tonight, if that's possible."

"Let me just see if she's available," said Charlene. She disappeared into the back again.

He read Tanya's statistics. She was twenty-one. She liked dogs and Dr Pepper. She disliked winter and "too much TV." Mark wondered how much it would cost, and if Tanya would charge different amounts for different things.

Tanya was unavailable that night. The earliest he could see her was the next day at noon.

Mark picked up White Castle hamburgers and two bottles of wine on the way home. He celebrated in front of the television. Then, feeling groggy, he went upstairs and lay diagonally across the bed. It was Susan's bed, really, California-king-sized, which is bigger than king-sized. He wasn't tired enough for sleep, just drunk enough to dream. Charlene interviewed him with a clipboard while he humped a hole in the mattress.

"How long have you been studying medicine?" she asked.

"Twelve years." It was a lie.

"Well, then, go ahead."

He looked down at his forearm, which was open. There was a slit from the back of his wrist to his elbow. He could see pink, capillaried tissue and a strip of bone emerging from underneath. He looked up at Charlene, who rose to answer the phone in the other room.

He opened his eyes. The pillow was wet with saliva and his forearm was numb from being at an angle under his body.

3

Back in the eighties, when they were still poor and happy, Mark bought Susan a thirty-five millimeter camera with all the adjustables and a tripod. He left it on the breakfast table for her to find. She woke him the next morning by jumping onto the bed. "Let's go! I want to try it out." Her small face with its sharp nose and thick black eyelashes wore surprise so beautifully!

They drove out through the meadows and marshes, then over a ridge, and Long Island Sound opened before them, still and gray under the white May sun, a great plain of steel that they could drive out onto if they wanted. Mark loved going to the water. Only then did he feel that he lived on the Long Island he had looked up in his atlas after his first date with Susan, back when they were sophomores at the University of Washington. (Where was she from? he had wondered, as he turned the heavy pages. Then he found it. Long Island was huge. It stretched away from New York City along Connecticut's underbelly. Mottled with bays, it splintered at its farthest end into smaller islands. It must be beautiful, he thought.)

Mark sped along the shore and Susan clicked a frame out the open window, advanced, adjusted, then clicked again.

"Those pictures aren't going to turn out, honey. Do you want me to pull over?"

"No," said Susan. "I'm experimenting. Go faster."

And he did, up onto the bluffs from which they could see Connecticut, then down through the little beach towns that were just beginning to wake up for summer. "Let's go all the way around," said Susan, so they drove out the North Fork, took the ferry to Shelter Island, crossed it, then passed down through the Hamptons. They didn't return home till after dark.

One morning a few weeks later, Susan told Mark she was pregnant. He was overjoyed, and as he rattled off plans and expectations, Susan smiled sadly.

"Susan, you aren't happy," he said.

"It just seems too soon. There's so much stuff I wanted to do first."

"Like what?"

"Oh, you know. My art and stuff."

"Susan"—Mark looked at her sternly—"whether or not we have a baby, you can do whatever in the world you want to do."

Mark was haunted by two memories: his mother sinking into depression when he was ten, and his father making him choose a career when he was sixteen.

"Thanks for saying that," she said. She was silent for a few minutes while Mark stroked her hair. Then she seemed to awaken. "You're so good," she said embracing him. "How did a selfish girl like me end up with such a good, good Dunford?"

People sometimes called him "Dunford" like that, usually when referencing how good or dependable he was. He couldn't remember when it had started. Growing up in a logging town near Puget Sound, it never occurred to him that his last name was odd or ugly. Some college friends had joked about it. And then, when he and Susan were planning their wedding he had tried out the name aloud: "Susan Dunford."

"Oh," she had said, "I was planning to keep my last name."

"Really?"

"Yeah. You don't care, do you? It's not the whole feminist thing, I just don't really like the sound of 'Susan Dunford.' Are you hurt?"

"No," he said. "I'm surprised, I guess. . . . No, I don't care."

The guys at the architecture firm used the name in a slightly denigrating way: "Have Dunford do it," when *it* was a particularly tedious task. Susan's family used it in a teasingly affectionate way: "How's Dunford treating you?" the only conceivable answer to which was "Just fine."

With their child, who was a wiry, gorgeous little boy they had named Pullman after the town in Washington where they had gone to school, Dunford was a character Mark would play. "Look at Dunford," Susan said to the toddler in her lap, and Mark ran into a wall. He backed up, rubbing his head and scowling, then ran into the wall again. The child squealed and giggled. Mark looked at the wall angrily and, with determination this time, ran into it. The child was in hysterics, writhing against Susan. The Dunford act never got old.

When Pullman was old enough for day care, Susan returned to work. For two weeks her eyes were dim, and she was quiet during the evenings. Mark worried that she was becoming ill. Then Susan made a proposal; "Let me try just doing my art for two years. If nothing happens I'll go back to work full-time. I'll even get some miserable high-paying job so you can have your turn; you can go back to school or switch jobs. . . ."

Mark agreed without reservation. He loved her pictures, and it would be good for Pullman. And, deep inside, Mark felt a quiet satisfaction that he need not, for the next two years, worry about the fulfillment of his dreams.

So in the mornings Pullman went to day care and Susan went to the darkroom. In the afternoon she picked him up, and off they went to take pictures. Pullman considered picture taking very serious business. He held lights for his mother. He moved lights for her. He ran around the yard with lights as she held down the shutter. He swam in the neighbor's pool with glow sticks. And in many of the resulting pictures he appeared, always blurred and floating mysteriously like a skinny little spirit.

At Susan's first solo show at a gallery in Bridgehampton the six-year-old Pullman led strangers around the gallery by the hand, pushing people gently out of his way. "This was when I took Christmas lights and shook them up and down like this while my mom took a picture."

Mark stood with a friend from work, drinking red wine and marveling at his wife and son. How did Susan know all these people? She was stunning with her bold rouge and wet-looking curls piled atop her head. She and Pullman were of a very different breed from Mark, two aliens sent from the planet of the bright and beautiful to live with him as some sort of experiment.

Susan sold five prints that night.

The eighties turned into the nineties, and the two-year agreement was forgotten, but Mark didn't care. He didn't want to be special and couldn't remember if he ever had. Susan could be special for them both. He worked longer hours and they paid him more. Then he came home and watched TV.

One day after work he went to a dealership and bought a blue Mercedes sedan with leather interior and a sunroof. He made a lot of money and he might as well show it. Susan was convinced that it was a company car. "You're telling me you just went and bought a big Mercedes?" she said, standing barefoot in the driveway with her arms folded.

"Yes, Susan, I did!"

"It's the firm's," she said.

"No, I bought it," he laughed. "Why don't you believe me?"

"Because you wouldn't! It's an old-man car!"

"I like it, Dad," said Pullman.

"Thank you," said Mark. "That makes two of us."

And it surprised Mark, as the years passed, how much he did

like the car. It was sturdy and ran well and everyone respected it. He took it to the car wash often because he loved the way it looked when it was spotlessly clean and brilliantly buffed. And, more than this, he loved going through the car wash—the gushing foam, the spinning brushes, the great, roaring blower that drove away the droplets like fleeing pests. The whole experience was like being in the eye of a hurricane, remaining untouched.

Pullman skipped the fifth grade and was soon acknowledged, even by the older kids, to be the brightest and best-liked in the class. Susan's photographs were being selected for one after another group show in New York City. And then, in what she described as her first big break, a nonprofit gallery in Soho invited her to show her photographs in their project room. "A room all to myself, Mark!" she said at dinner. "It's the next best thing to a solo show!"

Pullman bounced in his chair. He had already known the news.

"Sweetheart!" said Mark, coming around the table to hug her. "Congratulations."

They planned to attend the opening as a family and stay in the City for the weekend, but Mark knew from the beginning that he wouldn't go. He made up an emergency at work mere hours before it was time to leave. Susan burst into tears. "Do you have any idea how important this opening is to me?"

"Honey, yes! You know I wouldn't miss it unless it was absolutely unavoidable."

Her eyes were desperate. You're hurting me too much, you're breaking something, they seemed to say. But all she could manage aloud was, "Mark, what are you doing?"

"Susan, there'll be more and more of these openings. I just know it. And I'll be at every one, I swear."

He knew she suspected that he resented her success, but she was wrong. What he felt wasn't resentment, but something much more blank. His feelings were losing their shape.

He spent the weekend in front of the TV.

Years passed. Mark remembered, back when he first fell in love with Susan, thinking that the only way his love could possibly die was if he got to know her completely; if he knew every nook and cranny of her personality and there was no mystery left. But his love died for the opposite reason. She was becoming more complex, more beautiful, and more mysterious. Without meaning to, she had outrun him. His exhausted love was being pulled under by his drowning spirit.

When the blue Mercedes lost its shine, he traded it in for a new black one, a little bigger, with all the new features. Susan and Pullman nicknamed it "the hearse."

Mark began to masturbate in the car wash. He didn't know why he felt this urge, and didn't try to understand it for fear of killing off one of his last remaining pleasures. He did it in many different car washes. His favorite was twenty-five miles away in Huntington, a long, complex carnival ride of a car wash that afforded him time to relax and enjoy himself, imagining the girls from the escort-service commercials or from the pornographic Web sites he visited at work.

First, the car was doused from every side, then attacked by soapy, bristled brushes. Then came a long, steady rinse like a summer-afternoon thundershower. The car rocked as it was dragged to the next station where an electronic display off to the right said *"Wax."* The car was drizzled upon from above. The wax created squirming, braiding channels down the windshield. Then the buffers, spinning cones the size of large men and composed of thousands of felt flaps, made repeated passes from the sides and above. Next was his favorite: Two overhead carousels, with ten-foot strips of blue felt hanging from them, whirled back and forth. The car passed through as it would a room full of dancing ladies. Lastly, the blower.

The entire event took eleven and a half minutes. Mark had time to clean up before being ejected into the parking lot.

Susan and Pullman teased Mark about his overconcern with the cleanliness of his car but, as they were both very busy, didn't think much of it. When Pullman entered middle school, Susan bought him a video camera, and he began recruiting the kids from the school and around the neighborhood to star in one after another short film: horror films, mostly, with plenty of ketchup, or re-creations of Three Stooges vignettes. When the film was complete, there would always be a screening party in the basement, where Pullman, the stars, and dozens of other kids would gorge themselves on pizza and Coke and laugh themselves silly, Susan right there on the floor among them.

Once, Mark woke in the middle of the night, and decided to go to bed rather than spend the night on the couch. He slipped under the covers and heard a soft sound. For a moment he thought Susan was having a dream, but then he realized she was crying. He let her cry and soon fell asleep.

They were wealthy now. They built a house on a grassy hill farther toward the South Shore. Mark kept his clothes in the closet, but slept downstairs.

Pullman adjusted quickly to the new school and spent this, his sophomore year, making a feature-length video. He had left the horror and slapstick in middle school; this film was a simple story about a boy growing up in Long Island. Susan played a small role as a crusty but good-hearted meter maid. For months it seemed that Mark was always walking in on a scene being filmed in the laundry room or on the deck. Dozens of attractive teenagers went up and down the spiral staircase to Pullman's room, and adults, too—actors who had responded to a call Pullman had placed in the local paper.

When Pullman finished the film, the screening was not in the den, but in the high-school auditorium, attended by hundreds of kids, parents, and teachers. Schools in neighboring towns asked to screen it. And then, through a series of events whose description Mark only half-listened to, Pullman's film was accepted by a festival in California, something for kids.

That spring, the California trip was all Susan and Pullman could talk about. They would attend the festival for five days, then go to Los Angeles, where Susan would meet with some dealers who had expressed interest in her pictures.

Mark had to work.

4

In the morning, Mark felt very aware. The sound of his breakfast cereal crunching was too loud. He put the bowl aside for a while to let it soak. The leaves of the plants by the breakfast table were green, veined with yellow, and sharp at the tips. When he started eating again, he realized that he liked his cereal a little soggy. He had never put this into words for himself before.

He put on good-looking casual clothes and used some of Susan's foundation to conceal the red areas under his eyes. Then he went out to the car and realized that although it was sunny, there was a chilly wind, so he returned to the house. He had trouble finding the jacket he wanted. Then he went back out to the car, but had brought the wrong set of keys. These were minor setbacks. He set off into the clear morning.

He arrived at the Denny's in Ronkonkoma, where he was supposed to meet Tanya, twenty minutes early, so he drove on down the boulevard for a while. At one after another car dealership, the sun glinted on chrome as plastic flags snapped in the breeze. Power lines were etched black against the cobalt blue sky. The transformers on telephone poles and the antennae on rooftops interested him in a way they hadn't before. They were little pods we're connected to. Organs.

He returned to Denny's and parked. He flipped open the makeup mirror on the back of the visor, and the bars of light on either side glowed. This was the first time he remembered using this feature of his car. He fixed his hair and lowered his sunglasses to check his eyes. Then he slung his jacket over his shoulder and entered the restaurant.

As he passed the register, he saw Tanya leap out of a booth in the smoking section, which was separated from the rest of the restaurant by a glass wall. She approached quickly.

"Are you John?" she asked.

"Yes," said Mark holding his hand out.

She didn't shake his hand. She took it and led him out of the restaurant.

"Did you want something to eat?" he asked.

"No I just ate. I just wanted to meet here. Let's go."

She led him back to his car. She was not quite as pretty as the pictures. Her mouth wore the same loose expression, like someone had just told a joke she didn't get. But her eyes seemed wiser and more suspicious. Maybe the pictures were taken a year or two ago.

She smiled. "I was watching you primping, getting ready to come in. It was cute. You're cute."

Mark looked up at the restaurant. Tanya's booth was overlooking his car. In it, another girl whom he hadn't noticed was watching them and writing Mark's license plate number on a small pad of paper. When she saw Mark looking, she shimmied away from the window and out of sight.

"Who was that?" he asked.

"Who?"

"That girl. There was a girl and it looked like she was writing down my license plate number."

"I dunno." Tanya tossed her head. "Let's go."

Mark started the ignition, but didn't back out yet. "Look," he said, "you're not some sort of . . . investigator, are you?"

Tanya sat on her hands and laughed. "No. Why would I be?"

"I'm not imagining that there was someone in there with a notepad watching us."

Tanya released an exasperated sigh. "Look, that's my friend, okay? She's my safety. She comes with me when I meet new clients, just in case something bad happens. Satisfied?"

"Yes."

They drove quietly down the boulevard for a while. Mark wondered how to break the spell of that weird exchange, until Tanya did it herself:

"So, why don't we talk about what we want to do and get the money thing out of the way. Then we can have fun."

Mark smiled, keeping his eyes on the road. "That sounds fine," he said. She was chipper and girlish. He should be distant, yet kind, he thought. Mature.

"So, what are you into?"

"Well,"—how could he say this coolly?—"I want to do it in a car wash."

"Wow," she laughed, "you sure know what you want. But I don't know if that's really . . . realistic."

"Oh, not to go all the way in a car wash, just . . . with your hand."

Her expression opened slowly into a smile and she leaned toward him to whisper in his ear. "That sounds hot." She bit his earlobe. Electricity shot down the side of his neck, but he resisted the urge to cringe or laugh. He drove to a car wash he knew in the neighborhood.

He parked away from the entrance and said, "Let's get the money thing out of the way."

"My rate is two hundred. That'll cover what we're going to do."

"Is there a time limit?"

"No, I want you to take your time. We can even go somewhere else after this. I like you."

Mark took his money clip from his breast pocket, folded back ten twenty-dollar bills, and freed them. Tanya thrust her hips up in order to stuff the money into the front pocket of her tight jeans. "Let's go. I'm ready." She giggled and tossed her head.

I'll bet this sort of thing happens here all the time, Mark thought. I wonder if the other men bring such pretty girls. He rolled down the window and paid a short Indian or Pakistani man with acne pits. Mark recognized him from previous visits. He regarded Mark with a vaguely hostile stare.

They entered. As the first round of brushes closed behind them like curtains, Tanya opened Mark's pants and yanked them down. "I've never made it in a car wash before," she said. "Pretty hot. Ooh, you're nice and hard, I guess you like this, huh? You like me touching your big old hard-on in the car wash?"

Mark slid down in his seat. He liked the way she smelled and the heat of her breath. He slid his hand under her T-shirt and held her small, soft breast.

This was good, but it wasn't perfect. He had hoped the presence of the girl would meld with the effect of the car wash to take him somewhere new. Some unimaginable peak. But something was wrong. Maybe she was using the wrong hand. And her voice in his ear overwhelmed the sounds of the car wash. Something was slipping away, and Mark tried to hold onto it as the wax drizzled, but that made it slip away faster.

The blower descended and Mark pulled away. "It's almost over," he said. He pulled up his pants and zipped. The car rolled out into the sunlight, and two men approached with rags to dry it off. Mark opened the window a crack. "Thank you, that's not necessary," he called, and drove off.

"Wow, that was fun," Tanya said.

"You liked it?"

"Yeah. It was a turn-on."

"Do you want to go to another one?"

"Uh, sure," said Tanya.

Mark shot her a look.

"Yeah, let's go! Do you know where another one is?"

"I do," said Mark.

They drove down a long highway past superstores crouching in their vast parking lots. Tanya leaned against him and massaged his thigh. She gripped him playfully and he gave her a stern look that broke into a cool smile.

Mark decided it would heighten his pleasure if he confirmed what he had suspected when he saw her picture at the office. "You were in a commercial, weren't you?" he said.

"Commercial?" she said.

"For the escort service."

She looked at him blankly. Then she either remembered or pretended to. "Oh, yeah, that. You've seen that?"

"I was sure I recognized you when I saw your picture."

"Cool." She drew close again and slipped her hand between his legs. "You've seen me on TV, and now I'm here. Pretty cool, huh? Pretty hot."

They arrived at the car wash—an overpriced but satisfyingly long one that Mark visited whenever he was in the neighborhood. They had to wait in line for several minutes. Tanya kept her hand at the nape of Mark's neck. She massaged the muscles at the base of his skull and let her fingernails wander through his hair. Mark wondered if the drivers before and after him knew what he was up to. He was so pleased by this idea, as he paid the man, that he forgot the first rule of the car wash: He forgot to put the car in neutral.

"This time," said Mark to Tanya, "use your mouth."

This was much more successful. Mark leaned back and watched the foam swirl against the glass and listened to Tanya's irregular breath and occasional slurp. They entered the rinse, and Tanya started going fast. She seemed to want to finish him off so they wouldn't have to go to another car wash. Mark gently rested his hand on the back of her head to slow her, and concentrated on the descending, whirling buffer.

Then Mark adjusted himself to enjoy a better angle and, in doing so, hit the gas pedal. The car surged forward and the front wheels jumped out of their cradle. There was a loud groan of rubber against metal, and Tanya sat upright.

"What was that?" she shrieked.

"I don't know. I jumped the track."

Mark hit the brake and fumbled with the gearshift. There was a loud snap outside and the car ceased to move.

"You're supposed to be in neutral!" said Tanya. "It said so! Put it in neutral!"

"I know, I know, just hold on!"

"Why aren't we moving?"

Soapy water drizzled down the windows and a wall of brushes whirled behind them. Mark could see the belt inching along the ground, but the car was still.

"You better drive out," said Tanya.

"Just hold on!" Mark said.

Something bumped them from behind, and Tanya screamed. The next car, having emerged from the brushes, nudged them forward. The driver honked furiously.

"Put it in drive!" Tanya shouted. "We've got to move!"

Mark drove forward carefully, but now they were at odds with the car wash. Two vertical metal rods spraying water simultaneously struck either side of the car and scraped as they passed. Mark turned on the windshield wipers and saw the car before him exiting. All the brushes between Mark and the exit had stopped spinning. He surged forward, failing to notice the blower as it descended. He hit it hard. A bright crack shot down the center of the windshield. The blower rolled over the rest of the roof, and they emerged into the parking lot where an SUV stood dripping. Two men in blue coveralls rushed toward the car.

"What the hell are you doing?" yelled one.

The other directed Mark to the corner of the parking lot. "Move! Move!" He pointed again and again with both hands as if he were guiding a jet onto an aircraft carrier.

Mark pulled over to the corner. Before him was a short curb and an open road. In the rearview mirror, the two men approached. Mark stepped on the gas and flew into the road.

"Oh my God! Are you fucking crazy?" said Tanya.

"What, did you want to stick around?" asked Mark as he half-stood to close his pants.

"No." She looked away from Mark out the window. "That was totally humiliating. I should have known. It sounded too easy."

"Sorry," said Mark.

"You're gonna get in trouble for that, you know."

"That's none of your concern."

Tanya was silent, then she swiveled to face him. "Are we going to do this or not?"

"Do what?"

"What do you think? Fuck. Just regular fucking, no more car-wash stuff. I don't like it."

"I'm a little jittery now. My car is damaged. Maybe we should just park for a while."

"And do what? I'm telling you I won't do it in the car. I'm not sixteen anymore."

"No, just . . . pull over and talk."

"Talk? Oh, no. No way. I'm not your fucking shrink."

"I just need to gather my thoughts."

Tanya opened her bag and took a swig from a little bottle of yellow mouthwash. She gargled, rolled down the window, and spat.

"You know what, *John,* talking is the last thing you need. You need to fuck. You need to either fuck me nice and lovey-dovey to get back at your wife, or fuck me hard and slap my ass to get back at your daughter, or fuck my face then come on my tits to get back at your mother. All right? Whatever you need. Whatever bitch you want to get back at. But no car washes and *definitely* no talking."

"I don't even have a daughter."

Tanya groaned.

"No," insisted Mark, "You're talking to someone else—some other man you've seen—not me."

"Yeah we all think our midlife crisis is special." She lowered her voice into a dopey imitation. " 'No, I'm not having a midlife crisis, I'm just sick of my wife and my job, that's all.' You know what? It's not just you. I'm sick of my job, too." She took out a tiny red cell phone. "So are you going to take me to a hotel and fuck me, or am I going to call my friend to pick me up?"

"I never wanted to fuck you in a hotel," Mark said.

Tanya punched in numbers with her thumb, muttering, "Oh, yeah, you just wanted to get your car washed. . . . Jenny? Yeah, it's me. Could you pick me up at, um . . . the Burger King on Route 29 in Brentwood?" She tapped Mark's shoulder and pointed emphatically at a Burger King they were nearing. "No, it's fine . . . just kind of annoying. . . . Yeah. Thanks." She pushed another button and said to Mark, "Just drop me off here."

Mark pulled over, wanting desperately to reclaim ownership of the situation, but his thoughts had slowed. "You know," he said, "your attitude doesn't match your profile."

She stepped out onto the curb and slammed the door behind her. The wind gusted the smell of fresh landscaping into the car.

There was a child crying alone on the suspension bridge in the fenced-in Burger King playground. Tanya turned and hung into the still-open window like a street hooker. "I know you don't have a daughter, *Mr. Dunford*. You recognized me, but not from a TV commercial. You recognized me from your backyard. I'm an actress. I was in Pullman's film."

5

The police car pulled Mark over politely. No siren, just flashing lights. It parked at a respectful distance behind. For a few seconds Mark dreaded being arrested for hiring a prostitute. But the pink-cheeked policeman informed him that he had damaged the car wash and put a small dent in the car behind. He invited Mark to step out, and they went around to lean against the back of the Mercedes.

"I barely knew what happened, it was so fast," said Mark. "I thought the car wash malfunctioned. It never occurred to me to stop."

The policeman accepted this with a vigorous nod. "Of course, Mr. Dunford. It'll just take a few minutes to fill out these forms, then you can go on about your business." Mark had never been pulled over before. It was nothing like *Cops*. This must be how they treat guys in expensive cars.

Dozens, hundreds of cars were passing them on the boulevard, but there was such camaraderie between him and the young man that Mark didn't feel embarrassed. They must have looked like friends taking a moment to catch up. Racquetball partners. Uncle and nephew. It was a welcome break from the agony that had descended on Mark after Tanya left.

What insurance didn't cover, Mark would pay out of pocket. There would be no hearing. He would get his own car in and out of the shop before Susan and Pullman returned, and they would never know.

When the forms were completed, Mark lifted himself from the car to shake the young man's hand and experienced a flash of memory: his father lifting him out of the trunk of their old Buick.

When Mark was little and his parents were still poor and happy, they would sneak him into drive-in movies. He would lie nestled down where the spare tire should have been, covered by a scratchy old Mexican blanket that smelled like a wet dog. When the car paused, Mark knew they were there, paying admission. He would hold his breath. He always expected the trunk to open, and the fat old owl-faced theater manager to yell, and the police to come and put them in jail, Mark, mother, and father, all in one cell. But then the car would rev and bounce. His father would pull around behind the cinder-block bathroom building in the corner of the lot. There was the click of the lock, then the blanket would lift, and Mark's father would gather him from the trunk gently, like something precious.

Mark drove aimlessly on through the paved world, a car among cars. Despite the crack in the windshield and the scrapes on the sides, he didn't want to go home. He passed a mall with a restaurant at a short distance across the lot like a boat dropped from a great ship. He turned into the landscaped entrance. Three seagulls fought over a piece of trash on the pavement, flapping their wide wings. He parked facing the boulevard and watched the cars pass. Each one had someone in its trunk. Businessmen napping against briefcases. Old women unable to get comfortable. Girls, boys, waiting. The thought comforted him.

He'd rest here awhile, then drive on.

Disability

THE INSURANCE COMPANY sends me to a shrink because they think I've been on disability too long. They want to find out if I'm really still in pain or if I'm crazy or a liar. But he's not a very good shrink for any of these purposes. I tell him about my back pain and he just sort of nods and waits for me to go on to something else. He always acts like everything I say makes perfect sense, and I'm making all the right decisions. And if he's coming to the conclusion that I'm a liar, he must have some secret method 'cause whenever I lie to him, he acts like he believes it, no problem.

Maybe he's forgotten that I'm not one of his regular patients and that he's supposed to be finding me out rather than helping me.

He nods a lot. He crosses his legs like a girl, leans toward me, props his chin on his thumbs and nods. His thumbs fit neatly into the cleft in his chin. Maybe he wasn't born with that cleft, it's been worn in by years of leaning and nodding. At first I thought he was gay because of the way he crosses his legs, but then he says all these annoying straight-guy things. Like when I come in he shakes my hand and slaps my shoulder and says, Hey guy, how was your week? Then he nods his way through the session and doesn't say anything substantial till near the end of the hour, when he comes up with a weird summary of what he's been thinking, like Jerry Springer's Final Thought. But they never really have anything to do with my life. Like, last week he listened to me talk about this fight I had with some asshole bartender the night before that got me eighty-sixed, and this new ringing in my left ear, plus a few back-pain references. When I ran out of things to complain about he nodded at my quietness for a minute then gave his Final Thought which was something like, Frank, we can't be afraid to share our needs with those closest to us, because that's the foundation of love, and the amount of patience we measure out for their response is something we learn through trial and error. Which is fine, but it wasn't for me. Maybe that was the response meant for the guy before me, and the old lady who comes in after me will get mine.

I would even understand if I talked about all that shit and his response was something about the value of honesty and hard work—then at least I'd figure Insurance was feeding him lines. But it's just senseless. Is he getting away with being weird just because I'm not paying and because I've never done therapy before so I don't know what's appropriate and what's not?

I haven't talked to anyone about this. Maybe I should. Especially someone who's done therapy before. I'll ask around. I'll bet Rand's done therapy.

My Deal

Rand is rich—rich from his family so he doesn't have to work. But he doesn't know his family anymore and doesn't really have anything. Except for a big loft in Soho or Tribeca—down where it's fancy and I'm completely out of place. He says he thought about buying in Brooklyn and would have if it weren't for delivery. He can't live somewhere without good delivery.

So he owns the top two floors of an old, narrow converted factory, but he only lives in the top floor. He leaves the other empty, so he doesn't have neighbors. Once I asked if I could live in the empty floor. I asked it only half-serious, hoping that he'd be into it. But he said, Then I'd have a neighbor, wouldn't I?

Rand's deal is that he has a need to be held down. His hands can't be free while he's asleep, so he had a special bed custom-made. It has a twin-sized birch frame, and about halfway down either side, posts come up from the frame with supports attached at angles. At the top of the posts are little boxes, also made of birch. They open toward the head of the bed, and they're lined top and bottom with an inch of foam rubber, then cushioned velvet. His hands fit snugly into these two boxes while he sleeps. He says he's never had trouble sleeping in the years since he had this bed made.

He also has an old-fashioned, cushioned chair that has the same kind of boxes fastened to the armrests. It stands against the wall between the two huge, naked windows. It's always struck me as odd that, with all his privacy stuff, he can live without curtains. There's no one across the street, but still.

Once I sat on the floor drinking his expensive old scotch and watching him read in his chair. He propped this little wire contraption on his lap that held the book open (it was some book on Chinese art) and he sat reading with his hands in the boxes until he had to turn the page, which he did. He even paused, holding the page to look at a picture before turning it. Then he put his hand back into its box.

I told him he was one crazy motherfucker and he said, And?

Most friends have to laugh it off when I talk to them like that, but not Rand. He was born missing a sense of humor so he has to deal with stuff head-on.

Maybe you're thinking how can I hang out with someone who doesn't have a sense of humor? Well, he's an interesting guy. He has interesting things to say. And he's been sort of a project for me. First to figure him out. Then, when I got as far as I could with that (which wasn't far) to find him a boyfriend.

The first candidate was my friend Daniel Hamburger. Daniel's a waiter at a fancy restaurant, where all the other waiters treat him horribly. He's sort of an easy target. For one thing, his last name is Hamburger. And he's a talker. If you tell him to shut up, he won't. He'll ask you what he said that bothered you so he can avoid the subject as he continues to talk. And he's a little big around the middle, which makes him waddle. But his face is really cute and he means well.

I thought it would be perfect, since Rand never laughs and Daniel's never funny.

But before I could even begin to put my plan into action, Rand met him by accident. Rand and I were at a bar. (He does go out, but only occasionally, and he primly drinks little snifters of cognac and doesn't talk to anyone. That's how we met—I picked him up at a bar and we went to his place and talked ourselves out of the attraction before we could have sex.) Daniel came up and started blabbing to me, and then to Rand. I went to get us a round and came back to find Daniel in the middle of an involved explanation of an episode of *Star Trek: The Next Generation*. Rand was nodding, looking around the room. Daniel wouldn't try that shit with me because I made a rule that he can't go into explanations of his dreams or TV-show plots. But I hadn't been there to stop him this time.

Rand hated him. All the way home he walked a half-step behind me the way he does when he wants to complain more confidentially into my ear. I just despise the impulse in people to drone on and on about the mundane experiences of their lives, assuming that these are shared experiences, and that that somehow makes them funny, he said. If they are shared, that's cause for despair, not laughter.

Rand never complains about people one at a time. He complains about behaviors or types of people, which is his idea of being polite, but it makes him seem put off by entire populations rather than, say, only Daniel.

It was just as well, though. The next week Daniel was back onto girls. He's constantly going back and forth, wondering if he should go after men or women. I try to tell him to relax and go after both, but he says he has to decide. Daniel believes in that 1930s MGM sort of love. He thinks he has to narrow down the field by fifty percent if he's ever going to find the One Love that's meant for him. He thinks there's a right answer.

I just roll my eyes—not really roll them, because finding the One Love is Daniel's biggest concern. Just roll them in my mind.

Candidate number two, Hector, stands a much better chance.

But before I go summarizing and analyzing all my other friends, you're probably wondering what my deal is, right? Other than being in everybody's business. Well, here in a nutshell is My Deal:

Remember Chaka from *The Land of the Lost*? The squirmy little ape boy with buck teeth, friend of the humans, always running around his family's dusty cave? That was me at eight. My dad was usually out selling things or cheating on my mother. We lived in East Brunswick, New Jersey, and our living room with all its browns and wickers was like a dusty cave.

Then my dad left. My mother shut the curtains and started sleeping in the living room. That was 1976, the year Judy Collins came out with the album *Judith*. My mother sat for a year listening to "Send in the Clowns" again and again. Do you know the cover of that album? It's a head shot of Judy. Her hair is blowing and her hands gently frame her tilted head. Her lips are parted, just a little. She has these incredible gray eyes that are sort of vacant and knowing at the same time. If you added makeup and a tear, it could actually be a face from a sad clown painting. My mother wore that same expression as she listened to "Send in the Clowns."

I started missing school to take care of her. We went on welfare. She started sharing her pills.

That was before the invention of CD players, with their repeat function. My mother had to creep back and forth between the sofa and the record player all day. It was also before the government started cracking down on fathers who skipped out on child support and doctors who made a business of overprescribing sedatives to nervous women.

A few years later, my mother got into self-help. She read books and went to a group every Wednesday night in the rec room at the Presbyterian church. This helped her get off pills. She took a course to become a real estate agent and, over time, became beautiful again. She was too busy for me now, but I had my own business—I had appointments with the doctor and sold the surplus pills to kids at school. Remember Wesley from TV's *Mr. Belvedere*? The half-cute kid who's always conniving to either make a buck or get himself out of trouble, able to fool everyone but, of course, Mr. Belvedere? That was me in high school.

With my mother and me both making money, I didn't have to

go to the grocery store with those embarrassing food stamps any-more. She gave me real money to eat out.

By the time the doctor went to jail, it was no big deal because I had other suppliers to fall back on. Then, just a couple weeks after high-school graduation, I went to jail myself. My mother was shocked, and I was shocked that she was shocked. She was already trying to rewrite her own history. She hired me a lawyer, and when I was released after two weeks, she introduced me to all these creepy people who wanted to help get me off drugs. I said no thank you and quit by myself. My main connection had been arrested, too, and I was afraid of breaking my parole and going back to jail. I was satisfied to carry a thermos of vodka and ginger ale in my backpack. I still do, as a matter of fact. I don't know why people use flasks or, worse, paper-bag it. A nice old-fashioned plaid thermos holds more, keeps it cold, and is far less obvious.

My mother married an older guy who makes less money than her, and they moved deeper into New Jersey. I moved to New York City. At different points over the years, she would refuse to support me and I'd get some job. Then, three years ago, she said she'd had it, I was nearly thirty and it was time to quit hitting her up for money. She swore she'd never give me another cent as long as I didn't have a Career. I reminded her that she owed me for the years I took care of her. Her husband pounded his fist on the kitchen table and said how dare I speak to her like that, I was a deadbeat, and so on. I stomped out and didn't speak to my mother for over a year. I wasn't really mad at her, just waiting for her to give in and call me to offer money. But she didn't.

So I got a job as a courier of specimens for a medical lab in Queens. It was the best job I ever had. I got a decent wage plus benefits for driving around to clinics in Queens and Long Island picking up little insulated lunch boxes full of blood, urine, and stool samples, and bringing them back to the lab. I had a little plan in case a cop ever pulled me over and asked me to open my thermos. I'd say, Don't you want to open the lunch box first? One summer morning I was on my way out to a pickup in Levittown and a truck slammed me from the side and rolled me off the LIE. Luckily, the thermos was thrown from the car. When I woke up, I had a heavenly feeling that I recognized as heavy-duty painkillers. There was my mother's concerned Judy Collins face and, hallelujah, a muffled pain in my right lower back.

That was a year and a half ago. I'm still on disability. I go for physical therapy and get massages. I have doctors' appointments twice a month, and now this shrink. I tell them all I'm still in incredible pain.

I am in a little pain actually, but not like I say. You're getting the extra-confidential version here, 'cause I don't tell anybody I lie about the pain. *Nobody,* not even my friends. It's the one thing I lie about, and that's not so bad considering how most people wrap themselves in lie after lie after lie.

Remember, in *Hello, Dolly,* how Ephraim Levi, Dolly's dead husband, used to say that Money, pardon the expression, is like manure: It's not worth a thing until it's spread around, encouraging young things to grow? That's me now. I live on disability, but only because it allows me to give everything to others—friends and strangers. I don't hoard anything—my time, my things, nothing— for two reasons: because I'm driven to out of Love, and because it's actually easier for me if I don't have anything. It sounds like I'm joking, but I'm not. I've thought about this.

Nori

On Tuesday evenings I have to babysit the girls. Marcie and Bill go to their marriage counselor and then out to eat or to a movie by themselves—it's their weekly Marital Improvement Time. I stay home and watch TV with Missy and Tina. See, I live in their house for free in return for babysitting twice a week—Tuesday nights till ten or eleven and then Sunday afternoons when Bill goes for golf and Marcie sees her girlfriends. They've had this rigid schedule thing since they decided to try to work it out and he came back. That was a year before I moved in.

Marcie was a technician at the lab, and sometimes we'd have a drink after work. Just after the accident, my lease came up for renewal and, not knowing I'd get disability, I gave it up. Marcie offered me to live in the basement of her house out in Queens. It's sort of its own apartment—there's a little refrigerator and a hot plate. Separate phone line. The street winds back and forth, trying to make it seem like a roomier neighborhood than it is. All the houses were built at the same time and are variations on the same design.

Marcie said, You'd be doing us a favor as well, the girls adore you, Bill likes the idea and so on, but Bill doesn't really like the idea. It was just something he was giving in on to save the marriage. A concession.

I put the girls to bed at ten and go back to the living room. I pour myself a drink. Now I can watch what I want.

Bill and Marcie get home. They've been fighting. Marcie goes up to check on the girls and Bill stands in the dark living room with his fists on his hips watching the TV. He's thinking about something else, though.

Have a seat, Bill.

No, I think I'm going to bed. He stands there a minute, then sits down anyway. You want a drink, Bill? He looks at my glass of Stoli on ice. He hadn't realized I was drinking. I shouldn't have said anything, but I try to be friendly to the guy.

Um, no thanks, Frank. Then he says, Just out of curiosity, you weren't drinking when the girls were still up, were you?

Of course not, Bill.

No, I'm just saying, it's fine to have a drink sometimes. I mean, Marcie and I have a drink in front of them once in a while—they definitely know what it means—but we try to keep that at a minimum.

Understood, Bill. I've never even had a drink in the same room with the girls.

Oh, sure, he says, no problem. Just curious.

What a prick.

Well, I say, I'm actually feeling tired. I'm gonna go on down. I leave Bill watching TV and take my drink downstairs to watch my own TV, even though it doesn't have cable. But I'm restless. I slept in today and didn't really do much.

I call Rand to see if he wants to meet for a drink. The answering machine picks up and I leave a message, knowing that he's probably listening. Rand's like that. He'll tell you later, I heard you leaving that message but I didn't pick up. I didn't feel like going out.

He's been acting sort of odd lately. He gave me a set of his keys and told me that if he ever goes a few days without returning my calls, to come check on him. I guess it's because he does things like gag himself and shut himself in the closet for hours at a time. Sometimes he works with this older prostitute named Belinda, and I told him it would be safer for him to just stick with that. They don't have sex, she just comes over and ties him up or holds him down. I actually met her once. I was coming in as she was leaving. She was in her forties, very sturdy-looking, polite, professional.

He doesn't really know I'm trying to find him a boyfriend. He would just dismiss the whole thing. When I started my search, I sort of nonchalantly asked him if the guys he dates have to be into bondage. He said, Oh, definitely not. That's something I take care of on my own.

I would call Hector tonight to see if he wants to go out, but he never wants to go into Manhattan. He goes to the local straight bars or to the nasty gay bar on Northern Boulevard.

So I go in by myself. I park on Tenth Street and try to decide which bar to go to, then realize I'd really rather just go to the porn theater on Third Avenue.

It's a slow night—I count eight guys as I sit down in a dark corner seat and pour some Stoli and ginger into the thermos-lid coffee cup. On-screen, a bunch of skinny blond boys from the seventies are having group sex on a houseboat. That's what I like about this place—they don't just play the new-release video stuff. They show older porn too, stuff shot on film. The sex goes on and on and I wish it would end and the plot would progress. I'm completely immune to porno sex scenes. If I'm going to get turned on at all, it's by the in-between scenes, especially if there's a cute boy who stays dressed for a while, keeping me in suspense.

The secret about this place that everyone who comes here knows is that if you go downstairs, past the bathrooms and through a door marked Employees Only, that's where you'll find most of the guys. There're long dimly lit corridors lined with little dark rooms. They play tinny gay dance music and there're guys cruising the corridors or waiting in the doorways for someone to join them. Most of the guys tonight are old or ugly. (I take them twenty-five and younger unless I'm too drunk or bored to care.) Then I see him. Tall, square-jawed, Asian, probably Japanese, bored-looking, dressed in black. He walks down the corridor and I follow him.

I go for the direct approach, which is unusual for this place. I tap him on the shoulder. He sort of jumps and turns to me. I indicate an open doorway. He follows me in and I lock the door.

What's your name?

Nori.

What?

Nori, N-O-R-I.

Okay, I'm Frank.

Thick accent.

I kiss him. He's handsome, handsome, handsome, and I'm a little drunk. He smiles and puts his arms around me and I kiss him again for a long time. Then I offer him a drink. When I pull out the thermos, he says, Coffee? I pour him a little. He tastes it and likes it and drinks it down. I put my hand inside his shirt and feel his tight warm body. For a second I think he's calling me Papa which is weird, but he's actually just offering me poppers. I pass. They'd just make me weak-kneed and headachy. He puts the bottle to his nose and sniffs. Then he nuzzles me and groans.

We fool around for a while, light stuff, until the air in the little room is stifling with body heat and the smell of his poppers.

It is very hot in here, he says.

Yeah, do you want to go somewhere else? Your place?

He shakes his head. I have roommates, he says.

I can't take him all the way out to Queens. Do you want to go to a different room? I ask.

Uh . . . yes.

We pull on our clothes and step out into the hall. Everybody turns to look at us. I find us a new room, but Nori hesitates. Maybe I'll go home, he whispers, it's late.

I don't want to let him go, and I don't really care if I show it.

Oh, come on. Don't you like me?

Yes, I like you. He smiles.

Then come in here with me.

I don't like these little rooms.

Then I have an idea. It's a bad idea, but I do it anyways.

I know a place we can go. It's an empty apartment. We'd have to be quiet if we go there 'cause the neighbors are asleep.

Okay.

I think to myself, we should make the long walk down to Rand's instead of taking a taxi just to be more certain we get there past his bedtime.

It's late April and the streetlamps in Washington Square Park filter through the tree branches and their tender, light green leaves. I wish we could walk through the park but it closes at midnight. It used to not matter, I tell Nori, but now the place is crawling with police.

We have a halting conversation. He's an engineering grad student at NYU. He's from Japan but wants to stay in New York. We duck into doorways and kiss. My feet are like bricks and I'm walking unevenly. Watch out, he says and pulls me, but I've already stepped on whatever he was warning me about. It's stuck to my foot and I try to kick it off. Then I look. It's a glue trap with a mouse stuck to it. The mouse is still wriggling, trying to get free. Someone must have thrown it out the window.

Ugh! Pull it off! I yell, but Nori is laughing and won't come near me. I can't bring myself to touch it. I limp over to a metal trash can, lift it up, and slide the glue trap underneath it. I push the trash can down. It crushes the mouse, and I can pull my foot away. Good. Put the poor thing out of its misery.

Nori is still laughing, but he realizes that I'm really disgusted so he hugs me and says, I'm sorry, but you looked so funny.

When we get to Rand's, I can see that the lights on his floor are out. Remember, quiet. We climb the stairs and I turn the key very, very slowly but it still scrapes and knocks as it unlocks and I cringe. The empty apartment is lit by a streetlight. Rand stores some boxes and furniture down here, and they cast long shadows across the floor toward us. Wow, says Nori, this is a nice place. It's yours?

Sorta, I say.

I pull the dust cloth off a sofa, and we fool around for a while, mostly me doing stuff to him because I can't really get hard. He's affectionate, which I like. He looks me in the eye and touches my face.

At one point I think I hear something upstairs. I hold Nori tight and say shhhh. Rand is walking across his apartment. I'm terrified, because if he finds me out, he'll never forgive me. This is a shitty thing to do, and I don't know why I thought of it. The footsteps go back to the end of his apartment, where the bed is. He was probably just taking a piss. Maybe we should leave, I think.

Nori asks, What's wrong?

Nothing, I say, and go back to his smooth, narrow body.

It starts to get light outside and I tell Nori we have to go. We can't fall asleep here. We dress, put things back carefully as they were, and lock up.

We share a cab back up to the East Village. I'm so tired, says Nori. I have to get up soon and go to class.

I'm sorry.

Do you have to go to work?

No.

That is good.

Nori writes his number on a little pad he has in his pocket, and tears it off. He says, you can call me if you like, and I tell him I will.

The cab pulls up at his building. We kiss good-bye. We kiss and kiss until the cabbie says, C'mon!

Bonus

I'm not a morning person. Especially when I was up all night. The phone wakes me and it's Missy and Tina asking if they can come down. They're home from school so it must be 3:00. I tell them no, I'm still sleeping, I'll let them know when I'm up.

They used to just come down and pound on my door. Then Marcie told them that Frank's room is his own separate home and you have to call him before you go visit, just like your other friends.

The phone rings again and I let the machine pick it up.

Frank, it's Rand. Pick up.

Hi, Rand, I'm sleeping.

Frank, I'm freaking out here. Could you come over?

What's wrong?

I think someone broke into the apartment downstairs.

What? Why do you think that?

I thought I heard something in the middle of the night. I went down there this morning, and I could tell someone had been there.

Did they take anything?

I don't think so. They could have, though. I don't remember everything I had in there.

How did they get in?

I don't know.

Did you check the windows?

They were all locked.

And nothing was broken?

No.

Are you sure you're not just imagining this?

I think so.

You think you're sure, or you think you're imagining it?

I think I'm sure.

Okay, well, you're not in any danger now, are you? I'll come over tonight. I've got to go back to sleep.

All right.

I pull the covers over my head and feel ashamed. I never lie to my friends. You can never ever do that again, I tell myself.

The guilt won't let me sleep, so I call Missy and Tina. They come down and jump on the bed with me still in it. You sleep all day, they say.

I stay up late, that's why.

Doing what?

Stuff.

What kind of stuff?

Grown-up, none-of-your-business kind of stuff.

I go shower, leaving them to root around in my stuff and play my CDs. All the porno and booze is out of their reach, locked up.

Then Hector calls and talks me into meeting him for happy hour at the Broadway, this corny straight bar in Forest Hills decorated with posters from Broadway musicals. When I get there, he's slouched in front of a beer, but his face is beaming. Let me buy you a drink, Frank, he says. I got a raise today.

He does computer stuff. He's my most sensible friend. His face is shiny and his hairline is receding. He's short and has a strong little body. He lives in Jamaica, Queens, down the hall from his parents who immigrated from Guatemala before he was born. I adore his mother, but she has no patience for me. His dad works as a maintenance man, comes home, drinks a lot.

Hector goes to mass with his mother on Sundays. She goes to mass daily, and tells him he should, too; it's a ticket straight to Heaven, bypassing Purgatory, but he tells her he doesn't have time, and once a week is plenty.

Once he told me that a psychic that he trusts told him he would die before the age of thirty-five. I told him that's bullshit, and he just shrugged sadly. He's twenty-nine. Maybe that's why he goes to mass.

I think he and Rand would balance each other out nicely.

I've been hoping for this raise for a long time, Hector is saying. And they gave it to me as a reward for my one-hundredth contract. They also gave me these other bonuses. It was great. Hector stutters just a little. It's not really a stutter, his jaw just gets stuck on a few words and he has to push them out. You wouldn't even notice it the first time you met him. I think it's sort of endearing.

Like what? I ask.

A better parking space. And a gift certificate for a nice dinner. Do you want to go with me?

Where?

This restaurant in Tribeca. Nobu. Robert DeNiro owns it.

Actually, Hec, I know someone who could really use a nice dinner. My friend Rand.

What do you mean? he says suspiciously.

What do you mean, what do I mean?

Isn't he rich? Why would he need a nice dinner?

It would be good for him to get out, you know. Meet a new friend.

Wait a minute, he says. Isn't this that guy who's into bondage and stuff?

I think to myself, I should really keep my mouth shut, and I say, No, just forget about all that. Rand's really attractive—tall, thin, shaved head, very striking-looking. You'd like him.

Maybe, says Hector. I'll think about it.

Hector has a couple of beers and I have a couple of Stolis. Then he suggests we go hang out at his place. I've noticed he always stops himself at two drinks.

I sit on the couch in the living room of his dingy apartment and he plays these new records that he's excited about. Hector's sort of a record freak. He has hundreds and hundreds of them—lots of Latin stuff, all the old eighties New Wave he used to listen to, female jazz vocalists, and this weird stuff he's been collecting lately. He doesn't like CDs.

Now this is genius. There's nothing else in the world like this. It's a Disney movie from the fifties called *Grand Prize*. No one's ever heard of it, right? But they released this record of the songs from the movie and Cubby—remember, the littlest Mouseketeer, the one who plays the drums?—narrating the story.

He puts on the record and this cheery little boy's voice starts telling about the County Fair and how a little orphan goat named

Sissy hopes to win grand prize. Then Sissy in her little goat-voice sings a song. Hector sort of mouths the words along with it and laughs.

Hector, what in the fuck am I listening to?

Isn't it just bizarre? laughs Hec.

You have too much time on your hands if you find this stuff entertaining, I yell.

Oh come on, he says. It's wonderful. Listen.

You are in bad shape, my friend. You work these long hours and come home and listen to children's records all night. You've completely lost touch.

Frank, please don't start, he whines, taking off the record. He's used to this treatment. Sometimes I feel like I have to abuse my friends a little, especially Hector who isolates himself so much. He needs to be toughened up and sent out into the world.

You've got to get out more before you disintegrate into this totally reclusive Catholic hermit fuckup. And quit going to mass. Psychics are bullshit and you're not going to die at thirty-five.

Dios mio, he says, looking to heaven. Why did I tell you about that?

And don't start speaking Spanish like you're some native. You grew up in Queens, New York, and have never been anywhere. That's why you should go to dinner with Rand.

What sense does that make?

He might tell you something new, I say.

I'm not really serious about any of this. It's just for my fun and his betterment.

There's a knock on the door. Hector? It's his mom.

Oh allow me, I say and I open the door. Hello, Mrs. Cordova, how are you? I hold out my hand.

Oh. Hello, Frank. She shakes my hand faintly. She turns to Hector and starts speaking in Spanish, because she doesn't trust me. He answers in English out of politeness to me: Mama, call them on the phone. They're nice people. You don't need me. She speaks even more quickly and he answers her in Spanish. Back and forth.

Then she shuffles back down the hall to her own apartment.

What was that all about? I ask.

Oh, she wants me to ask the Puerto Ricans next door to her to turn down their music. She doesn't want to do it herself 'cause she's afraid of them. She says island people cast spells. I told her to call them.

She hates me, doesn't she?

She doesn't hate anybody, says Hector.

Did she say anything about me?

He hesitates. She said you smell like alcohol.

Shit! I put my hand over my mouth and try to smell my own breath. Do I?

Hector shrugs sadly.

I remember that I'm supposed to go over to Rand's, and this is a good time to exit.

I drive in, and Rand's wringing his long hands, though he says he feels better. He takes me down to the empty apartment and asks me what I think.

Well, what makes you think there was someone here?

He shows me faint streaks in the dust on the floor. Doesn't it look like someone walked across the floor?

That could be anything, I say.

And this is the other thing. I have a method for covering things. I fold the cloth here and here. He shows me a chair covered by a dust cloth. But this is just thrown over, he says, indicating the sofa.

Now that is sort of weird. But how do you think they got in?

I don't know. Maybe they picked the lock. It might have been a homeless person who just spent the night, then left, he said.

Maybe you should have another lock put on.

I already did. The man came today. Here, he says, handing me a key, keep this with those other keys I gave you.

We go back up to his apartment. He puts on opera, sits in the chair, and puts his hands in the boxes. I tell him we should go out to eat, but he just wants to order in. I call for Vietnamese, he pays, and we sit down to eat at his long, bare pine table.

My shrink says the weirdest shit, I say.

Like what?

Just stuff that has nothing to do with me and doesn't make much sense. Have you ever done therapy?

My parents sent me to a psychologist when I was young, but I wouldn't speak to him. Then I tried some different types of therapists a few years ago, but they didn't help me much.

Why?

I don't think it was their fault. They were just trained to deal with one facet of the whole, I felt, and I needed something more . . . inclusive . . . or nothing at all.

Mine, he acts like he's listening, but I don't think he really is. Or at least he doesn't take it into account when he sums things up. He just invents something. For a while I wondered if he had some big, different idea of what my problem was and how to fix it. Like he was using some technique on me. But now I just think he's making shit up.

Then you should quit, says Rand with his mouth full.

Well, I can't really quit yet. The Insurance Company is having me go. It has to do with my injury.

How is your back, by the way?

Ugh. It's awful. The pain is just horrible. But it's like second nature to me now, you know, I just live with it.

He nods and wipes his mouth.

We finish our food and when I'm about to leave I say, You know Rand, I have a friend who lives out near me, Hector, maybe I've talked about him. No? Well, he got this bonus from work—a gift certificate to that restaurant Nobu.

Robert DeNiro's place.

Exactly. He asked me if I wanted to go and I'm not really interested, too fancy for me, but I thought maybe, since you live so close . . .

Are you trying to set us up, Frank?

No. I was just thinking, you know. Just a friendly thing. He couldn't think of anyone else to invite, so I suggested you.

Does he think you're setting us up?

Definitely not.

Well . . . says Rand, and he fades away for a minute, face frozen . . . I've been meaning to try that place . . . and they don't deliver.

Good. I'll give him your number.

But it's a couple of days later, Friday, when I call Hector to give him Rand's number and he tells me he already used the gift certificate, for lunch with his mother the day before.

Damn it, Hector, you said you would go with Rand!

No, Frank, I told you I would think about it, he says. Well, I thought about it and decided I'd rather take my mom. Can't I just meet this guy for coffee or something informal? Or, better yet, why don't the three of us go do something together? That would take the pressure off.

No, no, no, that won't work.

Why?

I have to call you back.

I go to my PO box, where my trusty disability check is waiting for me. I cash it, then I drive into the city, down to Hudson Street, where Nobu is. It's pretty impressive with ceilings so high it's sort of echoey, huge, abstract paintings and all these yuppies lunching. I ask to look at the dinner menu, and the host says they're serving lunch right now and I say I know, I'm going to buy a gift certificate. He opens a dinner menu for me and, Jesus this place is expensive! Better make it for one-fifty. But I want them to have wine, too. Two hundred.

I buy the gift certificate and order a spring-roll appetizer to go, because it's the only thing on the menu I'm willing to pay for for myself.

It's sunny and breezy so I go sit on a bench in the park and open the little box they gave me. These are the littlest spring rolls I've ever seen. There are two—the size of my pinkies. They're pretty good, though.

I have to see my shrink uptown at four, so I have a few hours to waste. I haven't talked to Daniel Hamburger for a while, and I know he works the lunch shift on Fridays, so I walk up Hudson to the West Village to visit him. It's this fancy French place—the Something Bistro.

It's so good to see you Frank. I've been meaning to call you. I have big news. Big, big news. Here, sit at the bar, do you want anything to eat? How about a drink? He has a breathy voice and he doesn't pause between sentences.

It's sort of early, I say. Maybe a Bloody Mary?

Good. He steps around the bar and starts mixing. It's good that you visited. I'm bored out of my mind, it's been so slow. But anyways I've got big news.

Someone calls from the kitchen, which is just beyond the bar, Hamburger? Hamburger? Why am I the only one running food? Oh, I'm sorry. I didn't know you had a friend.

It's an ugly little waiter with red hair. He gives me a flirty smile, then says, Never mind Daniel. Take your time.

I wonder if he would have been so nice if he didn't think I was cute.

What's your news, Daniel?

Well, I met someone.

That's great, I say. Male or female?

Female. Her name is Ana, and she just moved here from Idaho. She's really pretty. Her attitude is sort of dark. She's quiet and you'd think she's brooding, but she's just shy. When you get talking she's so smart and nice! She's really getting me into shape. Wise beyond her years, you know?

How old is she?

Daniel pauses. Seventeen.

Oh my God, Daniel, what are you doing? That's not even legal. What, is she some NYU freshman?

No. She doesn't go to college. But she wants to. She dropped out of high school. She's gonna get her G.E.D.

I can't help but laugh. Seventeen-year-old dropout fresh from Idaho? Was she hustling on the street when you met her?

Don't talk like that, Frank, I'm serious.

Let me guess, I say. She's staying with you.

Well, yeah. She's been great. You know how disorganized I am, how I never get anything done. She's been helping me. I really like her a lot.

I think for a minute. Who am I to criticize, if he's happy? Especially when it's so easy for him to find people he likes, but so hard to find people who like him. So I say, Well, then, Daniel, God love ya. Whatever makes you happy.

He grins and goes on about her. And on and on. Everything spells disaster, but I bite my lip, and nod like my shrink. He asks me if I want some food, and I say sure, just bring me whatever's good. He brings me a big bowl of mussels in the shell and a basket of bread, and goes on and on about Ana.

When I leave, he hasn't asked me one thing about how I am, but that's typical. It's not that he doesn't care.

I tell my shrink about Nori and Rand and the guilt. I tell him the pain is so bad I can't even get out of bed some mornings.

He tells me about the beauty of released aggression and suggests I pile up the pillows on my bed, and punch them.

That night I give Hector the gift certificate. I put it in his hand and say, Here. This is another gift certificate to Nobu. Don't you dare say no, and don't you dare thank me. And here, I put another paper in his hand. This is Rand's phone number. You will call him tonight.

My friends are such babies, I think.

Jeez, Frank, says Hec. Thanks.

Fuckup

Marcie comes down to visit me one afternoon. The first time in a while. We have to talk, she says, and puts her hand on my knee. Is this working out for you? I mean, are you happy living here?

Are you happy with me living here? I ask, because I can see what's coming.

Well, yes. You're great with the girls and it's been a real help . . . her voice trails off.

But . . . I say to help her along. Out with it, Marcie.

But Bill and I worry that we're allowing you to stagnate. It's been a long time, and you haven't progressed as far as we can see. You're back's not getting better, you're not working . . .

Marcie, does Bill want me to leave?

Don't get defensive, Frank. It's not that we want you to leave, we just want you to step back and evaluate things. Think of why you're here.

Marcie, you've been very good to me, so let me make this easy for you. I've been here too long. I'll start looking for another place.

Well, she hesitates, do you feel okay about that? I nod. No rush, you know, she says. You're welcome here as long as it takes.

Thanks, Marcie.

She gives me a confused half-hug and gets up. We'll still be friends, right, Frank?

I don't know. Will we?

She smiles and says, Sure.

But we won't.

That night, I go out with Nori. We eat at a diner on West Fourth and in his bad English he tries to explain what he studies. It's engineering, but it also has to do with architecture, and for some reason he has to take sociology. It's about how people use space. He's obviously excited about it and he wrinkles his forehead as he tries to explain.

Then he sits there and eats while I smile at him. He's so handsome. And fresh and clean and smart. I'm so afraid that he'll ask me what I do and I'll have to say, Nothing.

I'm a fuckup, and I'm okay with that, always have been. There are very few moments when I'm not okay with it, and this is one of them. I'm ashamed of myself in front of Nori, and, although it makes me sad, that probably means that this isn't going to work.

We walk quietly toward his building. On the way there, I'm surprised to see Rand on a corner hailing a taxi. Rand! What are you doing out?

Oh, hello, Frank, he says nervously. Nothing, just heading home.

Rand, this is Nori. They both nod. Oh! I say. Did you go out with Hector?

Yeah. A cab pulls up. I'll call you and tell you about it. Nice to meet you, he says to Nori.

Nori nods, then says to me when Rand's gone, Strange man.

Yeah, I say.

When we get to his building he asks if I want to come up. His roommates are away. No, I have to get home. Sure? he asks playfully and nudges his face against mine. Yeah, I'm sure. I'll call you.

It would be easiest just not to call, of course. He still doesn't have my number. But that would be cruel, and I'm not cruel.

The next easiest would be to make up an excuse—I have a boyfriend or whatever—but that would be a lie, and I don't lie.

So I get home, put my keys on the dresser, and call before I even take my shoes off. Nori, I say, this isn't going to work. I can't go out with you again.

Why? he says. Don't you like me?

Yeah, I like you a lot. But I'm not right for you.

I don't understand.

That's okay, I say. You don't need to understand, all right? I'm sorry.

He doesn't respond.

Bye-bye, Nori.

He doesn't respond again, so I hang up.

I drink. I fall asleep with the TV on.

Next morning, two calls:

Dinner was delicious, says Hector, and don't worry. I didn't mention that I had just been there with my mom.

The place was a little overrated, says Rand. Places owned by celebrities get a lot of undue attention.

I liked him. He was interesting, says Hector.

He was very nice, but I don't know if there's really a spark, says Rand.

I mean, he's definitely a bizarre guy. I would have to think about it if he asked me over again. But I enjoyed myself. Very, sort of, friendly, you know? says Hector.

He's not really my physical type, but he was handsome, says Rand.

So you guys didn't sleep together? I say.

Yeah we did.

Yes, he slept over.

The sex was okay, says Hector. But he's very, you know, distanced. He kept me at arm's length the whole time. And I had the feeling that he was thinking about every little thing. Not letting go.

It was nice, at least, to have sex, says Rand. It's been a while.

His bed was sort of small, and it had these boxes . . .

I know, I say.

I couldn't fall asleep with him there, says Rand. But it was all right. I napped the next day.

I don't know, Frank, says Hector. Maybe we could all get together as friends. I don't know if there's a lot of excitement.

He says I can borrow some records, says Rand.

Maybe you should give it another try, I say.

Maybe, says Hector. I gotta go. My boss is coming.

You know who was attractive? says Rand. That Asian man I saw you with on the street. Are you dating him?

No.

Mother's Day

Not to be a Daniel Hamburger, but I'm going to tell you about a dream I had. It's a sad dream:

My mother, her husband, and I are all sitting by a swimming pool. They look like they normally do—my mother has big sunglasses and a wide-brim hat with her orangeish dyed hair curling up from underneath. Her husband's sleeping with a towel over his head. This is all from when they took me to Florida a few years ago. My mother tells me I should take a dip in the pool. So I get up and start to go down the stairs into the water when I realize, this is a special pool. It looks like a normal pool, but there's only an inch or two of water; then there's air underneath. I put my head down there, and sure enough it's dry and I can breathe. The sun shines through the ripply border of water above my head.

There's a woman lying on the pool floor, down at the deep end. I walk down and kneel beside her. It's my mother, but from when I was little. Her hair is long, straight and brown, she's wearing a seventies granny dress with crocheted sleeves. I touch her hand and it's cold. Her face is still and her gray eyes are open, but she's dead.

I wake up missing my mother. It's been weeks since I talked to her. I'm such a bad son, taking care of everybody but her. Not once in my life have I even bought her a Mother's Day present.

But Mother's Day is in May, right? I look at the calendar and see that it's just over a week away. I'll do something special for her this year. Then the idea comes to me: Why don't me and my friends all take our mothers to a nice brunch together on Mother's Day? That way I'll have my friends with me, and our mothers will be meeting each other, which will distract them from what fuckups their sons are.

I start making phone calls. Hector likes the idea. Daniel will call his mom in Philly and see if she wants to come up for the day. He also gives me some suggestions of restaurants with outdoor seating. I call them, but they're all booked so I put myself on waiting lists. Should I invite Rand? He's not in touch with his mother, but I don't want him to be left out, and it would be a chance for him to see Hector again. I call and leave him a message, thinking, he'll probably say no.

I call Marcie upstairs and ask her if I could take the day off from babysitting. She'll get her niece to do it, she says.

Then I call my mother, who I should have called first, and she says, That's such a nice thought, Frank, but we're leaving for Atlanta that afternoon.

Ah, really? What time is your flight?

Five.

That's plenty of time! We'll meet at noon. Just bring your luggage and leave it in the car. You can go straight to the airport.

You know I like to get there early, says my mother.

I know, but still.

Okay. Sounds wonderful. How's your back, honey?

It's so bad, I tell her, sometimes I can hardly get out of bed.

A few days later, one of the restaurants calls—Emily's, in the West Village. There's been a cancellation and they can take us. I go by the next day just to check it out. It's perfect—little courtyard in back with ivy growing up the walls and birds chirping.

Rand decides that he'd like to come after I assure him he won't be the odd man out.

My one worry is that people will sit in the wrong places and no one will mingle. I want Rand as close to Hector and as far from Daniel as possible. Would it be weird for me to make a seating arrangement with little cards telling people where to sit? Weird or not, I do it, seating Hector by Rand, me by Mrs. Hamburger, who I've never met, Hector's mother by mine, and so on.

But on Mother's Day, everybody ignores the cards I printed so neatly. Hector sits next to me and his mother, next to him. Then my mother arrives with her husband. Why'd you bring him? I ask her under my breath.

I told you—we have to go to the airport soon, she says. Don't worry, he'll just sit at the bar inside and read the paper.

I seat her next to Mrs. Cordova and introduce them. Before I can rearrange the name cards, Rand arrives, solemnly introduces himself, and sits next to me.

I glance inside and see my mother's husband sitting at the bar in his off-white suit, looking sort of like Blake Carrington in *Dynasty*. Then, at the opposite end of the bar . . . Hector, isn't that your dad?

Yeah. He had to drive us in. My car's in the shop and he doesn't let anyone else drive his car.

His dad was already having a beer. I tell Hector, at least go introduce him to my stepfather. Hector says that *he's* never even met my stepfather, but he goes anyways.

Daniel Hamburger arrives with someone much, much too young to be his mother. Hi everyone, he says brightly, I'm Daniel and this is my girlfriend Ana. Ana's scowl breaks into a momentary tight smile, then sours again. They sit in the two remaining seats, Daniel next to Rand, Ana next to my mother.

Why is everybody bringing all these extra people? I ask Rand. He smiles. Never before a sense of humor, but he thinks this is funny.

Everyone introduces themselves to Daniel and Ana, all visibly disturbed that this man in his late twenties is dating a teenager. Mrs. Cordova in particular finds it difficult to meet their eyes. When Rand introduces himself, Daniel puts his hand on his shoulder and says, Oh, yeah. We've met. Rand, who doesn't like to be touched, cringes.

Daniel explains to me that his mother canceled at the last minute, so, knowing we had a reservation for seven, he invited Ana.

Well, you're very welcome, I tell Ana, who ignores me because the waitress is here to take our drink orders. Brunch comes with a mimosa or Bloody Mary. Everyone orders mimosas except for me and Mrs. Cordova. I order a Bloody Mary, Mrs. Cordova asks for plain orange juice. The waitress doesn't card Ana, thank God.

At least the two mothers are sitting together, I think. I strain to hear what they're saying. My mother compliments Mrs. Cordova on her lovely black hair. Do you dye it? she asks, then chuckles, I hope you don't mind my asking.

Oh, I don't mind, Mrs. Cordova answers. And no, I don't dye it. She twists and strokes her cloth napkin.

My mother gasps. You don't have a single gray hair. If I didn't dye mine it would be as white as this tablecloth.

You want to know my secret? says Mrs. Cordova. Daily mass.

In at the bar, the men seem to be getting along as well. Mr. Cordova has bought my mother's husband a beer. They stand, elbows resting on the bar, chatting.

My Bloody Mary arrives and we all order. I propose a toast to mothers, Rand says Hear, hear! and my mother and Mrs. Cordova raise their glasses, smiling bashfully like homecoming queens. Everything's going well, so I relax and try to draw Hector and Rand into conversation. Eventually they're talking over me, so I tell Rand to switch places with me, so I can talk to Daniel who, so far, has been occupied with Ana.

Our food comes—lots of sausages, hollandaise sauce, runny eggs—everything's delicious. Ana is a dark little thing, and even though I'm perfectly friendly, she divides her attention between Daniel and her food, nothing else.

She doesn't like Mother's Day, Daniel says when she goes to the bathroom. You'll have to meet her again when it's just the three of us.

Rand taps my arm and whispers, There seems to be a dispute at the bar. Sure enough, Mr. Cordova is talking forcefully and throwing his arms about. My mother's husband is flushed red, answering him. All the nice people inside, all the mothers, are looking. Why did Hector have to bring him? He's got a horrible temper. Hector knows that better than anyone.

Hector, I say, go calm your dad down. But too late. He's stomping across the courtyard to our table. He starts speaking to his wife in Spanish. Hector tries to answer him soothingly.

Hector, what's going on? I ask.

He says we have to go now. I guess your father said something about immigrants.

Mr. Cordova, please, I say, standing up. I apologize for my step-father. But we're in the middle of our meal.

I don't care, he says. I'm leaving.

Mrs. Cordova starts to get up. No, I say, Mr. Cordova, you go ahead. I'll give them a ride home, all right?

He says something to Hector in Spanish, Hector answers, and he leaves.

Oh, my, says my mother, and goes to check on her husband who's still sitting red-faced at the bar.

I excuse myself, too. I find our waitress. Excuse me, I say, could you bring me a second Bloody Mary, only this time, give me twice the vodka, okay? They're a little spicy for me.

All right.

You can charge me for a double.

All right.

And use Stoli, if you don't mind. The cheap stuff gives me a headache.

Certainly.

I go back to the table, and people are getting over the excitement, but Mrs. Cordova looks upset. I hope you don't mind riding home with me, I say to her, trying to be kind.

No, Frank. That'll be fine.

Do you want another drink?

I guess, some more orange juice, she says. I call the waitress over.

My mother returns to the table and she and Mrs. Cordova sit picking at their food and apologizing for their husbands.

As soon as the waitress clears our plates, my mother lays her napkin on the table and says, Well, this has been just lovely, but we've got a plane to catch.

Mother, you've got hours. Sit back down and have some coffee.

I wish I could, honey, but they have these new rules at JFK since that plane blew up. You've got to get there very early.

Come on, Mother. Just stay for a little, then we'll all go. We've barely finished eating.

It was so nice meeting you, she says sweetly to Mrs. Cordova. She says good-bye to the others, and I follow her from the table. I can't believe you're leaving so soon, Mother, we haven't even gotten a chance to talk.

Now listen, Frank. I told you I was going to leave early. She takes my hand and changes her tone. Thank you very much for this, honey.

I take my hand away.

Don't spoil it, Frank.

I go back to the table. We all sip coffee and chat politely, but it's spoiled.

When we get the bill, the boys all put in their cash, and I count it up. It's not enough to cover even the food, not to mention the tip. But rather than make a big deal, I make up the difference, using most of my remaining disability money. Check comes in a few days, anyways.

On the way out of the restaurant Rand takes me aside and says, Frank, I want to ask you about something. Remember that guy Nori you introduced me to? I met him again.

Where'd you meet him? I ask.

At that porn theater on Third Avenue.

I didn't know you went to porn theaters.

He shrugs and goes on, We sort of fooled around there at the theater, and he gave me his number. I want to call him, but I thought I should ask you first. Do you mind? You said you weren't seeing him, right?

We're standing on the street corner now and Daniel and Ana are saying good-bye. I'm numb. What if Rand invites Nori home and, climbing the stairs, Nori says, Oh, I've been here before—that empty apartment.

So how about it? says Rand.

Um, sure, Rand. Do whatever you want.

You seem unsure.

No, it's fine. Do what you want.

What am I supposed to say? No?

On the drive home, Hector's mom is spitting out grumpy Spanish words, and Hector's answering in Spanish. It's driving me crazy. Could you guys at least speak in English when you're in my car? What is she upset about, Hector?

I'm upset because you were mean to your poor mother on Mother's Day, she says.

Mean to her? I planned this whole damn thing for her!

She had to go catch a plane, and you made her feel bad.

Look, Mrs. Cordova, you don't know about my mother and me, all right?

You should have respect for her, like Hector has for me, she says. Instead you yell at her and make her feel bad.

Hush, Mama, says Hector.

You don't know what it's been like for me, I say. I've had a hard time and this brunch was a big deal.

You don't have a hard time, she says. You don't even work for a living.

I'm injured! I yell. I'm on disability. I can't work.

Injured, she laughs. I'm in pain my whole life and still I work. You're lazy.

Hush, Mama.

I drop them off and drive straight to the nasty gay bar out on Northern Boulevard, where I drink myself silly.

Silly

Late that night, I park my car in front of the house. I get out and have to stifle a laugh 'cause the car's half on the sidewalk. I get back in and park it right.

Concentrating so hard on driving distracted me from the nausea, but now, walking across the lawn, it hits me in wave after wave and I don't want to puke in the middle of Bill and Marcie's lawn, so I jog over to the trees and let go. I cough and sputter and look up and, uh-oh, here comes the neighbor guy yelling, Get off my lawn, you drunk! He shoves me and I turn around to see Marcie coming across the grass, arms crossed to keep her bathrobe closed. Then Bill passes her, grabs me by the arm and drags me, tripping and stumbling, across the lawn.

What the hell do you think you're doing, Frank? You can't live like this. Not here in front of the girls.

Let go of me, Bill. I yank my arm.

I want you out of here tomorrow, Frank! Hear me? Out!

Out out out! I say and Marcie's crying as she takes me down to my bedroom. Fucking straight prick, I say. I feel sorry for you, Marcie.

Oh, shut up, Frank, she cries. You're drunk.

I feel sorry for all you straight women who have to marry straight men like Bill. I go on about it, but the light's out and Marcie's gone.

In the morning, Missy and Tina sit in the living room bawling as I take stuff out to the car. Bill's nowhere to be seen. I find Marcie paying bills at the breakfast table, and I ask if I can store some things in the basement closet until I'm settled. Sure, Frank, she says, with a complicated look on her face.

I hug the girls good-bye. Their narrow, warm little backs heave and sob. I tell them not to worry, that they'll see me all the time. They nod breathlessly.

I get in the car and head toward Manhattan. I'm crying a little too, now. Oh, well, I think. Maybe this will get them on the road to hating their father. And the earlier the better, you know?

Where should I go? If I still had a set of keys, I'd go out to Jersey until my mother returns from Atlanta. If I hadn't spent my disability, I'd treat myself to a night at the Mariott, just to cheer myself up. If I felt like seeing any of them, I'd call my friends.

I park in a garage and spend the day walking around to little shops and having meals at cheap restaurants. The weather is beautiful, and I love all the freaks in the street. I have conversations with the waitresses. I start to feel better, 'cause who needs entertainment when you live in New York? And who needs a place to go at night when you can sit in the porn theater on Third Avenue and watch the movies until you doze off? Till they turn the lights on at 6:00 A.M. and say, All right guys, time to go home.

Then you can go sit in the park by the Hudson and watch the sun glint on the windows over in Jersey. At 8:00 A.M., the city gym on Carmine Street opens, and you can show your membership card that you use next to never, and they let you in to shower.

Everything's okay, I think, 'cause if you know what you're doing, New York is like your own big hotel.

But by that evening, I've had enough so I call Hector, who has a roomy apartment and a fold-out couch. We sit in his kitchen and I tell him what happened. He just sort of shakes his head. He wants to tell me things, to drink less and so on, but he bites his tongue, and I'm grateful for that.

Instead he entertains me with records. He says he can make me cry by playing sad songs, and I say he's wrong.

He starts with Tammy Wynette and I roll my eyes. He tries Sarah Vaughan, then Frank Sinatra, and I say, you don't know me very well, do you? As usual, he's putting on songs and taking them off before they're even half-through.

I know what'll get you, he says. Back-to-back he plays "Vincent" by Don McLean, "You Needed Me" by Anne Murray, and "Superstar" by The Carpenters, each one all the way through. Nice technique, I say, but no.

He puts on "Careless Whisper" by Wham!, and takes it off almost immediately.

Then a lone oboe whines a familiar melody. It's followed by a rush of strings and a woman's voice whimpering that there ought to be clowns. It's Judy Collins, and my life comes rushing at me. Turn it off, I say. You win.

He walks over and there's a grunt as he takes the needle off the record. He slides it back into the sleeve. He can see that I'm genuinely sad, but can't help saying, quietly, *Softy*.

He turns on the TV, and I'm glad for the noise, but I'm not watching. I'm going over my life and thinking of how worthless everything is. I feel desperate, and I want to feel close to Hector, so I lie across the couch and rest my head on his lap. He lays his hand on my shoulder and we watch TV like that for a while. It makes me feel a little better—his hand is heavy and warm. In my mind, I try to spread that warmth through my whole body. Friendship is the one thing I need, and the one thing I've got. That's something I tell myself all the time. So I try to make Hector's warmth enough.

His hand leaves my shoulder and begins to stroke my hair. I close my eyes and he rubs my neck. Now my thoughts are melting into sensations, as if I were drunk. I roll onto my back and look up at Hector, and his hand rests on my chest. His eyes are glassy, still fixed on the TV, and his jaw shifts back and forth. He swallows. He's nervous. That's good, it means I don't need to be.

I touch his face, and pull him down to kiss me. I should be wondering if this is a good idea, considering how it'll change our friendship and so on, but I don't care. Good idea or bad, it's suddenly what I want. His hand moves across my chest, under my arm to my back. He lifts me and we really kiss.

We leave my stuff in the living room and spend the night in his bed.

Our Deal

And the next night, and the next.

The sex is surprisingly good. I guess I always imagined it'd be boring, but it's fun. It's like playtime; we laugh a lot.

We sleep in each other's arms which scares me just a little. If we were just friends fooling around for the fun of it, wouldn't we sleep on our own sides of the bed? But our bodies fit together so nicely, and I sleep so well when he's right up against me.

Mrs. Cordova hasn't been coming by since I've been here, and I feel a little weird about that, too, but Hector says, She's got to realize I have my own life.

I leave Rand the third message since Mother's Day. He isn't returning my calls. I have this horrible feeling that Nori gave away my secret, and that Rand's furious. But then, didn't I promise to come check on him if we went for a few days without speaking? If he doesn't call by tomorrow, scared or not, I'll go over.

Hector gets home from work, and before we can even order food, we're kissing in the kitchen, and I'm taking his clothes off, and we're fucking on the couch. Afterward, we lie there naked and he flips on the TV. I sip on the drink I already had going.

So Hec, I say, is this one of those situations where the guy's in love with his friend for ages and finally, just when he gives up hope, the friend sort of turns around and they start screwing?

I don't know, Hector says. Have you been in love with me for ages?

No, I'm saying *you're* the one in love, I say.

You sure talk about love a lot, he says.

Listen, I say, don't tease me. Just because we're having sex doesn't give you all sorts of rights and privileges, all right? I'm still the aggressor in this friendship.

He rolls over on top of me to prove he's the aggressor.

My shrink's response to all this is a Final Suggestion rather than just a Thought: I want you to close your eyes and return to that day when you were ten years old and your father left. I want you to pretend I'm your father and tell me what happens to me. Predict my life, Frank. Tell me where I went, and what I did. Tell me if I succeeded or failed, if I'm alive or dead.

No, I say.

What? he says, lifting his chin from his thumbs. There's a red impression in the cleft.

Look. I was eight, not ten, and besides, that makes no sense to me. The things you say never make any sense. This isn't working, so I think that I should quit coming.

Well, he says carefully, I'm sorry you feel that way. Maybe we should work on communicating more clearly with each other. You are free to discontinue sessions . . . but I should warn you, your disability payments are contingent on your attendance here.

Oh, I say, contingent.

On the way home, I consider going by Rand's, but there's tons of traffic so I decide to give him one more day.

I pick up the *Village Voice,* go to Hector's, and sit in the kitchen looking at the apartment listings. Everything's so expensive, even in the outer boroughs. Hector's going from room to room, picking things up, piddling around.

What are you reading? he asks.

I tell him.

He goes into the living room for a minute, then comes back. You know, he says, then his jaw locks and he pauses . . . I was thinking that maybe I'd offer to let you stay here . . . sort of, for a while. Like indefinitely.

You were *thinking* of offering that, or you *are* offering that?

I *am* offering that, he says, but with a condition.

What's that? I ask.

That you limit yourself to two drinks a day.

Hmmm, I say. I think for a minute. How 'bout this: I'll stay here, and I'll drink only two drinks a day if you quit going to mass.

He looks down at his shoe which is tapping on the brownish marbleized linoleum.

Okay, he says.

• • •

The following week, Hector's mother talks him into going to mass on Saturday night. The next night I go out drinking. I let myself get only moderately drunk, but the headache I didn't realize I had is washed away, and I recognize myself.

The day after that, we reinstate our agreement and say we'll try to stick with it this time.

It's a start, at least. Right?

Foray

THE FOURTH DAY of July passed like those that preceded it: I sat reading, and the wide, slate-colored Snake River rolled on. There was a nook to swim in by the beach, a slow eddy where foam circled lazily and where Grandy kept his speedboat, but just beyond that flowed the river, silent and powerful.

Did you know that the current was so strong here? my mother had asked her mother the day we arrived.

Gram had shrugged stupidly—a habit of Grandy's which had always exasperated her, but which she had picked up after they sold the farm, gave in, and became alike: two big Idaho people, stout and intrepid except when being affronted by one of their daughters—then they played dumb. We'd been on the river fishing so many times, Charlotte, we just knew it to be calm. We didn't notice on the map that the house was just below the confluence.

Well, all you have to do is look at the water! I just worry . . .

. . . about Vance, the three of us had said in our minds. And we had stood looking out from the deck—Mom, Gram, and I—at the jagged cliffs veiled in a cloud of twittering canyon wrens who then swooped down over the churning gray water and returned en masse. It was so beautiful, I thought, but I didn't say so aloud.

That had been late afternoon, when the canyon was cool. Now it was early afternoon and the sun shone powerfully. I lay in a beach chair like a pale six-foot-two scarecrow under an umbrella, knobby knees resting together, gigantic feet planted apart in the sand. The canyon wrens disappeared during the nearly three hours of direct sunlight, and my cousins, the screaming idiots, bathed in the eddy. I was the oldest grandchild, and an only child. There had always been a gulf of misunderstanding between me and siblinged children, especially my cousins, whose names I can hardly remember. They were a squirming orgy of fat brats, like a batch of piglets at the teat, and the moment just before noon when the sun touched the water, down from the house they rolled. Patchy-furred mountain goats, with aristocratic scorn, exited along a narrow ledge. Tall, stubby-armed river otters stood upright on a rock downstream in dumb amazement as the cousins splashed around the eddy, pulling each other by the foot, scratching, yanking ponytails, squealing with pleasure, then pain, then pleasure again, dunking each other, threatening, betraying, tattletaling. Handstanding in the water with their fat babylegs the color of honey-roasted ham gleaming in the sun. Motorboating each other around, blubbering engine-noise through their slack, spitty lips. Marco . . . Polo! Marco . . . Polo! Ollie ollie oxen free. Sugar Donut! screamed one, Let's play Sugar Donut! And they all charged out of the water and rolled in the white sand until their skin was thickly sugared. Hee-hee-hee, Sugar Donut, Sugar Donut!

And me trying to read!

Up on the porch, Vance, the second-oldest grandchild whined

and squirmed. How he wanted to join them! Couldn't he just go down and put his feet in the water? It was so hot. Couldn't he just wade, Mommy? Pretty please?

But Aunt May was firm—I told ya once, I told ya thousand times! Now, no more smack-talkin'. (Smack-talking. They were Idaho people. We lived in Oregon.) There'll be firecrackers tonight. You'll have your fun.

Awww, Vance whimpered.

I just worry . . . my mother had said that first day.

And her worries had been realized three afternoons later, when Vance had been pinched underwater and, backing away from the splashing throng, had been gently taken up in the current. There was a scream from the porch and everyone, even Gram with her wobbly ankles, ran down the stairs onto the beach. But I, under my umbrella with my book, was the closest. I dived in and swam swiftly to Vance. (No one but my parents had known what a strong swimmer I was, as I had given up sports in sophomore year in favor of Advanced Placement classes.) I reached Vance who was stiff with fear, held him around the chest with one arm, and sidestroked toward shore with the other. The churning water sucked at us, dipping us under water, then it swelled around invisible boulders, shouldering us aside. Still, it didn't take long to reach the border, where the river lost its power and there were just jagged rocks to chop the current and skin our knees as we swam-crawled toward shore. I let go his body, but kept a firm grip on his arm as he shivered and sobbed.

At last we climbed up on a flat sun-bleached rock, and sat panting. We looked at each other face-on for the first time that summer—perhaps the first time ever, as he had always embarrassed me and I suspect I had always frightened him. His eyes were set too closely in his concave face, and his gaping mouth was filled with an oversized pink tongue. A string of saliva dangled from his chin. His gaze was more than a gaze. Vance had Down syndrome.

A sob caught him and he turned away, sputtered and coughed.

I heard the whine of Grandy's speedboat, and at the same time as it appeared around the bend semicircling toward us, my father's voice came from the rocks upriver: Raymond? Vance?

We're here! We're okay!

Oh, thank God! cried my father. He crawled up a rock and into view, dripping wet, his big, hairy belly heaving and jiggling, and his eyes black with desperation. But of course he was desperate, I thought, suddenly realizing what had happened. They're all right, both of them, he called over his shoulder, and there was a faint cheer.

That day I became a hero in the eyes of the brats—not one to be rallied around, not a sports hero, but a mystical, holy one. A saint. They had assumed I couldn't swim, so it seemed a miracle, and afterward they gave me an even wider berth. It was perfect.

Mommy, I won't go far out. Just to get my feet wet. It's so hot.

His voice, though high-pitched, was dull and slurry. Aunt May simultaneously wrestled with him and carried on a conversation with Aunt June. (Yes—April, May, and June. So Idaho! But my mother, April, had always gone by her middle name, Charlotte.) Vance was May's alone; the younger three or four were her husband's responsibility, and since he was absent that summer, they fell to Aunt June and her husband, Rick, which seemed natural enough, as it was impossible to differentiate child from child in the boiling stew of the eddy: Tyler! Don't dunk your sister, er, cousin——!

May was firm with Vance, but forgave him everything and the others nothing. She had begun to live for him.

How embarrassing, their struggles! Once I had been sitting in the kitchen to escape the heat, and Vance, having again been thwarted in his attempt to leave the deck, marched angrily through the room and up the stairs, an erection impudently lifting the front of his lime green swimsuit.

The white sun on white sand, the shrieks from below and the whimpers from above, the cushion of adult conversation behind, and me in my little circle of shade perfectly content to turn my back on them all. Then the shadow fell. The brats ran shivering up the beach to be forgiven their crimes and embraced with towels. The adults started thinking about dinner. The cloud of canyon wrens appeared again, as if its lovely dipping and soaring had never been interrupted. And I took down my umbrella and read on, exempt from resentment and the threat of interruption for anything but dinner, because I had, a week before, saved my Mongoloid cousin, so there!

Exempt—or so I thought until that evening. My mother approached me on the deck as a Roman candle lit the circle of cousins red, then blue, then yellow, and the smell of sulfur rose from the beach. Raymond, honey, May and I were talking this afternoon. Vance is so unhappy here. He can't play with the others. He's too old, and they're mean to him. How would it be if, since you're spending your days reading anyway, you read aloud to him? Come on, Ray, try it just for one day as an experiment. He understands more than you think. And he looks up to you, especially after . . .

Unlike any other event of note that summer, whose story was told and retold ad infinitum, ever increasing in grandeur or hilarity, the story of the rescue wasn't repeated after the day it took place. It was the Gospel of Me; they kept it in their hearts, not on their tongues.

Ray, I don't want to have to insist . . . but I insist. Just a day or two, as a favor to me.

Oh, all right, Mother.

For a year or so, I had been trying out calling her Mother, although in my mind she was still Mom. It always made her wince. What a prick I was!

The wavering light from the beach went out with a hiss. Awww, said Grandy, don't throw it in the river! You're a litterbug!

It burned! cried the brat.

So the next morning, as mist rose from the river, Vance followed me across the scarred sand. It was chilly, but I always started early, and if he was going to read with me, he'd have to follow my rules. He knelt, and I reclined in the beach chair, put a towel over my legs, and pulled from my backpack, not whatever I had been reading, but my secret weapon, as heavy as a brick and twice as big. I heaved it into my lap, perhaps with a little grunt, and shot a sidelong glance at Vance to gauge his reaction. There was none. His glassy eyes rested on the book without fear. Maybe he was so overwhelmed by the situation itself that objects lost their meaning. I opened, skimmed through introductions and forewords, and began, *Call me Ishmael* . . .

For a while, I couldn't tell if Vance was listening. He watched the river blankly, and I wondered if he was hypnotized by the cadence of words he couldn't understand, or if he was considering the force drawing Ishmael toward the sea and comparing it to his own little daily struggle with his mother. The wind always blew upstream in the morning, moving the swiftly rising steam in the direction opposite the current, which made the water appear to flow twice as fast. If you watched it for long enough, the beach seemed to grind into motion too, and then the world was reduced to three planes—river, mist, and sand—spinning in opposite directions. It created that void in your belly of watching other trains in a railyard and wondering if they were moving this way or you were moving that. Maybe Vance spent the morning trying to steady himself against such forces.

After the mist dissipated, Vance got fidgety, scratching his thick neck then pouring sand from one cupped palm into the other. Ishmael made his way to New Bedford and took on the strange but happy bedfellow of Queequeg the cannibal. At one point, Vance realized that the edition I was reading from was illustrated, and he began checking over my shoulder each time I turned the page for a picture he could look at. Finally, close to noontime, I clapped the book shut on a just-revealed illustration and said, Vance, if you're going to read with me, you can't be hopping up and down looking at the pictures. You have to make pictures in your mind.

He knelt back down and nodded soberly. Then he closed his eyes and meditated, I suppose, on whatever pictures he could conjure of seedy inns and salty whalemen as I read on. When the brats made their screaming run for the eddy, he frowned and tilted his head toward me to better hear the preacher's wild retelling of Jonah and the Whale. Then we broke for lunch and Vance disappeared. Maybe, I hoped, he would be distracted by whatever quarreling or game playing was going on upstairs, but no—when I headed back out he reappeared behind me. That evening, when Queequeg, on the boat bound for Nantucket, dived into the sea and saved the greenhorn from drowning, Vance bit his lip, made white-knuckled fists, and leaned forward on them, slowly pushing them into the sand in an odd but undeniable show of excitement. I thought to myself, Maybe this is the wrong book. However, if I get up extra-early tomorrow morning . . .

But no. As I quietly gobbled a biscuit at the crack of dawn, one of the sleeping bags rustled (the cousins slept scattered around the downstairs like shoes on the floor of a messy closet) and out crawled Vance. He followed me down, staggered sleepily across the sand, and collapsed onto his knees next to the beach chair. This'll put him to sleep, I thought, as Ishmael and Queequeg negotiated their way onto a ship, but Vance remained looking alert as one could with one's eyes closed. Every so often, he would whisper, *wait,* which meant he had to pee. He must have had a bladder the size of a walnut. I would wait, perhaps stretching my legs and surveying the cliffs, as he made a limping sprint up to the house where he must have squeezed out the stream as fast as possible, slammed the door without flushing, and raced back down to the beach.

When, near the end of the third day, Captain Ahab toasted to his harpooners, *Death to Moby Dick! God hunt us all, if we do not hunt Moby Dick to his death!* I let my voice carry all the husky drama Ahab deserved, because Vance had come this far and, I supposed, earned it.

And so the days passed, Vance and I following the ghostly spout of the Great White Whale. There was no discussion, no explanation of difficult passages, no deciding of the next morning's starting time. He would simply follow me down in the morning, take a dozen pee-breaks, and follow me back up at night to be consumed again by the tumult of cousins. But even with this intensive schedule, I soon real-ized we would never finish the book before my parents and I left for home. I started skipping the chapters not directly related to the plot, then reading them quickly to myself in bed at night. Then I'd scan the next day's read for more chapters to skip.

One of these late nights I went down to the kitchen for a snack and found Aunt May on the phone with her husband. She shot me a pained look, turned away, and hunched over the phone. She was complaining about me! I thought as I returned to my room. I had noticed her grow quiet and sullen around the time I started reading to Vance. It had been her idea, and now she resented me!

In any case, Vance now disdained the same afternoon frenzy he had once begged to join. When the rays of the sun struck us, he would scoot under my umbrella and wrinkle his nose at the hoots and hollers, trying to shut them out.

One afternoon the brats were in rare form. They reached such a state of babbling ecstasy that the eddy could no longer hold them, and several came up onto land. They wanted to write a huge name in the sand, and they hopped around, each dragging one leg stiff like a fat pink pencil, debating all the while whose name it should be. A moment's attention convinced me that they would end up writing gibberish. I read on, and Vance leaned in to hear me. The argument increased in pitch, and their hobbling and scribbling took up more and more of the beach. Then, one particularly pinch-faced brat—her name was Trish or Treena—crossed into an imaginary circle that *I* had drawn at a ten-yard radius from my person. I ducked under my umbrella to stand at my full height, pointed at the girl, and in my low-pitched voice boomed, WILL YOU SHUT UP?

All the cousins froze except the offender, who looked up at me, arranged her jutting teeth and blubbery lips into a sneer and said, You're mean!

The other brats gasped. Wasn't she afraid? Didn't she realize that he was the River Wizard, and if she incurred his displeasure, tonight at midnight he would use his powers to levitate her from where she slept, float her down to the river, and dunk her?

Apparently not.

You're not my dad! she said.

I couldn't dispute so bafflingly true a statement, so I simply allowed my eyes to widen, then narrow.

She turned on a heel and marched back down to the eddy, flanked by cowering cousins.

I eased myself back into my chair. Where was I? Vance smiled and shut his eyes again, ready for a new round of pictures. Within a minute or two, screams were again rising from the eddy, but on we read.

I came to recognize that Vance wasn't fidgeting when he ran his cupped hands through the sand, but acting out in miniature whatever scene of whaleboats chasing whales that I was reading. He never failed to become breathless when Ahab emerged from his cabin—he feared him!—or to be lulled by descriptions of a mast-head lookout over a peaceful sea. He loved the story in a way that I couldn't, and it put me to shame. I had wanted to read this book because I knew in my upcoming Advanced Placement English class we would read *Billy Budd*. How delicious, I had thought, in discussing the novella, to make casual comparisons to the author's behemoth masterpiece! I never expected to actually *enjoy* the book. But now I did, and my enjoyment depended on Vance's.

It drew near the time my parents and I would head back to Oregon. One night, after the cousins had gone to their various sleeping spots, the grown-ups lit the bug candles on the deck and pulled chairs up to the railing. It was a last-quarter moon, and the hilltops downriver were outlined in silver. Grandy brought out his bottle of brandy. Hey there, Raymond, don't rush off to bed. Have a little brandy and watch the bats with us old-timers. Charlotte?

Well, my mother said, what do you think, Gary?

I looked from parent to parent.

Why not? said my father. Just a taste, though. Don't want him singing ol' Dixie and waking the little ones.

Grandy poured, and I tried the sweet and fiery liquid. It was like swallowing candlelight. Black bats, hundreds of them, were descending overhead to make their jerky rounds over the river.

The adults were discussing something in hushed voices.

I wish you'd reconsider, said May.

Sweetheart, said Gram, it's too much. We could take Vance for a little while. But the other three instead . . . it would just be too much.

We'd have to put them in school up here . . . added Grandy.

He needs more than you realize, May said.

We can handle him, said Gram. But to chase the little ones around—with my ankles?

How could he do this? said Uncle Rick.

I glanced at May and felt a throb of pity for this woman with silly combs in her hair. And I felt proud that the adults were discussing this in front of me. I sipped my brandy.

I really wish we could help you too, May, Aunt June said reaching over to squeeze her sister's hand, but we've got our hands full, 'specially once school starts.

My parents said nothing. Their faces were hard in the candle-light.

Years later, after I had gone east for college, and Grandy died, then Gram soon after, as if she was in a rush to meet him, when the family fought and broke ties, I wondered if this had something to do with their bitterness—that my parents, richer than May and with only one child, had sat silent when she was abandoned.

The discussion went late, and I made my brandy last. Vance would stay here with Gram and Grandy. May would return home with her other children. She pretended to shake off her sadness—Oh, these things will all work out, Lord willing; I still got my faith—but we knew that she would rather be left by a hundred husbands than leave Vance.

Not a word of this to the kids, said my father under his breath as we folded the chairs to go in.

Of course not, I said dismissively.

So I read on as if I didn't know, and Vance seemed happy.

Let me tell ya, Raymond, ya really got to see the sun set over the Wallama Hills, Grandy said over lunch a few days later. He took a gulp of his iced tea and ate a chip. Sometime we'll hike to the top of the canyon. It's not a hard climb—just a few rough patches of rock, but there's roots growin' out of 'em to ketch hold of. Only takes an hour or so. And then you pop out on top, and there it is—your old friend the sky, bigger than you remember. Like I always said, what us Idaho farmers missed in landscape we made up in skyscape.

Grandy had been advertising the sunset hike since I arrived, and although the idea appealed to me, the complacency that seemed a natural effect of living at the bottom of a canyon made me put him off. There was also the matter of which brats would be allowed to tag along, and the shrill negotiations that would doubtlessly lead up to the final cut. But it was three days before my departure, and this seemed my last chance.

Let's do it, I said, and Grandy's eyes lit up. We should bring
Vance, I added.

Well, I'll see what May has to say about that.

So the next evening, after an early dinner, the younger children
began a craft project involving pipe cleaners while Grandy and I
gathered flashlights and water bottles. Vance! said Aunt May. Lookit
what we're gonna make! She held open a *McCall's* magazine before
Vance, who turned away to see what I was up to. We're gonna do
this, then *this,* then twist *this* around *that.* . . . This was May's trick
and I had seen it many times. By animating her voice and waving
objects, she managed to captivate Vance while the others slipped
away. If he hadn't become so engrossed in her performance, I might
have insisted he be allowed to join us.

We piled into the speedboat and went a mile downriver to the
trailhead. Then we started the climb, Grandy leading the way, followed by me, then a few cousins, and my father and Uncle Rick
bringing up the rear. The cousins, probably sensing that this was an
adult venture that they were privileged to join in, concentrated on
their footing and said little while the two men provided a murmur
of pleasantries, and Grandy, in a voice breathless from both excitement and exertion, filled my ears with facts and guesses: These roots
are nice and pliant, huh? Good to hold onto. They all lead to that
one Russian olive clear up there. Get so little rain up here they have
to have ten times the roots as they have branches. When it does rain,
though, little blue blossoms pop straight up outa the bark.

We reached the cliffs and climbed a tilted, rocky stairway which
had been carved into a crevasse to emerge onto a gentle slope thickly
forested with gnarled old junipers. The trail was sufficiently wide,
but Grandy gave the bordering bushes a few whacks with his walking

stick, anyway. Then the brush abruptly ceased and we were standing on a rocky ridge from which we could see hundreds of miles in every direction. Westward, the rolling, treeless hills, sliced through occasionally by dry beds of ancient rivers, looked like ripples and channels left in the sand by the retreating tide. I could imagine the mirage along the horizon, a hazy glimmer under the small orange sun, to be the Pacific, and this expanse between us to be the waste laid by the eons, as the sea shrunk, leaving us high and dry.

I turned around, and beyond the blue gap of the canyon rose pine-covered mountains that in the orange light took on the appearance of mossy rocks. Everything seemed in miniature under the awesome expanse of the sky. High clouds made delicate pink loops over us in the pattern of wood grain in a plank of pine. To the south, the trails of two invisible jets made an X, and to the north, hundreds of miles away over Washington, there was a dark smudge—a storm that would certainly never rain on us.

Slowly, the pink cloud-loops turned crimson. The X in the south, being at a lower altitude, was the first to turn blue and, after a few minutes, so did the clouds.

The sense of smallness and desolation—of not deserving to see so much—melted into cool comfort as the blue of the sky drowned the colors of the world, and everything seemed closer. The show was over.

I looked around. We were all sitting on rocks at distances from one another. My grandfather said, Well, Raymond, what do ya think? and I answered in a word that, like all words, is very small: *Beautiful.*

When we reached home, the children were in their jammies and there was an ungainly collection of wiry objects lined up on the kitchen counter.

Vance, said Aunt May, come here. Show Raymond what you made him.

Vance looked away and tried to peel May's hand from his shoulder.

Come on, Vance, don't be shy. It's a thank-you present for reading to him.

Begrudgingly and without meeting my eyes, Vance handed over a tiny lopsided basket woven from pipe cleaners holding a white pebble from the beach.

I said nothing and Vance wandered off. It was silly and unnecessary, Vance and I both knew. I wished May hadn't forced him.

We would have to start early and go late if we were to finish the book the next day, so we headed down while the canyon was still pale with dawn. The air chilled us a little more deeply that morning, as summer was beginning to fade just a touch, and Vance wrapped himself in a beach towel and sat rocking in the sand. The *Pequod* and its crew had reached the Pacific and the sense of foreboding mounted with every ship they encountered, Ahab forgoing all decorum to demand, *Hast seen the White Whale?*

The brats were bathing by the time there was an answer in the affirmative, *Aye, yesterday.*

Vance froze.

My mother appeared and, with a wink, set brown-bag lunches beside us. I read on, my mouth full of white bread and bologna and cheese-dusted corn chips, but I had begun to worry. I knew how this story would end, and even if I hadn't, the sense of doom would have prepared me for tragedy. But wasn't this beyond Vance's power to detect and understand?

After lunch, Ahab himself, hoisted by ropes and pulleys to a lookout, cried, *There she blows!—there she blows! A hump like a snow-hill! It is Moby Dick!* Vance's gasp was further evidence—the book could have ended with Ahab never encountering his mortal enemy, and Vance might have felt neither surprised nor cheated. But the chase was on, and as the shadow climbed the canyon wall, whale-boats dropped from the ship and surged against hammering waves only to be capsized or snapped in two by the whale's enormous jaw. Vance put aside his pretend-world in the sand to stare intently down at his own fists nested between his knees.

Dinnertime! called Gram from the deck. C'mon, fellas, you can finish after.

We swiftly consumed an extra-special g'bye dinner of over-cooked steaks and soggy beans. Then, because my parents and I would leave early the next morning, I was forced to go through a receiving line of cousins, bidding each farewell and kissing their sticky, sunburnt cheeks.

My father suggested Vance and I read inside since it was so dark out—we could use his and Mom's bedroom where it was quiet—but this would have felt like a retreat. We had witnessed the whole adventure nestled in the same patch of sand, and that was where we would finish it.

So, without discussion, Vance and I returned to the beach, planted a ring of bug candles around us, and resumed our positions. I held a flashlight over the book as I read. Sharks snapped at oars, and with splintered harpoon-poles jutting from his side, the White Whale lunged at whaleboats and rolled—dived and reappeared. The wild, passionate language left my throat throbbing and Vance breathless.

During one of his pee-breaks, I actually wondered if I should make up an alternative ending. Ahab could throw his harpoon. It would disappear into the black sea. Moby Dick would turn and swim toward the azure horizon, churning the water into cream, and Ahab would howl some strange benediction to heaven—they had been worthy opponents and their contest had ended in a draw! It could convince Vance, if no one else. But here he came, shoulders hunched, scuttling down the stairway then staggering across the sand.

There was no moon, and the night was dark. Bats flitted above the river, and black frogs the size of large spiders made tiny hops in the sand outside our circle. Now Vance faced me, hanging on every word. Reading slowly, I let the horrible events unfold: Moby Dick rammed, Ahab was lost. Vance clutched the beach chair's armrest. The crew of the whaleboat turned and cried, *The ship? Great God, where is the ship?* and they watched, and Vance and I with them, as their ship and shipmates were swallowed by the sea.

Tears streamed down Vance's face and fell into the sand. His hands moved from the armrest to cling to my arm as if there were something I could do for all those men. For him it had been not tragedy, but disaster.

I did not cling to him as he clung to me, but I did what I could—I met his eyes. Again I felt what I had weeks before, when we two were dripping there together on the sun-bleached rock: that his gaze was more than a gaze. His close-set eyes, blank brow, and the curvature of his face made it a lens pinpointing the power of his attention, and this time I did not turn away. I let go the look of severity I had worn all summer and let him see what I was.

He continued to cry, and to cling, as I read the one-page epilogue. Ishmael alone escaped to tell the tale. Then I closed the book. Our foray was fulfilled.

Vance released my arm and hung his head. He rose and walked slowly into the darkness toward the house, crying in the way I wish I could now—crying for the world—as if he knew!

Nightwalking

"WHERE HAVE YOU been?" Angela asked her son.

"Why? It's only seven."

"Yes. That's two hours I haven't known where you or your father were. That's two hours I couldn't write."

Matt glanced beyond her, past the refrigerator, into the study, where the computer screen was glowing with a half-filled page. "If you haven't been writing, then why isn't the screen saver on? It kicks in after five minutes." He knew, because he had installed it. A little smile of victory spread across his round, sweet face, and he turned and mounted the staircase two steps at a time.

"I was rereading what I wrote this morning, smarty. I can read when I don't know where you are, but I can't write. I've explained that before." Her low-pitched voice crescendoed as his footsteps faded down the upstairs hallway. "Dinner in a half-hour, whether your father's home or not!"

Angela went into her study and closed the door. Why do I do this? she wondered. Why can't I leave them alone?

She picked up the phone anyway and tried her husband again on his cell.

At a mini-mart in Ohio, Calvin dumped onto the counter the following: jelly beans, unsalted peanuts, a bunch of bruised bananas,
and two cans of Diet Mountain Dew. Sarah didn't allow chocolate
or partially hydrogenated oils. Calvin held out his card. "I'm the
green Toyota. I think it was fifteen bucks, plus all of this."

"Shore," said the woman. She glanced out to the gas pumps.
"That's pump six."

A flash of this woman's life came to him: It was her little crusade
to get customers to take note of their pump numbers. Calvin looked
out to pump six and saw that Sarah was slumped down in the car,
laughing to herself. Maybe she had heard something funny on the
radio, or maybe she was thinking of a trick to play on him. He
smiled.

"Twenty-one twenty-five, sir. If I could git your autograph right
there you'll be on your way." She had written a large "6" at the top
of the receipt and circled it.

Calvin signed and took the bag out to the car. When he
opened the door, he saw that Sarah had taken off her shirt and
bra. She had reclined the seat to be out of view, and there she sat
in her jeans and socks with her Pollyanna braids falling over
either shoulder. She had round breasts that were set wide on her
chest, the nipples pointing in different directions. When he had
first seen them, two months ago, he had thought of his father,
who had a lazy eye.

"Holy shit," said Calvin, looking around to see who could see.

"Get in," said Sarah. "If we want to make it to Pennsylvania
tonight, we can't dilly-dally." She was biting her lip, doing a bad
imitation of herself when she was clothed and serious.

"Holy shit," said Calvin, climbing in. He pulled out of the gas station and up to the traffic light. He reached over to run his fingers over Sarah's ribs, but when he went to touch her breast, she slapped his hand. "Oh, no you don't. Drive. The light is green."

"You are a cruel woman," said Calvin.

Last night they had fallen asleep watching the local news in an Illinois motel. This morning they awoke kissing and touching, neither of them knowing who had started it. Calvin rolled on top of Sarah, but she said, "Not this morning. You're lazy after you come. I'm gonna make you wait." And she went to take a shower.

Back on the interstate, Sarah brought her seat up and leaned forward to fiddle with the radio. She found an old Journey song that she knew all the words to. She sang and swayed back and forth. "Hey," she barked. "Keep your eyes on the road!"

Calvin laughed and drove on, watching her out of the corner of his eye. Swaying and singing, she began to unbraid one of her pigtails. Then she took out her lipstick and, rather than using her own mirror, jerked the rearview mirror toward her, and leaned over.

"Jesus Christ."

"Stay in your lane, Calvin."

When she had applied her lipstick, she sat back down, leaned against the door, and, facing Calvin, put lipstick on her nipples, one by one. Then she burst out laughing.

Half of her hair was flying around in the wind, the other half was still in its braid. She had red lips and red nipples. Her laugh was musical and free, like a soprano singing arpeggios.

Sarah was thirty-one—two years older than Calvin. She taught trigonometry at a school for gifted teenagers in San Jose, and her last boyfriend had been a biker. Calvin had never imagined a woman like Sarah could exist in real life. She was his dream girl, and she would leave him the moment he bored her.

Late at night, Meg was awakened by blotches of light winking and nodding on her ceiling like the blurry faces of angels. She rolled over and saw the same pattern of lights, but smaller and in sharper focus, on her curtains. Wallace, her cat, leapt to the floor with a soft thud. It was 2:30 A.M.

They forgot again, she thought. Whoever is in charge of turning off the lights after the business league's baseball game keeps forgetting. Or no one's in charge, and the last one to leave is supposed to do it. But then he doesn't know where the switches are, and his wife and kids are waiting in the car, and a chilly wind is starting to blow down the hillside, rattling the leaves which are just starting to dry and turn yellow.

Milroy, New York, was in a shallow valley on the poorer side of the Berkshires just west of the Massachusetts border. At the bottom of the valley was a creek, and Main Street was just above it. About the level of the shop rooftops, the slope leveled off, and there was the high school. A step above that was the baseball field, and then on the top step, just below the crest of the hill, were several old houses with chipped paint. Meg's was the closest of these to the edge of the step, only a hundred yards up from the baseball field. She grew up in this house, falling asleep to the sound of baseball games, but she didn't recall the lights ever being left on afterward.

It was September. Sean had left in June. That was a little over three months—about one hundred days. So a hundred times she had lain down wishing he was there. A season of nights. How many times—thirty, forty—had she awakened in the middle of the night wishing it again?

She turned again to watch the lights on the ceiling and wait for sleep.

Over breakfast, Angela reminded Matt and her husband, Andy, that she was leaving that afternoon.

Both of them looked at her, astonished. "Where are you going?"

"I'm driving out to Milroy to visit Meg and Dad."

"Why?"

"Calvin's coming through town, so I figured I should go. It's our first chance in a long time to all be there together."

"When will you come back?"

"Tomorrow. I told you guys about this weeks ago."

They returned to their breakfast with sulks that Angela knew were for her benefit. She *had* told them about the trip weeks ago, but then intentionally had not reminded them until now so neither of them would expect to accompany her. She felt as if she should keep Andy and Matt, her simple family, away from her complex and troubled family.

Angela was a poet who had worked in obscurity for many years, writing odes on flowers, love poems to her husband, and celebrations of pregnancy, childbirth, and motherhood. She got the occasional adjunct position at colleges around Boston and left the mortgage payments to Andy, who was a contractor and believed in her art. Then, five years ago, Angela's mother had become seriously ill. Angela sank into depression and stopped writing. Her younger sister, Meg, moved from New York City back to Milroy to help their father take care of their mother. Angela visited often, but always felt ill at ease. How could Meg and Dad carry on their regular banter with Mom, when she was bald and frail and veiny? All evening Angela would be on the verge of tears, choking out paltry contributions to the conversation. A few times she sneaked out after dark and drove back to Boston.

When her mother died two years ago, Calvin, the youngest, too handsome and bright-eyed for their family, had flown in from California and spoke poignantly at her funeral, recalling humorous stories from his childhood and drawing wistful, life-affirming conclusions. Angela hated him for it.

She went home and began writing again, but now she wrote a different type of poem: the death poem—honest, painful expressions of guilt and anger and horror of the unknown—dust in one's palm, skies empty of stars, nightmares of drowning. She published a collection which, for poetry, became a huge seller. It won a prize. An expanded second edition came out the next year with new poems on the same subject and an introduction by a famous novelist.

Now Angela had a full-time position at Suffolk University, and had already gotten an advance from a big publisher for a memoir. She was successful, but she was a mess.

"There's a broccoli casserole in the freezer. I know you're not going to eat it. You're going to order pizza and watch R-rated movies on HBO, which is fine, I suppose. We'll eat it tomorrow night, or Sunday."

Her husband winced, and her son laughed and shook his head, but neither looked up from his breakfast.

"I'm sorry," she said.

They both turned pitying smiles on her. They looked alike, both round-featured, with thick eyebrows. Matt had inherited all of

Andy's Armenian blood and none of her Austrian. They were like Papa Bear and Baby Bear. But who was she, then? Certainly not Mama Bear. Not Goldilocks or Grandma. She must be some witch. She chuckled aloud at the thought, then caught herself and frowned. She was a witch.

She rose from the table. Andy and Matt looked to each other, bewildered.

Calvin and Sarah camped out in a tent in the woods above a rest stop in western Pennsylvania. They zipped their sleeping bags together and slept in each other's arms, but awoke too sore and cold to have sex.

Now Sarah was driving fast through the misty hills and the heater was blasting. "I hate this song. Find something good," she said.

Calvin scanned through the stations and found an old Fleetwood Mac song.

"This okay?"

"I guess."

She slowed as they entered a mining town wedged between two hills. They passed a rusted old water tower, then a warehouse with all the windows broken out. The song ended and a quick-talking announcer said, "Mix 95.5 plays the hits of the sixties, seventies, and eighties. We're in the middle of a rock-block Friday morning— you know what that means, four Fleetwood Mac hits in a row on Mix 95.5. From 1979 here's 'Sara.'"

"Oh, no," said Sarah.

"I love this song!"

"Don't," whined Sarah, but Calvin was already singing in an

exaggerated Stevie Nicks vibrato, "Drowning in the sea of love, where everyone would love to drown . . ."

"You're awful," laughed Sarah.

Now his song became a serenade. He put his hand under her hair and held the delicate cords of muscle at the nape of her neck singing, "Sarah, you're the poet in my heart. Never change, never stop . . ."

"Do you know how many people have sung this song to me in my life?"

He turned down the volume a little and said, "But no one meant it like I do."

She smiled at him incredulously and furrowed her brow. He kissed her shoulder. She turned back to the road and her smile faded a little.

Had he said too much?

She reached over and squeezed his hand.

Maybe not.

The sun was shining at such a slant that it reached down between the hemlocks and warmed the back porch. As Meg strolled around, pinching dead leaves off plants and throwing them over the rail, she could hear the kids calling, "Heeey, batter batter batter batter, swing!" then breaking into laughter when the batter swung at air and the ball struck the catcher's mitt with a sharp *pock*. Through the trees, she could see flashes of their bright red uniforms.

Kids in the afternoon, she thought, then grown-ups at night, playing under bright lights swarming with bugs. Pretty soon she would take the plants inside. Next week, maybe.

She heard tires on gravel. She stepped off the porch and walked around the house to see her father climbing out of his red truck holding up three bottles of wine.

"Rioja for us"—Dolf held up a single bottle—"and Merlot for the sissies." He held up the other two.

"Sounds nice."

"So, who all is coming?" Dolf asked, although Meg had already told him.

"Angela and Calvin and his new girlfriend, Sarah," said Meg.

"Sarah. I'll never remember that."

"Calvin just called. They'll be here around eight."

"Kind of a late dinner, don't you think?"

Meg shrugged.

"Are Matt and Andy coming?" asked Dolf.

"No. I had hoped so, but when I talked to Angela this morning, she said no."

They stood for a moment looking up at the trees.

"Is this going to be dreadful?" asked Dolf.

"Of course not," laughed Meg.

She had inherited her mother's job of curbing his hyperbole. Dinner might be hard—it would be the first time they were all together since the funeral—but not dreadful. She looked at his tired gray eyes and lipless mouth. He had a habit of chewing on the inside of his cheeks.

I'm the only one he actually likes, Meg thought with a twinge of sadness.

"You know, Meg, you are the only one I like," Dolf said.

"Don't say that, Dad."

"Well it's true. You are the only one that turned out normal. They are just weird. I wish Matt and Andy were coming."

"Do me a favor, Dad. I'll take these," said Meg taking the wine bottles, "and you go out to the garden and start picking some kale. I'll bring you a colander."

"What the hell is kale?"

"Oh, come on, I'll show you."

"What have you done with my garden? Is this going to be another one of your squeaky dinners? I hate food that squeaks when you eat it."

Angela shouldn't have tried to squeeze in an hour of writing before leaving, because when she shut down her computer and went to feed Bony, the dog, she couldn't find him. He had escaped from the backyard, as he always managed to do when he felt neglected.

She called all the neighbors she knew, but got only answering machines. So she put a handful of dog biscuits in her pocket and set off down the street, peering over hedges and wandering into the woods between properties, calling, "Bony . . . Bony . . . Wanna treat?" The street ended in a busy road with a golf course beyond. He never would have gone this far, would he? "Bony, goddammit! . . . Wanna treat?" She headed back. Maybe he had gone in the other direction.

At last she found Bony pretending to sleep on someone's porch in the cul-de-sac at the opposite end of her street. She leaned over the gate, waving a biscuit. "Wanna treat? Good boy!" He didn't budge. She hesitated to open the gate and walk up a stranger's pathway, even though no one seemed to be home. "Come on, Bony. You can't live here. They don't want you. We want you. Wanna treat?"

Cautiously, she opened the gate, and realizing, apparently, that it was inevitable, Bony rose and trotted down the path. "Good boy," said Angela, scratching his rump. This he tolerated, but then walked a few paces behind her all the way home.

She quickly packed an overnight bag and headed out, shutting Bony inside the house. It was three-thirty, a full two hours later than she had wanted to leave, and when she got to the turnpike, it was packed. It starts earlier and earlier, she thought. She opened her bag between the seats and groped around for her phone.

"Meg, I'm going to be late. It was Bony—he ran off and I had to go find him."

"What time should we expect you?"

"I'm not sure. There's tons of traffic. I'll call you when I'm closer. Shit, someone just cut me off. I've got to go."

The sun had fallen behind the hills by the time Calvin drove down Main Street, past the secondhand bookstore where he had once found a *Penthouse* from the seventies, hid it in a *National Geographic,* and spent the afternoon with it in a dusty corner; past the tiny storefront law office where Meg worked; past city hall with its little fountain in front, where kids used to throw pennies and dimes for good luck. He wondered if they still did. Once, after a day of shopping on Main Street, he and his mother had climbed all the way back up to the house when, helping him off with his coat, which must have been suspiciously heavy, she reached into his pocket and took out a handful of wet coins. Down the hill they trudged, his mother lecturing all the way, then she stood with her arms tightly folded as he pitched the money back into the fountain as hard and spitefully as he could. A group of high-school girls in jean jackets had laughed as they walked by.

"So this is where you grew up," said Sarah.

He made a sharp left and zigzagged up the hill, past the high school, to the house. Only his father's truck and Meg's shabby old Volvo were there. "Good," he said, "Angela's not here yet."

"Why? What's wrong with Angela?"

"Nothing, it's just better to do it bit by bit, you know."

They got their bags from the trunk and walked up the pathway.

"So, you grew up in this house."

"Yep."

"And now your sister lives here and your dad lives . . ."

"In the next town over."

"Welcome!" said Dolf, emerging onto the porch, letting the screen door bang behind him.

"Hi, Dad. You look great," said Calvin, setting down his bag to embrace his father.

"It's been too long, son."

"This is Sarah. Here, I'll take the bags in."

"Welcome, Sarah." Dolf shook her hand and one eye wandered over her as the other remained gazing over her left shoulder.

"It's good to meet you. . . . What can I call you?"

"Oh! Dolf, Please. It's an ugly name; my parents were Austrian . . ." His voice trailed off. "Well," he said, releasing her hand, "this is the first time we have seen Calvin in a long while. Maybe you can tell me, what does he do for a living? I can never understand it."

"He writes programs that tell computers how to talk to each other over the Internet. It's more boring than you can imagine. That's probably why he doesn't explain it well. The company knows how boring it is, so they pay him more than he deserves, and he knows too much to ever be fired, so he can just tell them that he's going to take a month off to drive around with me, and they just say, 'Okay. Don't forget us.'"

Calvin, who was still standing in the foyer, smiled proudly at this description, then went into the kitchen to see Meg.

"You know," said Dolf, "all the times he has explained it, I have never understood until now."

He has no accent, thought Sarah, but he doesn't use contractions. They must have spoken German at home. "What do you do, Dolf?"

"Well, I work for the county telling people whether or not they can chop down trees to build additions to their houses and things like that."

"Have you ever taken a bribe?"

Dolf laughed loudly. "It's chilly. Let's go in." He put his arm around her and took her to sit in the drafty parlor.

Calvin was already standing at the kitchen sink beside Meg, snapping the ends off beans.

"Is she pretty?" asked Meg quietly.

"Very," said Calvin.

"Well, keep an eye on Dad, then. He loses his cool around pretty women these days. It's the only evidence of senility so far."

"She can handle him. When is Angela getting here?"

"I don't know. She's supposed to call."

"Is she bringing Andy and Matt?"

"No."

"Shoot."

Nearly an hour passed and Angela had still not called so they sat down to eat.

"Sarah, may I pour you a little Merlot?" asked Dolf.

"Um, what's that other one?"

"That is Rioja."

"Ooh, I'd love a glass of Rioja."

"Me, too," said Calvin.

Dolf hesitated.

"Pour them some wine, Dad," laughed Meg.

"What, aren't we allowed?" asked Calvin.

Dolf poured and Meg explained, "The past few months, Dad and I have been educating ourselves about wine. We started with French, but then discovered that California wines are cheaper and easier to understand."

"Then Chianti," said Dolf.

"I couldn't really get into the Chiantis the way Dad did. But for the past few weeks it's been Rioja. We both like Rioja. Cheers. To Milroy, I suppose."

"Mm," said Sarah. "Nice and peppery."

"Makes you warm," said Meg.

The phone rang. "That's probably Angela," said Meg, rising.

"So you got this nice Spanish wine for you and Meg, and you were going to stick us with a cheap California Merlot?" said Calvin.

Dolf cleared his throat. "Exactly."

"Well, that's not very nice."

"Bring your own damn wine. Beans, Sarah?"

"Yes, please."

"That was Angela," said Meg, sitting down. She'll be here in ten minutes." Then she added with a tinge of remorse, "She says to go ahead without her."

Calvin snorted.

"Well, we might as well finish this off," said Dolf topping off everyone's glass.

As soon as Angela turned onto the Milroy exit, she began planning what kind of impression she would make. I'll be casually apologetic, and I'll be very friendly to this new girlfriend. I'll ask her what she does before she asks me. Remember: Ask her what she does!

She looked at her watch. Shit, I'm so goddamn late! She sped through the town and up the hill.

I'll mention the book, but not go into the subject matter.

She parked and walked quickly up to the porch. She was out of breath from her speeding and self-coaching, so she stood a moment smoothing the front of her slacks. She didn't want to enter gasping for air.

Meanwhile, everyone at the dinner table had heard her climb the stairs to the porch, and was quietly wondering why she hadn't entered.

Finally, she rushed in. "Sorry! Sorry! Oh, don't get up!" She went around the table giving half-hugs. She gave Sarah a firm handshake. "Hi, Sarah, I'm Angela. It was Bony! Blame Bony! He always runs off." She collapsed into a seat between her father and Meg.

"Merlot?" said Dolf as Meg filled Angela's plate.

Calvin resumed his description of their journey across the country and their plans to take a southern route back home. Then Meg and Dolf filled the others in on happenings about town, mentioning name after name that called up dim recollections in Calvin's and Angela's memories, but no faces. Then there was a short silence.

"So, Meg, is Sean around?" asked Calvin.

"Oh, no. He moved out."

"Oh, I'm sorry."

"You have got to keep up on the news, Son," said Dolf. "He left, what, three months ago?"

"More or less," said Meg.

"That's too bad," said Calvin, "I liked Sean."

"We all did," said Angela.

Meg pushed a cauliflower floret around her plate with a knife. "Yeah, things are . . . I don't know. It's weird. We still talk, though."

"He lives in Cameron," said Dolf. "You know, I saw him just yesterday from across the street, but he didn't see me. I keep telling Meg that they are being silly. She should just invite him to one of our little dinners. Get him back over here."

"Well, I doubt it's that simple, Dad," said Angela.

"It probably is that simple! When people are young they go out of their heads. Convince themselves of things. They are of two minds—or many minds. You've just got to, sort of, corral them back in, them and their minds. That is what your mother did. I left her once when I was young, and she just talked to me straight and brought me back."

"Really? You left Mom?" said Calvin.

"It was before you were born," said Dolf.

"That's so funny that neither of you ever mentioned it," said Meg.

"They didn't mention it"—Angela laughed incredulously—"because it was a secret. You were too young to know, Meg. Dad, I can't believe you're telling them now!"

"Why not?" said Dolf. "I've decided it is better to say these things. I didn't even know that you knew, Angela."

"Of course I knew!" she said with the same strangely high-pitched laugh. "I was seven years old."

"But your mother . . ."

"Told me you had gone camping, but I knew. I had heard you taking all your things out to the car in the middle of the night. I was a smart kid. I knew you didn't need all your things to go camping."

"Your mother told you I'd gone camping," Dolf said again, quietly. "She knew better than I did that I would come back. I was only gone a week."

"Wow," said Calvin.

"I was a different man back then. She was pregnant with you, Calvin. Can you imagine, leaving a pregnant woman with two little girls? I was a different man. I am ashamed."

There was silence, until Sarah saved them.

"Angela, I've been excited to meet you. Calvin showed me some of your poems. They're very powerful."

"Thank you."

"What are you working on now?"

Angela seemed disoriented, as though she had just been startled out of a nap. "Well, it's a memoir of the last five years, sort of focusing on the death of my mother . . . of our mother. It's about half-done. I'm on a deadline, which is an odd feeling. I wrote my poems without deadlines."

"What's it called?"

Angela swallowed. " 'Dying to See You.' Meg, is this tarragon?"

"Basil. From the garden."

"Delicious."

"Well, it is good that you're writing about Mom, Angela," said Dolf. "You know," he chuckled, "I told Meg a funny story the other night. Should I tell them? The one about the fishing trip?"

Meg laughed. "Oh, this one's good."

"Back when we were newlyweds, we used to go fishing a lot, down near Pittsfield. It was summer and we were at our favorite fishing hole, deep in the woods, and she took off her shirt!" He laughed breathlessly. "We were sitting on a rock in the sun, I was baiting a hook, and when I turned around, there she was, topless! I said, 'Katie, what are you doing?' And she said, 'I just felt like letting my breasts out.'"

Everyone laughed but Angela, who began eating very quickly.

Dolf went on with watery eyes, "Can you imagine? 'I just felt like letting my breasts out,' like they were little animals. I will never forget that till the day I die. It was so unlike her. She was usually so conservative."

"No, she wasn't. Neither of you were conservative," said Meg.

Calvin and Sarah were still laughing.

"You are right; that's the wrong word," said Dolf. "She was careful. Caring."

"Caring is a good word," said Meg.

"But she was careful in the way you are, Meg, sometimes too much so."

"You know," said Angela, mouth full and fork in hand, "maybe it's just me, but, doesn't it seem inappropriate to be telling all these stories about Mom that were never told?"

Calvin caught Sarah's eye and they laughed again.

"I mean, if we're going to . . . memorialize her . . . it shouldn't be in this jokey, gossipy way," said Angela between bites.

"Angela," said Meg. "For the first year, Dad and I didn't really talk much about her. When she came up, we'd just tiptoe around her, because it was hard, and we were worried for each other. But then we decided we needed to start talking about her again, in this way. It was Dad's idea, and I agreed. So we've been trying."

"You're right," said Calvin, who had realized the gravity of the conversation and stopped laughing.

"Maybe I'm the odd one, then," Angela said. She gulped the last of her wine as she stood. "It just seems wrong. I'm sorry. I need to deal with this for a few minutes."

She took her bag, which had been leaning against the door-jamb, and climbed the stairs to her room.

"Sorry, Sarah," said Meg.

"Don't apologize. People in my family storm away from the table all the time. I have to say, though, they never gobble up the end of their meal before they go."

Calvin snorted.

"She thinks she's smarter than we are," said Dolf.

"Don't worry about it, Dad," said Meg.

"She thinks she has all these lofty emotions, and we are just peasants. 'Dying to See You,' for Christ's sake."

"Let's have dessert," said Meg. She went to the kitchen, brought out a pound cake, whipped cream, and blueberries, and served it.

"These have got to be the plumpest, sweetest blueberries I've ever tasted," said Sarah.

"I don't remember all this good stuff coming out of the garden," said Calvin.

"That's because all Mom and Dad ever grew was cabbage and onions."

"That is all you need to grow," said Dolf.

"Oh, come now, Dolf," said Sarah, "you have to admit this was an amazing meal."

"Meg knows I like her food. I shouldn't tease."

"Um, you guys?" Angela called from the stairway landing.

"Yes?" said Meg, leaning back in her chair to peer at her from around the corner.

"I'm sorry. Really. It's good for you guys to talk about her in that way. It's good for you. I wish I could do it, too."

"Well, come back to the table," said Dolf, his mouth full of cake.

"No, I'm just going to stay in my room for a little while. I'm just—I'm sorry."

"All right," said Meg.

Angela climbed the creaky stairs as quietly as she could.

Everyone at the table was quiet for a while, until Sarah, again, broke the silence.

"So, do you all mind if I claim my right as visitor and skip out on dishes?"

"Not at all," said Dolf.

"I thought I might go down and watch a little of the baseball game."

"I'll come with you," said Calvin.

"No, you stay and help. I'll just be a little while."

As others began clearing the table, Sarah put on a sweater and stepped out onto the back porch. She paused to admire Meg's little jungle of plants, all of them, it seemed, ready to burst from their pots. Their stalks leaned against the railing and their leaves tangled with one another's leaves. The chirping of crickets, which she had noticed the moment she stepped out of the car, was louder now that night had fallen. This must be their silence, she thought. The rustling of leaves, the chirping and buzzing—they never knew real silence growing up, so this must be their version of it. Sarah had grown up on a street crowded with little houses and manicured lawns in the southern California suburbs. She had known real, silent silence.

There was the crack of a bat and a cheer. She left the porch and climbed down the path through the woods.

"Angela," said Dolf, tapping on her door. "I am leaving."

Angela opened the door and stood in the doorway. "Sorry, Dad. I found some of my old school papers. I kind of got lost in them." She nodded toward some papers spread on the bed. "I should have come back down."

"Will you stick around tomorrow?"

"No, I have to leave in the morning. I've got some appointments."

"Well, next time, then."

"Next time," said Angela. "And I'm sorry about dinner. All these things—everything will be all right."

"Of course it vill."

"Vill?" chuckled Angela.

"Will," corrected Dolf.

"Bye-bye, Dad." Angela kissed him on the cheek, thinking it strange how something from so deep in his past still clung to the hem of his consciousness.

Meg and Calvin followed Dolf out to the truck.

"How long will you be around, Son?"

"A day or two."

"Good. I like your Sarah."

"I thought you might."

"I'll drop by tomorrow. Good night, Meg."

"Drive safely."

As the truck pulled away, Meg shivered.

"Cold?" asked Calvin.

"A little."

He put his arm around her—she was shorter than he remembered—and rubbed her arms, warming her as they walked back to
the porch. "I might join Sarah down at the game. Wanna come?"

"No," she said. "I'm going to read a little before bed."

"All right."

Calvin walked through the house and out the back door. Meg
went to the kitchen and put away a few of the bigger dishes which
had dripped dry.

It was always so strange to watch her father leave his own house.
He had moved out after her mother died, saying he couldn't stand
living with all the memories, but Meg knew it was also a way to get
Sean to move up from the City, and thereby keep her around. She
had laughed to herself when he made the offer, because only a few
years earlier he had wanted to keep it a secret from her mother that
Meg and Sean were living together in their one-bedroom on Avenue
A. But he had come around to Sean, as most people did—enough
to offer them his house.

Meg had met Sean at the Night Owl, an East Village bar where
he still worked. It was around the time she discovered she liked to
drink a lot and see rock shows in the little clubs, and began to
modify her plans to be a lawyer into plans to be a paralegal. Sean
was a big, tattooed Irishman who knew all the band members and
gave them free drinks. He had a potbelly, but Meg loved his accent.
It started out in the most casual way—a drunken one-night stand,
then another, and another. Then one day he just didn't leave.

Meg's mother got sick and Meg moved back to Milroy. Then she died and Sean moved up. He still went down weekends to work at the Night Owl. Meg worked for a lawyer down on Main Street. She never expected either of them to like living in Milroy, but they did.

For a long time, Meg had been turning into a more and more serious person and not wanting to drink so much. And, she supposed, her mother dying made her even more serious. Some strange things started happening. Meg would walk down to the kitchen in the middle of the night—sometimes even out to the gardening shed—and take things out of drawers. Sean would come down and find her, and take her back to bed. Meg didn't want to call it sleepwalking, because that sounded crazy, so they called it nightwalking. They joked about it, but it scared Meg. They were always her mother's things she was taking out and lining up on the counter: a potato masher, a wooden spoon, a tin measuring cup in the kitchen; a trowel, gloves, and the mossy shards of broken pots in the shed.

At times Meg thought to herself, Maybe Dad is wise not to live here.

Then, suddenly, things with Sean fell apart. Maybe it was her sadness. It was hard for her to understand. It was Sean's decision to leave, but she pretended it was mutual, out of pride.

She felt that lately she had been coming out of her sadness. How could she show this to Sean?

She went to the parlor, got her book, and sat in the big, comfy chair. She could scan the bookshelf and remember which books she had read when her mother was sick—in which waiting rooms, in which hospitals. Wallace, her cat, who had been hiding during dinner, jumped into her lap and curled up. Meg sat for a long time, her book open and resting on Wallace, without reading.

● ● ●

Calvin had showered. Now he felt clean and happy, lying naked between the cool sheets, waiting for Sarah. Meg had offered him the big bed in the master bedroom, but Calvin had declined because he liked the idea of having a girl in his old room.

Sarah came in, her hair wet and limp, wearing a big brown bathrobe. "Do you think it's okay for me to wear this? It looked so comfortable."

"Why not? It's too big to be Meg's. Maybe it's Sean's."

Sarah threw her wad of clothing into a chair, slipped out of the robe and slid into the little bed beside him. They kissed. Calvin touched Sarah's face, then let his hand run along her soft neck and down under the sheets.

"Everyone's still awake," said Sarah in a strange voice.

"Just Meg, and she's downstairs."

"No, your dad's reading the paper on the porch, and your sisters are right next door playing with their dolls."

Calvin grinned and pulled her toward him. "I don't care."

"Calvin, shhh! We have to whisper." She started to say something, then hesitated. Then there was a shade of caution in her eyes as she said it anyway: "Your mother's in the sewing room. What if she heard and came in here?"

Calvin's grin didn't falter. "She'd blow her top. She'd call you names and never let me see you again," he whispered. "We have do it without making a single sound, so even if she comes and listens at the door, she won't know."

Sarah climbed on top of him and whispered, "Then we'll have to do it very, very slowly."

Next weekend I'll have my friends over for dinner, thought Meg, still sitting in the parlor. Most of her Milroy friends were ten or fifteen years older than she, but nice people who knew her father. Then I'll see if I can visit Miriam in the City the following weekend. I'll get drunk two nights in a row and feel like there's still a wild girl in me. Then I'll come home.

She looked down at the circular rug in the middle of the dark hardwood floor with all its cracks and grooves letting cold air up from the basement, and had a memory of Sean.

He had been making wooden crates for his record collection, because he and Meg agreed the plastic milk crates were ugly. It was an evening like this one. He had rolled up the circular rug and was kneeling on the floor, clumsily sawing a plank of wood. Meg was trying to read, but also just watching him.

He cut his thumb.

"Ah, sweet Jesus!" He squeezed his thumb as dark blood filled the cut and dripped to the floor.

Meg ran and got a wet towel. "Come here." She sat back into the chair. He knelt before her, and she wiped away the blood. The cut was only a half-inch long, but deep. "Should we go to the emergency room?" Meg asked.

He looked at the cut. "No, I think it'll be all right."

She wrapped his thumb in the towel, held it in her hands, and squeezed her hands between her knees, hoping the pressure would stop the bleeding.

"Are you sure, Sean? I'd feel awful if you needed stitches."

"Don't worry, my darlin'," he said. He always called her "my darlin'." It was one of those things that was hard for Meg to quote, because Americans couldn't say it without sounding silly. It was one of those rich Irish things to say. "It's just a flesh wound."

There was a pause. Meg looked at him and they both burst out laughing.

"A flesh wound, as opposed to what?" she said. "Rupturing a vital organ in your thumb?"

"Just a flesh wound, my darlin'. I suppose I'll survive it and your laughing at me, both."

She put gauze on his thumb and taped it up. Then she went back to reading. Sean gave up on the crate and spent the rest of the evening playing songs off his old records and quietly enjoying the memories they brought up.

How could he not miss nights like that?

Meg decided to call Sean, and pushed Wallace from her lap with an apology.

"How are you, dear?" said Sean.

"Fine. I had the whole family here for dinner, and they all asked about you."

"Ah, the whole bizarre clan. I saw your dad from across the street the other day, but he didn't see me."

There was a click on the line. Then Angela's voice said, "Hello?"

"I'm on the phone," said Meg. "I'll be just ten minutes."

"Oh, I'm sorry. No rush. I was just going to call home, but I'll use my cell."

"Is that Angela?" asked Sean.

"Oh! Sean! Hello."

"How are you, Angela?"

"I'm all right. I'll let you get back to your conversation."

"Say hello to Andy and Matt for me."

"Sure."

There was another click, and Sean giggled.

Meg asked, "So, how are you?"

"Good. I've been busy at the studio." He worked at a little studio in the woods outside Cameron, a town ten miles away, making expensive handmade paper that people used for wedding invitations. He used to leave his big rubber boots, splattered with dried paper pulp, on the porch. "I'm working there four or five days a week now."

"That's a handful—with going down on Fridays."

"Oh, I don't go down on Fridays anymore."

"You quit the Night Owl?"

"Do ya believe it? After all these years? I figure it isn't worth the commute. Can't stay a rock-and-roller all your life, when you live out in the woods."

Meg's heart felt as if it was being squeezed up her throat.

"Well," she said, steadying her voice, "don't be a stranger. Come over here some afternoon and make me your baked beans."

"I will. Meg? Are you all right?"

"Fine, fine. I'm gonna go. I have to get up early."

"All right, darlin'. I love ya."

"Don't say that, Sean."

"I know. I'm sorry."

Meg went upstairs, brushed her teeth, and put on her blue flannel pajamas. She lay down and Wallace curled up at the foot of the bed. The baseball game must have ended. There was no more cheering or taunting, just the murmur of voices, and occasionally a laugh that sounded like the clucking of a bird.

All through their last year together she had begged him to stop going down to the City to work weekends at the Night Owl. He would stay on friends' couches, sometimes even driving back up in the middle of the night after his Saturday shift. Then he'd lie down next to her with his whiskey breath.

"It's so dangerous, Sean!" Meg would say in the morning. "I'd rather you stay down there half of Sunday than drive home after a shift."

"Sweetheart, give me a little credit. I wouldn't drive if I weren't sober. And, after all, I do it so I can come home to you."

"Then why go down at all? It's so crazy! Ask for more shifts at the studio. Or bartend somewhere up here! It makes no sense for you to go down every weekend!"

He would laugh. He could always find a laugh in the middle of an argument. "My darlin', let me have my one indulgence. Don't make me feel old."

Since he left, Meg had been expecting him to move back to the City. It would make sense; he'd be returning to his old friends, his old girlfriends, his old life of tending bar and seeing rock shows. But now he had quit the Night Owl.

It was me he was leaving, Meg thought.

The room was dark now, and Calvin and Sarah lay side by side enjoying sleepy conversation punctuated by long moments of silence.

"Do you want to leave tomorrow, or can we stay another day?" asked Calvin.

"We can stay."

"My family doesn't scare you?"

"Scare me? No. Of course, no one asked me about me . . ."

"I'm sorry. We're all kind of self-involved."

"That's all right. I love your sisters."

"Really?"

"Yeah, they're so beautiful."

"Really?"

"And so sad."

"Yeah. I guess they're both still sad about my mom."

"And you aren't."

Calvin thought a moment. "No, I never really was. I mean, I miss her, I wish she didn't die, but she did. So I just remember her and I'm not sad. I loved her. She had a nice life that had a beginning, and a middle, and an end. If you're sad, that means you think you've been cheated and she should still be here. It's pointless."

"Or," Sarah suggested, "you're feeling sorry for yourself?"

"Exactly. If my dad were sad, that would make sense to me, because he's all alone now. That's a real reason to be sad. But Meg and Angela seem . . . addicted to it. Meg's getting better, but her eyes are still dim."

There was a pause. Then Sarah asked, "So, you never cried?"

"No," said Calvin. "I expected it to come, but it didn't."

"I'm sorry," said Sarah.

Calvin found her hand under the sheets.

They were quiet for a long time and Calvin thought Sarah had fallen asleep. But then she started a story in a dreamy voice: "When I was in Lisbon, I would go to a bar where they had fado singers, these women who wrap themselves in black shawls and sing old songs about losing their husbands to the sea and wanting to die. There's just one guitar accompanying. The singer stands still and throws her head back and wails out the song in an achy, nasal voice, very controlled and beautiful. It must be the most mournful sound a human being can make. I was there one night. The bar was packed because they had a really good singer. The people would sing along sometimes, or just wail when she sang the saddest line. I loved going there. Then she sang a song that no one sang along with. It was a beautiful song. Everyone just looked down at their drinks. Afterward, she seemed like she couldn't go on. She took a break and everyone clapped. The man next to me spoke English, so I asked him what the words of the last song meant. He said, 'She sang a new song. I have not heard it before. She sang about the worst type of pain—the sadness of being unable to feel sad.'"

In the silence that followed, Calvin thought to himself, I will ask her to marry me. Not soon, but someday.

The creaks of footsteps descending the stairs broke the silence. "What was that?" Sarah asked.

"I'll bet it's Angela. She's probably leaving."

"It's so late, though."

"She does this all the time. She gets herself all upset, then sneaks away. She's such a freak."

He rolled over and pulled himself up to peer under the window shade above the bed. There was the driveway, the three cars. Sarah knelt beside him and they both watched for a few minutes, but no one appeared.

"I guess not," said Calvin.

"Probably someone going down for some pound cake," said Sarah lying back down.

Calvin continued to watch for a while. There was a wind in the trees, and he could hear coyotes howling in the distance. "Hear that?" he whispered, but Sarah had fallen asleep.

There was a strange light shining past the house from the other side. But there were no streetlamps there, just the woods. It must have been the lights of the baseball field, but the game had been over for hours. Fluttering in this light, the leaves of the aspen looked like silver coins.

Angela called home and assured Andy she would return by early afternoon, although he encouraged her not to rush. Then she stayed up for a while, trying to make some notes for her manuscript. When it seemed that everyone had gone to sleep, she was tempted to leave. She was certain she could stay awake for the drive home; she had done it before. But no. She would stay and spend the morning with them being normal and charming, as if nothing of consequence had happened at dinner. But as she practiced possible breakfast conversations in her mind, even this took more strength than she could muster. She gathered her papers and rose from the bed, meaning to leave, but instead she put the papers into her bag and took out her sleeping pills. She had to stay.

The mere act of swallowing the pill put her at ease. She undressed and got into bed. No more decisions now, just thoughts, she said to herself, and experienced a wave of relief. Her mind wandered over her day, and things didn't matter so much now. Stupid Bony. And what had it been at dinner that upset her so? It certainly wasn't the story of the fishing trip. Even she could smile at the image of her mother in the sunlight. . . . It had been what came before— her father revealing that he had left that night. Angela's bedroom bordered the stairs, and all her life she had awakened whenever someone walked down those stairs at night, not thinking that he was leaving again, but remembering that he had. She had closely kept the secret. She had written poems about it, veiling it in symbols. It had become precious, and he had given it away.

Now the pill was doing its magic. It made falling asleep really feel like falling, down and down, yet still feeling the bed like the palm of a great hand.

For a moment she was awakened by the sound of her father descending the staircase. Then she told herself, I'm just remembering.

Meg had a wonderful dream. It was a simple dream. She was standing in some bright heavenly place. Around her, at a distance, was a ring of darkness, but she was in the center of the light. She lifted her eyes and opened her arms. It was cold, but her lungs breathed in the light and sent it to her heart, which turned the light into warm red wine and pumped it through her veins. She was in heaven, but she wasn't dead. This breathing and pumping were something new. She was new.

She woke up. Her feet were cold and wet. A little fear crept in. She lowered her hands and looked around, confused, and then she realized.

Meg laughed quietly and shook her head. Then she put her hands over her heart to try to hold in that last bit of joy. She could still feel it.

She walked out of the light and climbed carefully through the woods, thinking, How did these sticks and pebbles not wake me on my way down?